SWIMMING WITH THE DEAD

SWIMMING WITH THE DEAD

Peter Guttridge

Severn House Large Print
London & New York

This first large print edition published 2019
in Great Britain and the USA by
SEVERN HOUSE PUBLISHERS LTD of
Eardley House, 4 Uxbridge Street, London W8 7SY.
First world regular print edition published 2019 by
Severn House Publishers Ltd.

British Library Cataloguing in Publication Data
A CIP catalogue record for this title is available from the British Library.

ISBN-13: 9780727829504

Severn House Publishers support the Forest Stewardship Council™
[FSC™], the leading international forest certification organisation. All
our titles that are printed on FSC certified paper carry the FSC logo.

Typeset by Palimpsest Book Production Ltd.,
Falkirk, Stirlingshire, Scotland.
Printed and bound in Great Britain by
T J International, Padstow, Cornwall.

'Oh, would I were a little fish,
Upon the water skimming,
Oh, let me be one, 'tis my wish,
I am so fond of swimming'

– From a popular Victorian song
about J.B. Johnson, who failed to
swim the English Channel in 1872
(but briefly pretended he had)

'Ever tried. Ever failed. No matter. Try
again. Fail again. Fail better.'

– Samuel Beckett, not best
known for his swimming abilities

'So we beat on, boats against the current,
borne back ceaselessly into the past'

– F. Scott Fitzgerald, *The Great Gatsby*

For Jessica, Channel Swimmer *par excellence*

Prologue

The tug of the tides in her. Swept away on surges of emotion. Impetuous, foolhardy . . . feckless, fickle – these last words he chose for her as their relationship floundered and he cast her adrift.

The tug of the tides here in the slow deep. The soft swell comforting her. Cradling her. Carrying her away.

Soon she is far from anything she knows, or recognizes, or loves. Her senses awash, her treacherous limbs heedless of her brain's dim commands. Ponderous. Sinking.

She rises, snuffling for air but sucking in the sea. Slowly she sinks. Tiny bubbles swim around her head. She sinks deeper.

She does not rise again.

One

Something stirred the blackness. Sarah Gilchrist, awake in an instant, lay still, on her side, her head pressed into her pillow, one fluttering eye trying to see through the darkness enveloping her.

She took a breath and sat up, reaching for her watch. Five a.m. She heard someone on tiptoe move from her balcony to her flat's front door. She held her breath until she heard the thin rattle of the chain, the squeak as the door opened, the dull click as it closed again.

She switched on the bedside lamp and picked up her phone, glanced across at the crumpled second pillow where the man had slept. Five a.m. was acceptable. The time she would have left a stranger's flat. She hoped he hadn't left a note saying he would call or thanking her for a great night. She didn't want him to call and it hadn't been a great night.

It had been another lost night. But unlike other recent one-night stands she had invited this one into *her* home. Her refuge. Why had she done that? Too much wine? Too much lust and her flat had been nearest?

Her phone rang. She cleared her throat, took a sip from the water glass beside her bed. 'Morning, Bellamy,' she said, her voice only a little croaky. 'Bad news, I hope.'

'Morning, ma'am,' Detective Sergeant Bellamy Heap said, his voice sombre. 'The worst I'm afraid. Murder. Salthaven Lido.'

'Good,' Gilchrist said. 'Come for me in ten.'

'I'm here now, ma'am,' Heap said. Which meant he would have seen Gilchrist's midnight rambler leave. Well, okay. She ended the call and hauled herself out of bed, hoping the water in the shower would be hot.

Heap passed Gilchrist a coffee and a small bottle of still water once she had her seat belt on. She could smell his hot chocolate and a hint of his aftershave. She seemed to be more conscious of male fragrances on him since he had started dating her friend, Kate Simpson. She assumed he'd come straight from her bed. They weren't actually living together but he seemed to spend most of his time in her flat rather than in his own place in Lewes.

'What do we know?' Gilchrist said, sipping at the hot coffee.

'Male, Caucasian, found outside the lido. Multiple stab wounds. No defensive injuries.'

'Identification?'

'Not carrying any identifying papers, ma'am. In fact, not carrying anything.'

'The attack was frenzied?' Gilchrist said.

'I understand not, ma'am.' Heap glanced at her. 'On the phone, when you said "good", ma'am . . .'

'It was in bad taste, Bellamy,' Gilchrist said. 'But have you actually enjoyed the last few weeks? Is it what you trained for?'

4

'It's important work, ma'am,' Heap said. He saw her face. 'But no, ma'am, I haven't enjoyed it.'

For the past month Gilchrist and Heap had been part of an inter-agency examination of teenage violence and vandalism. Gilchrist had been putting off participating in the task force for months but had finally run out of excuses.

'So this is our ticket out.'

'But a man has died, ma'am.'

Gilchrist leaned across and squeezed Heap's arm. 'I'm sorry, Bellamy. I do care about this poor man.'

'Ma'am.'

Gilchrist was too tall to lean back into her seat, although that's what she wanted to do. Instead she leaned forward. 'Sometimes I get brittle.'

'Ma'am.'

'I do care about this man.'

Heap put the car into gear. He looked across at Gilchrist. He gave her a small smile. 'Ma'am.'

Gilchrist had been expecting the man to be sprawled on the pavement, limbs akimbo. But he was curled up tightly against the wall of Salthaven Lido. His arms were wrapped round his drawn-up knees, his forehead resting on top of them.

'He hung on to life,' she murmured.

'Tried to,' Heap agreed.

Gilchrist looked around, scanning for pubs that were nearby. 'Bad night in the pub?' she said.

'We'll know that when the blood levels have been taken,' Heap said.

'You don't have to be drunk to have a bad night, Bellamy,' Gilchrist said.

5

Heap nodded. Gilchrist stepped around the crime scene gingerly. 'It's just a post-pub argument gone wrong,' she continued. 'It's Saturday night in Brighton.'

'It's Monday,' Heap said quietly.

Gilchrist snorted. 'I know that, smartarse. The principle is the same.'

'There's a Save Salthaven Lido campaign going on at the moment, ma'am.'

Gilchrist stopped pacing and looked from Heap to the body. 'You think this is linked to that?'

'This man is quite well dressed, ma'am. Linen. Nice haircut. He's not the kind to get involved in a pub brawl, I wouldn't have thought.'

Gilchrist nodded slowly. 'My brain hasn't fired up yet, Bellamy. Good points all. Thank you.' She looked up at the Art Deco frontage of the pool. 'The council are closing this down, aren't they? I don't see how closing down a lido would lead to murder. I don't think it's going to hire hit men, ludicrous as its hiring policy often seems.'

Heap looked around them.

'With respect, ma'am, the lido is being pretty much pulled down not closed down. And by the businesswoman who bought the freehold off the council for some token amount – one pound or something. She intends to redevelop it with flats, offices and restaurants. That means money and money usually does mean motive. In light of that, the lido would seem the most likely link to this death.'

Gilchrist looked up at the sky and sucked in air. 'Then you work on that assumption, Bellamy.'

She looked around. 'Now where the fuck is Frank Bilson?'

The pathologist was not long in arriving. He parked a little way down the street then walked over to them in long strides, his battered leather forensics bag slung over one shoulder, dragging his suit jacket askew.

'Sarah – the delight I have in seeing you almost makes the unfortunate circumstances in which we meet worthwhile.'

'Almost,' Gilchrist said.

He nodded to Heap. 'Bellamy.'

'Mr Bilson.'

Bilson tilted his head and looked down at the dead man. 'So, Roland Gulliver stabbed to death in front of the wonderfully exuberant Salthaven Lido.'

'You know this man?' Gilchrist said.

'Of course. We swim together. Well, not together but in the same pool up on campus.' He gestured at the Art Deco frontage of the lido. 'He's part of the Save the Lido gang.'

Gilchrist glanced at Heap. In his place she would have been preening but he was po-faced.

'So you think this is somehow linked to that campaign?' Gilchrist said.

If Frank Bilson had had glasses he would have been looking over them.

'Not my area of cognisance,' he said. 'I'm just here to tell you how he died.'

Gilchrist looked across at DS Heap.

'Bellamy?'

'I'd like to work with the evidence, ma'am, before hypothesizing any further.'

Yeah, well fuck you too, Gilchrist thought but didn't say. She shook her head. Boy, was she in a bad mood. Swimmers. She hated men who did a splashy front crawl barging through other swimmers in public pools. She was willing to bring back the death penalty for anyone doing the butterfly.

'So tell me how he died, Frank,' Gilchrist said.

Bilson leaned in. 'Sarah, I *love* it when you're bossy with me.'

Gilchrist raised her eyes. Heap was working his iPad.

'He lives in Salthaven,' Heap said. 'Perhaps we should leave Mr Bilson to his work and go round to Mr Gulliver's house.'

'Is there a family waiting to be given terrible news?' Gilchrist said.

'Divorced,' Frank Bilson called from where he was squatting by the corpse. 'No kids. Might be a boyfriend though.'

She nodded at Heap. 'Come on then, let's visit his abode.'

There seemed to be nobody home at Gulliver's modern semi-detached house.

'Shall we check round the back?' Gilchrist said.

There was a big terracotta pot beside the kitchen door. Gilchrist tilted it and Heap picked up a key.

'People never cease to disappoint,' Gilchrist said.

The kitchen was small but tidy. The living room had an almost empty bottle of wine and two glasses on a table in front of an old sofa.

Heap leaned down to sniff the wine in the

8

bottle. Gilchrist was looking at a certificate in a frame on the wall.

'Mr Gulliver has swum the English Channel.' She snorted. 'Doing bloody butterfly. Fourteen hours and a bit.' She turned to Heap. 'How is that even possible? Butterfly is the daftest stroke around but to do it for fourteen hours non-stop? Or do they stop, Bellamy?'

'For liquid food intake and for the odd float I think but, no, they have to keep going.'

'Well, that's bloody unbelievable.'

Heap had put on a latex glove and was riffling through a pile of post on the fireplace. He pulled out one envelope. It had been opened. He took out the sheet of paper inside.

'Mobile phone bill.'

'See if we can locate his phone,' Gilchrist said.

Heap dialled and listened for a moment.

'Voice mail. I'll get his recent calls from the phone company.'

Gilchrist nodded, glancing once more round the room. 'Let's leave this to SOCO.'

'Kate's training for it, ma'am,' Heap said.

Gilchrist frowned. 'SOCO?'

'No. The Channel.'

'Swimming the Channel? Really? I know she's in the diving club but I didn't imagine her as a long-distance swimmer.'

Heap shrugged.

'She's swimming the length of Lake Coniston this weekend and in a couple of weeks there's a big open-air swimming event in Brighton when she's going to try for her six-hour qualifier. She needs to put on a couple of stone in weight so she's eating like a pig.'

'A woman trying to put *on* weight?'

'Swimmers need blubber to deal with the cold.'

'Eating like a pig? So there are some perks attached to doing it then?'

There was a buzz at the door. Heap glanced out of the window. 'SOCO,' he said.

'Let's leave them to it. Better get onto the Save Salthaven Lido folk. I'm going to talk to Frank Bilson again.'

Bilson was looking out to sea, smoke from his cigarette wreathing his head. A tall, lean man in his forties, he had that air of arrogance that comes with knowing a job inside out.

'Contemplating your next Channel swim?' Gilchrist called as she came up to him.

He turned, at the same time pinching the end of his cigarette between finger and thumb to extinguish it.

'That must hurt,' she said.

He smiled. 'Certainly, it hurts. The trick, Sarah Gilchrist, is not minding that it hurts.'

'*Lawrence of Arabia.*'

He tilted his head.

'You know the film? I wouldn't have thought it was your kind of thing.'

'No – I know a science fiction film called *Prometheus* where Michael Fassbender does an impersonation of Peter O'Toole. He's a robot.'

'Peter O'Toole?'

'Michael Fassbender. In the film.'

Bilson frowned. 'I'll take your word.'

10

'You don't see contemporary films, Frank?'

'Art house stuff at the Duke of Yorks.' He put on a familiar leer. 'But if you're asking me out, Sarah, I'll happily try some other fare. We'd be sitting on the back row I presume?'

She laughed. 'You presume too much. Tell me about Mr Gulliver.'

'We both attend the swimming pool at the David Lloyd up on the university campus. We both hog the fast lane, although he stays in much longer than I. Stayed in longer.'

'He swam the Channel.'

Bilson glanced over to the horizon. A couple of tankers from Shoreham were making their slow way to France.

'Ah – now I understand your comment. I didn't know that about him. And it is certainly not my intention to emulate him.'

'He did it butterfly.'

Bilson frowned again. 'Indeed. That's curious. I never saw him do the butterfly in the pool. Always crawl.'

'What else do you know about him?' Gilchrist said.

'Only a little. Our conversation was desultory, in the changing rooms or, occasionally, the sauna. That's where I heard his name – in the sauna. He didn't introduce himself to me but to someone else.'

'Anything I should know about his death?'

'As always, I'll know better after I've got him on the slab. At first sight, however, he has indeed been stabbed to death.'

'Drink or drugs involved?'

11

'I'll know that after the toxicity tests.'

'Time?'

'Somewhere between midnight and three in the morning.'

'You said you thought he might have a boyfriend?'

'Terrible, isn't it, eavesdropping at my age? But in a sauna it's difficult not to.'

'This emerged in that same conversation with the man he introduced himself to?'

'Yes. Actually, it wasn't quite an introduction, more of a re-introduction. He was reminding this man who he was. He then gave him a one line account of his marriage break-up and subsequent acknowledgement of his "true nature".'

'He used those words?'

'Yes. Rather old-fashioned, wasn't it?'

'How did the other man respond?'

'This was a couple of months ago, Sarah.'

'You don't remember?'

He smiled. 'Actually, I do, though I don't know exactly why. He said something like – no, exactly like – "your true nature has been known to the rest of us for a long time". Then they both laughed.'

'Gulliver wasn't offended?'

'Didn't seem to be but I wasn't looking at them, just listening.'

Gilchrist nodded. 'I don't suppose you remember the name of the man Gulliver was talking to?'

Bilson thought for a moment.

'There might have been a first name but I don't really recall.'

'A regular at the pool?'

12

Bilson shook his head. 'Actually, no. I'd never seen the man before. Or since.'

'Description?'

'You think this man might have had something to do with the stabbing? Bit far-fetched, isn't it?'

'I have no idea whether he did or not, Frank. I'm just trying to build up a picture of Gulliver's life.'

'Paunchy, but strong-looking arms. Not gym work out pretend – properly exercised. Tanned. Dark hair, neatly cut. Late forties, early fifties.'

'Facial features?'

'Didn't really notice. So regular featured, I'd guess.'

'Tell me about the Save Salthaven Lido people.'

'It would seem to me you might find it more profitable to investigate the businesswoman they are opposing.'

'Do you know her too?'

He shook his head. 'I think she's based up north somewhere. Scarborough, perhaps.'

Gilchrist followed his look out to sea. One of the tankers had disappeared. The other was just slipping below the horizon.

'It's my birthday today,' Bilson said.

'A significant one?'

'I don't regard any of them as significant, Sarah. We're born, we suffer and we die.'

'Jesus, Frank.' She nudged him. 'Don't be such an optimist.'

He smiled. 'Realistic, Sarah. That doesn't mean I don't make the most of life.' He raised an eyebrow. 'So if you were inclined to give me a birthday treat . . .?'

She laughed. 'I'll buy you a bag of Percy Pigs.'

Bilson shrugged.

'I don't know what they are but I'm sure I wouldn't like them, even coming from your fair hands.'

Gilchrist squeezed his arm. 'Best offer you're going to get from me.'

She saw Heap approaching in their car. Bilson saw it too.

'Bright lad, that Bellamy. He'll go far.'

'Yes, he will,' she murmured, thinking about him going out with her best friend, Kate. She looked back at Bilson. 'Anyway, happy birthday, whether you like it or not.'

'Do you mind if we put the windows down, Bellamy?'

'I have bathed this morning, ma'am.'

'I like the wind blowing in off the sea.'

They were high up on the cliff road, driving past Rottingdean School on their right, Brighton bay spread out below them to their left. The sea looked jolly, like something out of a children's picture: against a backdrop of fluffy white clouds and bright blue sky, the sun darted off the water and dozens of sail boats flitted back and forth.

'The negative ions,' Heap said.

'Something lifts the spirits, that's for sure,' Gilchrist said, pushing her face into the breeze flapping through the window. 'But actually I think it's just the salty tang.'

'Do your spirits need lifting, ma'am? If you don't mind my asking.'

Gilchrist kept her face towards the sea.

'I think sometimes we all get in a slump or take a wrong turn. Don't you, Bellamy?'

'Of course, ma'am. But what makes us special, it seems to me, is our ability to work our way through such slumps by force of will or change of ideas or whatever the solution might be.'

Gilchrist nodded, although Heap's eyes were on the road, so he wouldn't see. Perhaps Heap wasn't the person with whom to discuss late-onset promiscuity. Not that she had anyone else to discuss it with. In the past she would have talked to Kate, but if she did that now it would only get back to Heap anyway because of the way that couples share other people's secrets. So maybe she should just cut out the middle-person and go straight to Bellamy, after all.

'There's a Yorkshire woman owns the freehold on the lido, ma'am. Tough-sounding cookie called Alice Sutherland.'

'Bilson mentioned her. Based in Scarborough, he said.'

'She's a developer. There's a big old hotel in a dominating position in Scarborough she wants to buy but the owners are resisting. She looked at a development at the West Pier but backed out when the i360 got the go-ahead. Her usual model is conversion into flats with some offices and a couple of restaurants.'

'Doesn't sound a bad model,' Gilchrist said. 'But what makes you say she's tough?'

'She was married to Harry Henrickson, that guy from the telly who runs all the spas? He's thirty years older than her. They'd been living together and a year after they married she left him. Screwed him for £30 or £40 mil and used it to set up her own chain of health shops.'

Gilchrist nodded. 'She's the one who put up a billboard directly opposite his HQ in Canary Wharf advertising her shops?' she said.

'She's the one. Well, now she's diversified into these kinds of developments. There'll be flats and offices in the lido if she has her way.'

'I don't see what's wrong with that. The lido is pretty much derelict anyway. No investment for decades, hardly anyone wants to swim in it because the water is so bloody cold. Far too expensive to keep up. What are the Save the Lido gang proposing to do with it?'

'Community use. Gym, heated pool, couple of restaurants, hiring out spaces. The local library is already there and will stay.'

'Same sort of idea then with a bit of community use thrown in. The two sides don't seem so far apart.' She smiled at Heap. 'You have been a quick worker this morning.'

Heap shook his head. 'I knew most of this stuff anyway. Kate is a signed-up Save the Lido person.'

'You?'

'I'm a copper, ma'am. Not allowed personal opinions.'

'Is the future of the lido enough motive to kill though?'

'Money is always a motive to kill, ma'am.'

'Yes – but linking it so obviously to the lido? Shouldn't he have been gift-wrapped too with a card from her attached to him?'

'Perhaps when we've spoken to some of the Save the Lido people it will make more sense.'

Gilchrist nodded and closed the windows as they approached the aquarium and the road junction at the bottom of the Old Steine. As usual, the area in front of the Palace pier was thronged with people.

Gilchrist yawned.

'I'm knackered and the day hasn't even started yet.' She flushed when she remembered Heap had seen her last night's visitor leave her apartment. Heap kept his eyes on the road.

Two

The chair of Save the Lido, Mrs April Medavoy, worked in Brighton, as most people from Salthaven did. She arranged to meet them in Browns café opposite a church that had been converted into an art gallery. Last time Gilchrist had wandered into the gallery she found herself in the middle of an exhibition comprising layer after layer of washing lines hung with hundreds of shirts. There was a lot about the arts in Brighton she didn't get.

'I thought it would be more private,' Mrs Medavoy said, as cutlery clattered and waiters and waitresses bustled around them.

'Not entirely,' Gilchrist said.

'My office is definitely not private,' the woman said. 'Open-plan.'

17

'This is fine,' Heap said as their drinks arrived. Two coffees and his mint infusion.

'So, Mrs Medavoy,' Gilchrist said. 'How well do you know Roland Gulliver?'

'Please, call me April – if you're allowed to, that is.'

'I don't think that would be seen as fraternizing with a witness,' Heap said, sipping his infusion. The smell of mint spread around them.

'Is that what I am? A witness? Witness to what?'

Gilchrist glanced at Heap. He shot her an apologetic look. Gilchrist scanned the woman's face. Well preserved fifties, she judged, carefully made-up and with an expensive haircut. Good figure.

'What kind of business are you in, April?' Gilchrist said.

'We wholesale alternative therapy products,' she said.

'Interesting,' Gilchrist said, without conviction. 'And how long have you known Roland Gulliver?'

'Well, I've known of him for longer than I've known him,' she said, blowing on her latte before taking a sip. 'You know – his Channel swim using that bullying stroke.'

'Butterfly,' Heap said.

'Yes. Personally the Channel or some other massive area of water is the only place I'd allow anyone to do it. *So* antisocial.'

Gilchrist nodded. She might end up liking this woman. 'A remarkable achievement though,' she said.

'You have no idea,' Medavoy said. 'Do you

know how many muscle groups are involved in that ludicrous stroke?'

'I'm guessing you do,' Gilchrist said.

Medavoy smiled. She had good teeth. Artificially whitened. Gilchrist had been thinking about having it done.

'Actually, I do. I used to be a county swimmer, though backstroke was my preference.'

'Did you get near to the national team?' Heap said.

'I trained with them but, you know, life got in the way . . .'

Medavoy smiled again, more brightly. Gilchrist smiled back, not persuaded by the brightness.

'And then you met Roland?'

'Only when we launched the Save the Lido campaign.'

'Which was when?' Gilchrist said.

'Six months ago, in the Salthaven library. He turned up drunk.'

Gilchrist forced herself not to glance at Heap.

'Was he difficult?'

'Not in the least,' Medavoy said. 'In fact he made some very good points.'

'In a slurred sort of way,' Gilchrist said with a smile.

'Actually, I don't recall him slurring. But his exuberance indicated he was drunk.'

'Why was he there?' Gilchrist said.

Medavoy shrugged. 'He didn't want the lido to close,' she said.

'Did he say why? Was it the swimming?'

'That and the beauty of the building. It's pure 1930s Art Deco. We're trying to get it listed.'

'Did Roland Gulliver have something special to offer the campaign to save the lido?' Heap said.

'Enthusiasm. Some expertise in building development.'

'Building development?' Gilchrist said. 'What's that? Refurbishment?'

'Sort of – more about finding new uses for old buildings.'

'Isn't that what Alice Sutherland is proposing?' Gilchrist said.

Before Medavoy could reply, Heap asked: 'Had he lived in Salthaven long?'

Gilchrist pursed her lips at the interruption.

'I don't believe so,' Medavoy said. 'I hadn't seen him around and it's a pretty small community. But perhaps he kept himself to himself.'

'So he joined your committee,' Gilchrist said. 'Was he helpful?'

'Efficient. He did whatever he was given to do efficiently. Helping draft letters to councillors and English Heritage, working on the news sheet and keeping the website updated. And he helped organize the security rota.'

'Security rota?'

'He persuaded us that we couldn't expect to rely on the police to prevent vandalism at the pool. There are grown men and women who regard that man who defaces buildings in Bristol and elsewhere with graffiti as an artist.'

'Banksy?' Heap said.

'I believe so. Roland believed that the best communities were most safe and secure if the community worked in partnership with the police and other appropriate agencies.'

Heap glanced at Gilchrist, whose face had gone stony, and she saw him hold down a smirk. That was the kind of rubbish she and her detective sergeant had been wading through for the past three months. As far as she was concerned, such collaborations just diluted the effectiveness of both preventative and reactive policing. However, she knew that Heap disagreed with her.

'Did Mr Gulliver have policing in his CV, do you know, April?' Gilchrist said.

'Not so far as I'm aware,' Medavoy replied, 'but he was a highly intelligent man. Highly intelligent.'

'Is it possible he was at the lido because it was his turn on the security rota?'

'I don't think he was usually on it. But perhaps if someone had dropped out at the last minute . . .?'

'Do you have a copy of the rota?'

'Probably – somewhere. Roland was very good at copying the committee into everything.'

'If you could find that as a priority when you get back to your office, Mrs Medavoy,' Gilchrist said.

'April,' Medavoy repeated quietly.

Heap leaned forward. 'Did Mr Gulliver have dealings with Alice Sutherland?' he said.

Medavoy looked from one to the other of them. 'Has something happened to her?'

'Why would you think that?' Gilchrist said mildly.

Medavoy wrinkled her nose in an oddly girlish expression. 'Hope, not think. She is a very

21

difficult customer who cares nothing for our community – or, I imagine, any community – but only for her own profit.'

'You have had dealings with her?'

'Yes, through our lawyer. I have tried to arrange meetings with her but have been rebuffed on each occasion.' Medavoy clasped her hands in front of her. 'But I shouldn't have said what I said. I wouldn't wish harm to anyone.'

'I'm afraid it's Mr Gulliver who has come to harm,' Gilchrist said gently.

A look Gilchrist couldn't read – alarm or fear – crossed Medavoy's face.

'What's happened to him?' Medavoy said breathlessly.

'I'm sorry to tell you he's been killed,' Gilchrist said. 'He was discovered this morning on the steps of the lido.'

Medavoy took an audible gulp of air.

'An accident?'

'We don't know the circumstances, but he was stabbed.'

Medavoy almost shrank back in her chair.

'Are you all right, Mrs Medavoy?' Heap said.

She flashed a look at him. 'Of course I'm not, you stupid boy,' she said. An instant later, she put her hand to her mouth. 'I'm so sorry,' she stammered. 'The shock . . .'

'Just take a moment, Mrs Medavoy,' Gilchrist said. 'Such things *are* a shock.'

Medavoy looked from one to the other of them. 'Perhaps not to you,' she said weakly after a moment. 'But in my world . . .'

'In anyone's world,' Heap said quietly.

'Can you think of any enemies Mr Gulliver might have had?'

'I didn't know him well enough, Detective Inspector.'

'Can you think of any particular friends – maybe on the committee?'

'Not that I'm aware of. But then we're not the kind of committee that goes down the pub after a meeting. We have a job to do and that's what we concentrate on.'

Gilchrist pressed her palms on the table and started to stand. 'I think we're done for now then,' she said. 'If you could let Detective Sergeant Heap have contact details for other committee members and, indeed, anyone who has signed up to save the lido.'

'Well, we have a petition of three thousand people but I'm not sure we can release those names. Isn't that against Data Protection or something?'

'If it's a petition, the names and addresses are public anyway, Mrs Medavoy,' Heap said, his voice still quiet.

Medavoy gave a little laugh. 'Of course.'

Heap passed her his card. 'My email address is on here. We need the security rota too. If you could send everything through by lunchtime that would be great.'

These days Gilchrist and Heap had an office to themselves. The dreaded DS Donald Donaldson, who had a somewhat combative relationship with Heap, was on loan to the Gatwick Airport division. Gatwick had the biggest arsenal of weapons in the whole force. Gilchrist was too professional to say anything to Heap but she seriously wondered if putting the fiery-tempered Donaldson so near to it was wise.

They discussed April Medavoy on the way in.

'There was something off about her,' Gilchrist said.

'You think she's a suspect?' Heap said.

'No, not that. Just something not quite right. What about when she snapped at you after she'd been all nicey-nicey?'

'I think it's understandable in the circumstances,' Heap said. 'But let's see what Bilson has to say when he phones.'

He phoned on the landline half an hour later.

'And?' Gilchrist said.

'And hello again to you, Sarah,' Bilson said. 'How quickly they forget once they have used you.'

'I haven't used you yet, Mr Bilson.'

'And first names go too, even on one's birthday.'

'Sorry. I forgot it was your birthday. What are you doing with the rest of your day, *Frank*?'

'Scuttling beneath a silent sea. You haven't seen my ragged claws, have you?'

'That's a bit over my head, Frank, but then many things are. What do you have?'

'Alcohol in the system though nothing excessive.'

'We found an empty bottle of wine with two glasses at the house.'

'I know. The DNA on one glass is his. The second glass does not match the DNA splashed around his body. I hope you have a budget for turning those DNA tests round so superhumanly quickly, by the way. And as yet there's no match with anyone on the database for either.'

'Drugs?' Gilchrist said.

'None in the system. No indication of recent use of any.'

'Cause of death?'

'Two causes.'

'Two? Is that possible?'

'It is when I'm not yet sure which takes priority or if they were equally contributory.'

'Go on.'

'Bled out from multiple stab wounds, front and back.'

'Frenzied?'

'I think not. But not precise. Only one vital organ was pierced – the liver – and that was probably by chance. No anatomical knowledge was shown by the pattern of the stab wounds.'

'And no indication that Gulliver attempted to defend himself?'

'None. Which is odd.'

'What do you deduce from that?'

'My dear young woman, no pathologist has deduced anything since the heady days of Sir Bernard Spilsbury.'

Gilchrist, phone still to her ear, walked to the window and looked down on the busy seafront. She noticed a stocky, paunchy man wearing a trilby with two feathers sticking out of the head-band, his grey hair flowing halfway down his back. He was arguing with two women, jabbing his finger at each in turn.

One was a sharp-featured girl with long black hair, tattoos all down her left arm and wrapped around her left calf. The other was a short woman, whose hair came down to her bum. It was meant to look wonderful but because her legs were short it made her look a bit like a Hobbit.

'Who's Sir Bernard Whatsit?' Gilchrist said absently down the phone, growing angry at the way the man was haranguing the women. She turned her head and gestured to Heap to come over to her.

'The most celebrated pathologist of his or any other day,' Bilson said. 'He did the autopsy on the Brighton Trunk Murder victim, among many other autopsies. Unfortunately, someone likened him to Sherlock Holmes and he rather enjoyed the comparison so consistently went far beyond his remit to conjecture causation and train of events. In actuality, he was more Dr Watson in that most of his speculations were dangerously erroneous. I think at least two men were wrongly executed because of him. His knighthood, you see, unduly impressed juries.'

'OK,' Gilchrist said, now with Heap beside her. She pointed down at the group and Heap nodded. He retreated to his desk and she heard him murmuring into his phone.

Bilson cleared his throat. 'So, my dear Sarah. I give you the bricks, you get the mortar and construct the building.'

Gilchrist grimaced down the phone line. 'How very B&Q of you. OK, oh, wise one, do you have any thoughts you *could* share? Can you tell from the angle of the incisions whether he was standing or lying down?'

'You have been watching too many television

crime shows, Sarah. I would wish to tell you his assailant's height, weight and the size of his feet but alas I cannot – though I hope I'll know soon.'

'You're making further tests?'

'No. You are going to catch the person and tell me.'

'Ha ha. Any thoughts about the gender of the assailant?'

'I could give you some Golden Age guff about poison and knives being women's weapons but these days knives are definitely for boys and grown-up men.'

A policewoman Gilchrist didn't recognize was striding across the road towards the hectoring man and his women.

'Golden Age?' Gilchrist said. The policewoman reached the trio. Gilchrist turned away from the window. If only all policing could be so immediate. Heap raised a quizzical eyebrow. Gilchrist nodded.

'My dear Sarah, do you mean you're not a reader of crime fiction?' Bilson said.

'Wouldn't that be a little like coals to Newcastle?'

'I've never really understood that phrase – I think I went to the wrong school. But you're missing a treat with the Golden Age crime writers from the 1920s and 1930s. After a long day examining dismembered bodies, coming home to read a country house mystery where someone's cocktail has been poisoned and they are lying dead in their dinner jacket or, depending on the time of day, plus fours, is a wonderful way to wind down.'

'You're talking about yourself.'

'I don't wear plus fours.'

'The reader, I mean.'

'I'm presenting myself as a model for you, yes.'

Gilchrist saw Heap leave the room. 'Thank you, Frank,' she said gently.

'Don't you want to know the other possible cause of death?'

'It would be remiss of me not to ask. Not to mention rude.'

'Right on both counts. OK, are you ready?'

'My breath is bated.'

'He drowned.'

When Heap returned he joined Gilchrist at the window. The arguing trio were long gone but Gilchrist was looking beyond the promenade at the grey waves rolling in.

'Drowned and stabbed to death, according to Bilson,' she said without looking at Heap.

'I think the word *overkill* was invented specifically for this occasion,' he said.

She smiled. 'When I dared to query it with Bilson he got sniffy and said: "He had water in his lungs: he drowned."'

'But Gulliver wasn't noticeably wet,' Heap said.

'I don't think he was wet at all. When I asked Bilson to explain that he repeated his B&Q line about him providing the bricks so we can construct the building.'

'They don't sell bricks in B&Q.'

Gilchrist gave Heap a look. He coughed and reddened.

'So Gulliver was perhaps rendered unconscious

by submerging at least his head in water then he was stabbed to death,' he said.

'That was my thinking, Bellamy. That would explain why he didn't defend himself when attacked with the knife. But drowned until unconscious rather than dead would also explain why the blood flowed from his wounds for so long.'

'So he'd come round to find himself bleeding to death.'

'If he did come round. Perhaps he just went from one state to the next as he bled out.' Gilchrist gave an involuntary shudder as she said it.

'I think perhaps the way we found him hugging himself suggests he may have come round but he was too weak to do anything but somehow try to hold his life in.'

'Good point, detective sergeant. But if we accept your premise then he was drowned elsewhere and moved there. It was fresh water, incidentally, so we can discount the sea. What do SOCO have to say about that?'

'No sign of a struggle in the house. No immediate sign of blood anywhere. Plenty of blood at the actual scene so he definitely died there.'

'Could he have been drowned in the lido?'

'Saltwater in the lido I believe, ma'am, from the sea then purified.'

Gilchrist frowned. 'They use seawater in the lido?'

'Regular practice in seaside lidos, ma'am.'

'But why would people pay to swim in seawater in a lido when a few yards away they could swim for free in the same water in the actual sea?'

'I think you've spotted the crack in the business

model, ma'am. The reason lidos in coastal resorts only had a limited shelf life in the thirties. The SS Brighton – where the big cinema is now situated on the seafront? – Only lasted a year before it was turned into an ice rink.'

'OK, is there *any* fresh water in any pool in the lido?'

'I believe not, ma'am.'

She frowned again. 'Any thoughts?'

'Waterboarding, ma'am.'

'You think the CIA is involved.'

'They have never been the only ones to use the method. You'll recall from the Cambodian antiquities case that Pol Pot used it in the seventies.'

'I was being flippant, Bellamy, which was totally inappropriate. Sorry. That still requires a bath or something, doesn't it?'

'A wet towel over the mouth and nose does the trick, ma'am. With perhaps another dry towel acting as a bib to prevent water going anywhere else.'

'Jesus.'

They both looked out of the window.

'You know that petition Mrs Medavoy mentioned?' Heap said.

'The three thousand?'

'It's a bit dodgy.'

'Fake names?'

'Obviously I haven't gone through them all but some households seem rather overcrowded.'

'Wouldn't the fraud turn up by checking the electoral register?'

'Not until it was too late, ma'am. You get the

headline and by the time the truth behind it is revealed it's too late.'

'You say that but wouldn't the subsequent bad publicity be a problem for the campaign?'

'By then it would be too late because decisions would have been made that the council couldn't go back on.'

'Fake news,' Gilchrist murmured.

She looked out of the window again. She must have been staring out longer than she realized because Heap said: 'You OK, ma'am?'

Gilchrist turned and smiled down at Heap. Sometimes she felt like she towered over him. The Little and Large tag was heard less around the station these days but it was still heard.

'Hunky dory. Why do you ask?'

'Was there something else in your conversation with Mr Bilson to make you . . . thoughtful?'

'I didn't realize how lonely he is until today. He's so well hidden under his flirtatiousness and over-the-top bonhomie.'

'We live in a lonely world, ma'am.'

Gilchrist narrowed her eyes. 'The Philosopher Policeman,' she said, more dismissively than she intended.

Heap flushed, as always. 'Just my view ma'am.'

Gilchrist regretted her sharpness. She just wasn't used to thinking – and certainly not speaking – in those terms.

'Sorry, Bellamy. I'm a bit off-kilter today.' She glanced back out of the window. 'Bilson said he was going to spend the rest of his birthday scuttling in a silent sea or something. Is that a quote, Big Brain?'

31

'T.S. Eliot I believe, ma'am, especially if ragged claws were involved in his remarks.'

'I believe they were,' Gilchrist said, smiling again.

'*The Love Song of J. Alfred Prufrock.* It's a poem about loneliness – a man who measures out his life in coffee spoons.'

'Don't ever change, Bellamy.'

'Noted, ma'am,' he said, nodding gravely. Then he said: 'Are you lonely, ma'am?'

She jerked her head back. 'I'm not sure my apology entitles you to ask such a personal question, Detective Sergeant.'

'No, ma'am,' Heap said but held her look.

She raised her eyes. 'I'm alone but not lonely. OK?'

'Most people rush into often inappropriate relationships because they don't like the thought of being alone.'

Gilchrist thought he was either alluding to last night's one-night stand or her recent inappropriate affair with a man who turned out to be a villain. She bridled again.

'You're right. It was rather foolish of me to sleep with a man who turned out to be the crook we were chasing.'

She recognized that falling hook, line and sinker for that creep some months ago had been a major lapse in her judgement. The embarrassment when it came out was bad enough but it had somehow triggered her recent flurry of one-night stands in ways she was dimly aware of but didn't want to analyse too closely.

Heap flushed again. 'I was speaking generally,

ma'am.' He looked out of the window. 'Or maybe about me.'

'You think your relationship with Kate is inappropriate?'

'Before her, I meant.'

'How is Kate? Has she heard much lately from her shitty father, William Simpson, corruption personified?'

Before Heap could answer, Gilchrist's landline rang.

'To be continued,' she said to Heap. 'Or not.'

She picked up the phone. It was a woman's voice.

'Tracey here, Detective Inspector Gilchrist. The Chief Constable would like a word. She wonders if you could come straight away. Please bring Detective Sergeant Heap.'

'Sarah, come in,' Chief Constable Karen Hewitt said. She nodded at Heap. 'Bellamy.'

'Ma'am,' Gilchrist and Heap both murmured.

Hewitt went round her desk and sat down. She was spruced up in a smart turquoise suit today. *Actually, more trussed than spruced,* Gilchrist thought, wondering how Hewitt could feel comfortable in it. Maybe she didn't like to be comfortable.

'I hear you've snagged a murder,' Hewitt said.

'Yes, ma'am.'

'I want to be sure that it doesn't interfere with your important work on teen offenders and the other inter-agency work you're doing.'

'Well, actually, ma'am, the teen offender work

is drawing to a close,' Gilchrist said. 'We know who the ringleaders are.'

Hewitt nodded. 'Very well, but the initiative must continue.' She clasped her hands in front of her on the desk. 'The murdered man—'

'Roland Gulliver, ma'am,' Heap said.

'Could it be a hate crime?'

'Gay-bashing, you mean?' Gilchrist said. 'Too early to say. We're following several lines of enquiry, including his link to the Save the Lido campaign.'

Hewitt scowled as best she could within the limits of her Botox injections. 'The leader of the council was banging on about that the other day at lunch. What an embarrassment it's been to them. You think it's somehow linked?'

Gilchrist glanced at Heap. 'Bellamy might have more insight than I do about that.'

Heap looked puzzled but then twigged. 'The petition they got together looks fraudulent. Perhaps Gulliver was implicated in that in some way?'

'Would that be enough to get him murdered?' Hewitt said.

'It's a potential line of enquiry, ma'am,' Gilchrist said.

'Will you need to talk to Alice Sutherland?' Hewitt said.

'Probably,' Gilchrist said.

'Tread carefully – she has links with the town.'

'Ma'am?'

'She was involved with a consortium that lobbied very hard to get a development at the

West Pier not dissimilar to the one she proposed for Salthaven. They were somewhat miffed when the West Pier Trust favoured the i360.'

'I didn't realize there were competing projects,' Gilchrist said, aware that she was woefully ignorant of vast swathes of things that went on in her own town.

'Sarah,' Hewitt said, sounding exasperated, 'that sand on the beach is not for sticking your head in, you know.'

'It's shingle, ma'am. I'm sorry but the West Pier doesn't really interest me. I'll be glad when it finally falls into the sea.'

'Which it almost has. And there are some who share your sentiments. Even so don't say that too loudly around this town or you might end up murdered by the zealots' wing of the Regency Society.'

'I thought they were all zealots,' Gilchrist murmured.

'Zealots on the side of right, for a change,' Hewitt said. 'On the whole.' She sat back – stiffly because of her tight jacket. 'Anyway, i360. Terrible name but there it is and very popular it is. But what Sutherland's consortium was hoping to do was build a new pier, as happened in Hastings, using Lottery funding.'

'I see,' Gilchrist said, bored.

'But it just didn't seem economically viable.'

'Ma'am.'

'Clearing away the wreckage would have cost a fortune.'

Hewitt must have seen Gilchrist's eyes glazing over because she leaned forward with difficulty and said, exasperation in her voice: 'What it boils down to is this: handle Alice Sutherland with kid gloves.'

Three

The sun was up behind a skyscraper on Park Lane, and Hyde Park was already busy with early morning joggers, riders and squads of people in shorts and T-shirts doing regimented squats and running on the spot. There were about thirty swimmers already in the water at the lido on the Serpentine, the large lake in the centre of the park. Over half were in wet suits: there was a big triathlon event at the weekend and competitors were having their final swim.

Police Commissioner Bob Watts slipped on the slimy gangway down into the water so was in before he had time to worry about how cold it was. He lay on his back for a moment then rolled over. Putting his face in the water was hardest. He wished he had a bathing cap like everybody else. And ear plugs. As he swam a fast crawl to get his circulation moving, his forehead started to ache with the cold.

Years earlier, in his army days, he'd done a good deal of cold-water swimming as part of a survival skills course. He used to know the ratio of body temperature to water temperature to energy loss. It was usual to advise people who were in the water because their boat had sunk not to swim but to conserve energy and therefore body heat by staying put until someone came to get them.

But here at the Serpentine Swimming Club most of the swimmers seemed to embrace the cold. Christmas day here was like the first day of the January sales, with a throng of swimmers eager to get in, though Watts didn't think the freezing water was much of a bargain.

Many of the people here were cross-Channel swimmers. In cross-Channel swimming and its pre-Channel qualifiers, the hardcore world in whose shallows Watts had been paddling for a few weeks, only ordinary swimming costumes, a single rubber bathing cap and ear plugs could be worn.

Watts had been intrigued to read that in the early days of all-male open water swimming the swimmers had preferred to go totally naked to ensure no artificial aids were being used.

Captain Webb, the first man to swim the Channel without the help of any aids, had worn his famous striped woollen swimming costume but he had presumably been thoroughly searched first.

It had been Jimmy Tingley's suggestion that Watts should take up what was known as wild-water swimming with an eye to doing the Channel. Watts, heading for his mid-forties, was fit enough but, naturally, slowing as he got older.

'Stamina counts for more than speed on a cross-Channel swim,' Tingley had said over a beer in a new bar in an old building at one side of the tracks in Brighton railway station. Watts had just come in from London; Tingley, his old companion-in-arms, had come in from Worthing, for reasons unspecified. Watts had long known it was best with Tingley, living in his ex-SAS shadow world, that things remain 'unspecified'.

Watts happened to know that this L-shaped room had long ago been the left luggage office where the Brighton Trunk Murder victim had been discovered in the sweltering summer of 1934. More recently it had been converted into the station's toilets. Now, it was brightly and stylishly laid out with sofas and armchairs among the more formal tables.

Although the bar had rum it didn't stock peppermint, so Tingley's signature drink of rum and pep had not been possible. Even so, as usual Tingley had laid out his cigarette packet and lighter in a neat line beside his drink – a beer. In a glass. He was a neat man in every way: medium height, slender physique, unobtrusive. He was occasionally looking with a mixture of bemusement and distaste at the younger people lounging on sofas and soft chairs in an outside area chugging on e-cigarettes or sending vapour trails drifting to the ceiling.

Watts saw Tingley staring at a couple of people with vaporizers.

'They are the ones I don't get,' Tingley said in a low voice.

'They're vaping – though I believe it's called "grazing" among aficionados,' Watts said. 'Trying the different flavours attached to the nicotine.'

Tingley looked at him suspiciously. 'How come you know all about it?'

38

'Article in the *Observer*,' Watts said.

Tingley nodded, straightening his already straight cigarette packet a little more. He gestured to Watts's stomach.

'Anyway, you might as well make use of some of that blubber you've put on sitting on your police commissioner arse all day.'

Watts had no paunch but sucked in his stomach anyway. 'I'm the same weight I've always been,' he protested.

Tingley chuckled. 'Yeah. Except now it's fat not muscle. But that's good. Channel swimmers need a layer of blubber as protection from the cold, given the amount of time they're in the water.' He touched his own chest. 'Someone with my physique wouldn't last an hour.'

Watts thought about Tingley's suggestion over the next few days, in budget meetings and drinking wine on his balcony looking to the horizon, knowing France was just beyond it. He usually ran most mornings along the seafront beyond the West Pier and back the other way along Madeira drive as far as Black Rock. But he also liked to swim up at the pool on the university campus.

Sometimes he bumped into Frank Bilson, the pathologist. Bumped into him literally, as Bilson did an arm-waving front crawl without goggles. With his eyes closed he assumed everyone else would get out of the way. He looked quite indignant when some didn't.

Watts disliked splashy swimmers. Usually they were men who slapped the water hard with the palm of their hands instead of sliding their arms in with each stroke. He prided himself on being un-splashy, unlike many men of his size.

For better or worse, Watts knew he was a man with drive, the drive that made him the country's youngest chief constable back in the day. But the truth was, his job as police commissioner was boring as hell. He had power over areas he wasn't interested in and no power over the areas he was.

He had inheritance money in the bank – a lot of money by most people's standards – so actually didn't need to work again. But he was not the retiring, life-of-leisure kind. He liked challenges and swimming the Channel was a pretty big one.

He'd been astonished to read on one of the Channel swim websites that many more people had climbed Everest since Sir Edmund Hillary's successful ascent in 1953 than had swum the channel unaided since Captain Webb's accomplishment in 1875.

Now, in the Serpentine, he did half an hour, keeping his mouth shut to avoid the duck, goose and swan shit he knew was in the water. He had a close encounter with a swan and a slight squabble with a coot as he did his lengths between a couple of buoys and the enclosed lido area.

The triathletes were generally messier swimmers, hitting the water hard and wide as they powered along. For most triathletes he'd met the swimming was the least favourite part and it showed in the inelegant way most of them tackled it.

He climbed out behind a man in Serpentine Swimming Club trunks with his name written on the back across his buttocks – a peculiarity of the club he didn't quite get. He'd joined for just a few pounds for the year because the lido was for club members only between around six and 9.30 a.m. After that you had to pay a daily fee to swim.

The small, mixed changing room was crowded, with no privacy for man or woman. As Watts towelled off he listened in on random conversations, cockney voices mixing with posher ones. He liked the friendliness here.

'Good swim?' the woman next to him said as she wriggled out of her costume behind a towel that didn't actually conceal her left breast. She had long dark hair and a wide mouth. She was probably mid-twenties.

He looked her in the eye and nodded.

'You know your heel is bleeding?' she said.

He looked down at his left heel and blood was indeed pouring out of two parallel cuts either side of the tendon. The woman reached into her rucksack and produced a couple of tissues.

'Use these. Did you scrape yourself?'

'I felt something when I went in,' Watts said. 'I slipped and pushed my foot down hard to balance myself.'

The woman bent to peer closer and now Watts could see both her breasts.

'Crayfish,' she said, straightening up. 'Pincered you.'

'Crayfish?'

'Yes, there are loads of them in the Serps. Have you not seen the seagulls whacking them against stones to crack open their shells?'

'I'm pretty new here.'

'Some Mayfair restaurant used to have baskets here to catch them so it could serve them at lunch.'

'I must have trodden on it.'

'I suppose.' She grinned. 'Big man like you – savaged by a prawn.'

He chuckled. 'I've had more embarrassing things happen to me, I assure you,' he finally said.

'I'd like to hear,' she said, then turned away – perhaps out of embarrassment.

Watts looked away too. Jesus, this woman was almost young enough to be his daughter.

They finished dressing at about the same time.

'You fancy a cup of tea next door to warm up?' she said.

He nodded. 'Sure.'

There were two cafés on the Serpentine and usually he preferred the other one, at the far end. But he knew the club members mostly favoured the café immediately next to the lido and not just because they got a discount.

'Out or in?' she said.

'You choose,' he said.

'In then – I've had enough cold for the time being.' She held out her hand. 'I'm Margaret, by the way, Margaret Lively.' She grinned again. 'And try to say something original about my last name.'

Gilchrist and Heap had a raft of phone numbers from Gulliver's mobile account to keep them busy. His lover's number was the most frequent one called, of course. His name was Francis Shaw and he was in Paris on business. He broke down when he heard the news, and Heap gave him half an hour to compose himself.

'When did you last see him?' Heap asked when he called back. He'd put the call on speakerphone.

'Two nights ago.' Shaw sounded brittle now.

'And he seemed all right then?'

'You mean, had anyone stabbed him?' Shaw said. 'I think I would have noticed.'

'I mean, did you have a row?' Heap said, more sharply than he perhaps intended. Gilchrist saw him flush.

'No, nothing like that. He was disappointed I was going away but it's only for a few days.'

'Did he have any enemies, Mr Shaw?'

'That disliked him enough to kill him? None that I can think of.'

'Did he ever put himself in risky situations,' Heap said.

There was silence then a gruff laugh. 'You mean cottaging? Stereotypes don't change much in Brighton, do they?'

'Mr Shaw, he was found stabbed to death in a street. There is, sadly, some homophobia in certain sections of Brighton. It's a reasonable line of inquiry for us to follow.'

Shaw sighed down the phone line. 'Roland had never been into cottaging even when he was keeping his sexuality secret from his wife and family. Once he had come out, as far as I'm aware, he was faithful to me. Sorry to spoil your caricature.'

43

'When you return we'll need a DNA swab, Mr Shaw, to help eliminate you from the enquiry. When are you home?'

'You might want to talk to his wife. Vindictive bitch.'

'Thank you for the suggestion, Mr Shaw. When did you say you were back in England?'

'At the end of the week. I'll come into the police station, shall I? Where is it?'

'We'll come to you, Mr Shaw, if you don't mind confirming your address.'

Gilchrist and Heap put their phones down at around the same time.

'Fancy a trip to the seaside, Bellamy?' Gilchrist said.

He frowned.

'We're at the seaside, ma'am.'

'No, I mean proper bucket-and-spade, candy-floss, windbreak, freezing-water seaside, not Pinot Grigio with *fruits de mer*.'

'You get the old style here too, ma'am, down on the boardwalk, but I assume you're meaning somewhere *northern*.'

'Alice Sutherland can see us in Scarborough but it has to be today.' She looked at the wall. 'Scarborough. I haven't been there for donkey's years.'

'I'm sorry to say I've never been, ma'am.'

Gilchrist laughed. 'Some would say that's nothing to be sorry about but they would be missing out on its essential charms. I have fond memories of visiting my pen pal there. The castle, the boating lake with the pagoda on an island in the middle . . .'

'Should we take some Brighton rock to trade with the natives?' Bellamy said. Gilchrist gave him a look she couldn't hide the fondness from.

'Probably a good idea.'

Four

Gilchrist and Heap caught the next train up to King's Cross just in time to catch the high-speed train from there direct to York. Within four hours they were sitting outside a Victorian pub on platform three at York station, tannoy messages of arrivals and departures echoing across the high-roofed station. They had half an hour to kill before their train to Scarborough arrived.

'Do you know the north, Bellamy?'

'I'm more of a West Country person, ma'am. I'm not sure I've been further north than Nottingham.'

'A lot of Viking stuff up here, I seem to remember.'

'I didn't think you were interested in history, ma'am.'

Gilchrist gave him a look. 'You'd be right. I don't actually know anything about the Vikings, I just know that they were here.'

'There's a link with Sussex, of course,' Heap said, sipping his beer.

'Of course,' Gilchrist said, smiling.

'Battle of Stamford Bridge – the one a few days before the Battle of Hastings?'

'Oh, that one,' Gilchrist said, watching a man walk along the platform opposite with his trouser cuffs buckled round his shoes, dragging on the floor at his heels.

'King Harold was up here defeating the Vikings at Stamford Bridge, a few miles outside York, when he heard the news that the Normans under William the Conqueror – as he would prove to be – were heading across the Channel to Hastings. They think the forced march Harold's soldiers had to make just after fighting one battle exhausted them so much before the next battle in Hastings they didn't really stand a chance.'

'That's interesting, Bellamy,' Gilchrist said, thinking that it kind of was.

'Of course, the Normans were Vikings too,' Heap added. 'Originally.'

Gilchrist rolled her eyes.

'Enough already, Bellamy,' she said.

'Ma'am.'

Heap had a great knack of keeping a straight face that broke Gilchrist up – if she allowed it to.

She coughed, then: 'So we're meeting Sutherland at Scarborough yacht club.'

'I thought the way you described the town they'd just have pedalos,' Heap said.

The journey to Scarborough on the local train took about fifty minutes through a flat but pretty landscape. The sky seemed massive, with black clouds gathering in the east. There was no Wi-Fi and only intermittent phone signal so Gilchrist gazed out of the window until Heap was shaking her awake.

'Did I drool?' she said immediately.

'I was too distracted by the snoring to notice, ma'am,' Heap said.

She looked at his straight face and he allowed himself a smile.

'You neither drooled nor snored, ma'am. You were an exemplary train snoozer – would that others were so placid.'

There was a uniformed police inspector on the platform waiting for them. Gilchrist had called ahead to the local constabulary to clear them coming up. It was a formality really but an important one.

The inspector – his name was Evans – was medium height with wavy black hair and a friendly manner. In his forties, carrying a bit too much weight. Introductions made, he ushered them into a waiting car that swept them across a bridge and down a steep road to the seafront. Another iron bridge towered high above their heads.

Evans saw Heap and Gilchrist both craning their necks for a better look.

'It takes you along to the spa from the town centre. Bit hilly is Scarborough.'

'You don't sound like you're from round here, inspector,' Gilchrist said.

'Been here fifteen years but my heart is still in the Valleys,' the Welshman said. 'My fault for marrying a Yorkshire lass.'

'Major problems here?' Gilchrist said.

Evans shook his head. 'The problems poverty and drugs bring, of course. A couple of fatal stabbings; too many among youngsters. No big crime families or hassle from the Tyneside gangs. Although we're keeping an eye on the Manchester connection – the train line is pretty quick.'

'What do you know about Alice Sutherland?'

The car was driving slowly along the front, Heap in front with the driver, Gilchrist and Evans together in the back. On the left, a series of cheap and cheerful amusement arcades, rock and candy shops, gift shops and fish-and-chip and burger outlets, with a couple of nice cafés with tables set outside. On the right, a long stretch of sand with the tide out and a harbour with a lighthouse at the end.

'The yacht club is in the building attached to the lighthouse,' Evans said. 'They lease it from the council.'

'Alice Sutherland?' Gilchrist repeated.

Evans took a breath.

'She's a big cheese around here and in the north-east generally. Generous giver to local causes. Has a fair bit of sway with the council and the county council – she knows how to play the game. On a few tourism committees. She was very involved in getting the Tour de France to the UK, here in Yorkshire, for the first time. That earned her a lot of kudos. What are you thinking she's done?'

'Brighton had it first, Inspector Evans,' Heap said, twisting round in his seat. 'The Tour de France. Brighton council brought it over in the 1990s – cyclists went over Ditchling Beacon. Brighton's precedence seems to have got lost in the shuffle though.'

Evans grinned. 'That a fact?' Heap nodded.

'Well, it's a fact you'd best keep to yourself, detective sergeant, when you meet Ms Sutherland, or you'll find your meeting going rapidly downhill.'

'I'll bear that in mind,' Heap said, smiling back.

'This big hotel she wants to redevelop here?' Gilchrist said.

'It's back there looking down on us – you'll see it clearly from the lighthouse. Beautiful, massive place, dominates the skyline from down here on that upper part of town. She has big plans for it but so does the hotel chain that owns it. And, to be honest, I don't think Scarborough can sustain the kind of development she's talking about – not without a better infrastructure.'

'With respect, sir,' Heap said, twisting in his seat again, 'that's what they said about Margate.'

'Bellamy, isn't it, detective sergeant? Why not call me Wynn? We're less formal up here. If that's all right with you, detective inspector . . .?'

'Sarah,' Gilchrist said. 'But don't you be getting any ideas, Bellamy.'

Bellamy chuckled.

'No, ma'am.'

Evans looked at her.

'We tried that, Bellamy and me,' she said to him. 'Using my first name. Didn't work. Bellamy is just too formal. It's in his genes or something.'

'That right, Bellamy?' Evans said.

'Afraid so, sir.'

Gilchrist laughed. 'See what I mean?'

The car had gone round the small harbour by now and pulled onto a narrow causeway running between boat docks and heading for the lighthouse at the far end. There were nowhere near as many boats in here as in Brighton Marina – and no big ones – but there were fishing boats and larger vessels to take tourists out to sea with a couple of drinks and a barbecue thrown in.

'You'll have to explain to me about Margate another time, Bellamy,' Evans said as the car stopped just before a short bridge from the dock to the lighthouse complex.

'Happy to do so, sir.'

The lighthouse was small – some fifty feet high – and was attached to a double-storey rectangular building. Evans led the way to a low door at the near end of the building. He opened it.

'Commodore!' he called. 'Commodore?'

'Come aboard, Wynn,' a strong female voice from the floor above called back.

Evans led the way up a short flight of stairs to a long bar with a balcony over the yachts on the left. A porthole at the far end seemed to peek through into a small circular space in the lighthouse proper.

A woman in her mid-thirties was sitting on a stool at the bar. She was the only person in the room. Her skirt was perfectly tailored, her tan lacquered, her shins shiny with close shaving. She stood and smoothed down her close-fitting skirt and gave a little tug to her fitted cropped jacket.

Gilchrist was a bit of a middle-of-the-night-boxset woman, thanks to Netflix. She recognized that the Commodore's style – haircut, clothes and tightly packed look – was based entirely on the *House of Cards* character Claire Underwood, played by Robin Wright. But far browner – northern-style brown.

The Commodore flicked her blonde hair as she clacked over in tall high heels. Her smile was whiter than white. As usual in the company of slender women, Gilchrist felt like a heifer.

'Alice Sutherland,' the woman said, extending her hand. Gilchrist took it and introduced herself and Heap. Sutherland disengaged and hugged Evans, air-kissing him.

'So?' she said, scanning the three of them.

'Commodore?' Gilchrist said.

'Honorary title for whoever is chair of the yacht club,' Sutherland said, gesturing to a table for four. 'I do have a motor yacht out there but I'm not qualified in any way to sail boats. Would you like a drink?'

A man appeared from out of the shadows behind the bar.

'This is Billy,' Sutherland said. 'He's our steward.'

'Quiet tonight,' Gilchrist said to him smiling pleasantly. She saw Evans look down with a small smile on his face.

'Closed tonight,' Billy said, walking back to the bar to fill their orders.

Gilchrist looked at Sutherland.

'Perks of the job,' Sutherland said.

'We're here to talk about Roland Gulliver,' Heap said. Gilchrist looked at him. He was being abrupt but she understood why.

Sutherland looked at him too. 'Don't know him, detective sergeant.'

'He was murdered the other night,' Heap said.

'I'm sorry to hear that but I still don't know him,' Sutherland said, crossing her shiny legs. 'Is that why we're here?'

'He was involved with the Save Salthaven Lido campaign,' Gilchrist said.

Sutherland frowned and leaned forward from the waist, very straight-backed. Gilchrist instinctively straightened up.

'I'm still no wiser,' Sutherland said.

'Salthaven Lido is a place you're trying to buy and develop just outside Brighton,' Heap said. 'That's why we're here.'

There was something in Heap's tone Sutherland took exception to. All warmth and smiles a moment ago, she hardened her expression.

'As we speak I'm trying to buy and develop around fifty properties, *detective sergeant*, so forgive me if I can't immediately remember one of them.'

Heap was looking at the table as he said: 'Understood, Ms Sutherland. Perhaps you recall your involvement with a West Pier project in Brighton. In partnership with William Simpson? Among all your other projects?'

Gilchrist looked at Heap sharply. What the hell was this? William Simpson? The shitty, corrupt father of Kate. She looked at Evans, who was looking down at the table, perhaps embarrassed by the change of tone.

'Your point is?' Sutherland said coldly.

'Your focus on Brighton and its environs,' Heap said.

Sutherland recrossed her legs. She addressed Gilchrist not Heap.

'As I said, I have many projects. But this swimming pool you mentioned . . .?'

'Did you have any dealings with a Roland Gulliver?' Gilchrist said.

'My business team or my lawyers may have done but I really don't know. The name doesn't ring a bell.'

'I understood you to be very hands on with all your projects,' Heap said. Gilchrist glanced at him. He might appear shy but he was a persistent little bugger.

Sutherland looked at her perfectly manicured hands. 'Usually.'

'But not in this instance?'

'Brighton went . . . sour for me.'

'In what way?'

Sutherland glanced at Evans. 'Do I really have to talk about this stuff?'

She wasn't particularly addressing him but he gave a little shrug and looked across at Gilchrist. Sutherland looked back at her.

'I mean, you want to know about this Roland Gulliver, don't you? And I've said I never had any dealings with him. I don't see why you need to know anything else.'

'A murder inquiry needs to cast its net wide, Ms Sutherland; it's not immediately apparent what is and is not relevant.'

Sutherland stood.

'Talk to Philip Coates. He headed up our Brighton team. But anything else you want to ask me should be done in the presence of my lawyer.'

Gilchrist stood too, enjoying towering over this

perfect-looking bloody woman, despite the additional six inches Sutherland's heels gave her.

'Is there a reason you would require your lawyer to be present?' Gilchrist said.

'I understood that to be my right,' Sutherland said. 'But perhaps you're concerned because I have very good lawyers.'

Evans had stood too but was still looking down – at the ground now. Heap was taking his time.

Gilchrist locked eyes with Alice Sutherland. 'I know they get a bad press from crap newspapers but I'd match the Crown Prosecution Service against the best you can muster anytime. I repeat: this is a murder enquiry.'

'What are you up to, Bellamy?' Gilchrist said as she hung back from Evans on the causeway back to the promenade. 'Do you think you might have warned me about William Simpson?'

'She's not involved,' Heap said.

'And you know this how?' Gilchrist said. 'Policeman's intuition? At what stage did you segue into Inspector Morse?'

'The fact she had no idea what the Salthaven thing was,' Heap said. 'That's when I realized she was not involved.'

'You really think she doesn't? You mean it really is just one of her projects?'

Heap nodded.

'Then we've had a bit of a wasted journey.'

'Not necessarily. This West Pier–William Simpson thing . . .'

'Yes, thanks for the heads up about that.'

54

'Sorry – I'd looked at Company House records and his name popped up.'

'And you went into Defend Kate mode. The penny has dropped.'

'Not exactly. But it means there's something else going on that isn't to do with this case that we should look at in due course.'

'OK,' Gilchrist said as they stopped by the police car that had brought them there. 'But let's talk to this Philip Coates, shall we?'

They had time for a quick dinner in an Italian restaurant at the harbour edge. As night fell and lights winked on over the water, Gilchrist thought it looked quite magical.

Evans hadn't joined them. He'd been rather stiff with them, probably because of whatever dealings Sutherland had with the local authorities. Nothing illegal, just the usual mutual backs-cratching. It worked the same way in Brighton but Gilchrist never got directly involved. That was more the job for Karen Hewitt. Gilchrist idly wondered if Bob Watts was now obliged to do that in his new role of police commissioner. She couldn't see it. He was too upright.

'So we should leave Sutherland alone?' Gilchrist said. Heap had his mouth full of pasta so took a moment.

'For this, I think so. I see no reason to think she's the hiring-a-hit-man type.'

'You *are* using intuition, Bellamy!'

Heap pushed his pasta round on his plate.

'Possibly, ma'am. It just seems unlikely to me that anyone mischievous enough to pull that stunt with the advertising hoarding in front of her ex-husband's office would also be ruthless enough to have someone killed. I'm sure she's tough as nails, as we saw, but she uses her brain, her nous, to sort stuff.' He picked up another forkful of food. 'In my opinion, ma'am.'

Gilchrist was eating Caesar salad. She chomped on it for a bit thinking about what Heap had said.

'Wasted journey, then,' she decided. 'You'll still call Philip Coates tomorrow?'

Heap nodded and looked at his watch. Gilchrist followed suit.

'We'd better hustle if we want to get that train back.'

'We could always stay over, ma'am.'

Gilchrist gave him a mock-shocked look. 'Is that a proposition, detective sergeant?'

Heap, inevitably, flushed.

York station was echoey and deserted when they arrived back there. A few sleepy people were on the platform for the last London train. Gilchrist was pretty sleepy herself. She slept until Peterborough. When she woke, Heap was looking out of the window at the black night but his hands were resting on his keypad.

'Never stop working, Bellamy?' she said, her voice a little thick.

'Just catching up on William Simpson – he's one of the backers for the West Pier project that lost out to i360.'

'I thought he was a globe-trotting international consultant on peace now?'

56

'He spins bad news for oppressive dictator-ships,' Heap said. 'Not sure that constitutes advocating for peace.'

'What do you know about Simpson?'

'That he's Kate's dad and was somehow involved with events around the Milldean Massacre before my time in Brighton. That he was a big friend of Bob Watts before he turned Mr Watts over. His wife left him for reasons she has never shared with Kate. The rest I only know from newspapers.'

'Did you know I was part of the armed response unit involved in the killings in Milldean?'

Heap nodded. 'You were exonerated.'

Gilchrist sighed. 'And I still don't know what really happened.' She sat up and leaned across the table between them. 'You think we should be looking at William Simpson?'

'For this stabbing? I don't think so. But he's probably dirty, don't you think?'

Gilchrist nodded. 'But he's not our focus now. We need to focus entirely on who stabbed Roland Gulliver to death. Thoughts? Do you think it was random?'

'Unlikely with the partial drowning first.'

'What about his ex-wife?' Gilchrist said.

'Well, she's on the list to interview.'

Gilchrist nodded and looked out of the window but as it was so dark saw only her reflection. She grimaced and turned away. She didn't much like herself at the moment.

Heap was watching her. She swore that some-times he knew exactly what she was thinking.

'So . . . Kate and the Channel?' she said, to

change what she thought might be the unspoken subject.

'Yes – it's stupid, isn't it?' he said. 'I can't imagine anything worse. But Bob Watts is doing it too.'

'He would,' Gilchrist said. 'He has that Iron Man thing going on.'

Heap nodded slowly. 'Seems a waste of energy to me.'

Gilchrist stretched a little in her seat. 'To me too, Bellamy. To me too.'

Five

'How are you feeling about this, Kate?' Police Commissioner Bob Watts looked down at the young woman standing beside him, muffled up in a bright blue tracksuit. She had a towel wrapped round her neck and her hair scraped back.

Kate Simpson looked out from the jetty in front of the Bluebird Café up the length of Lake Coniston. She couldn't see the far end of the lake, over five miles away, and the nearest end was concealed behind the tree-fringed bay to the left of the café.

'Terrified,' she said.

'It's warm, at least,' Watts said.

'For the first hour,' she said. 'I've got two and half hours more to go after that. Possibly longer. This is my longest swim by far.'

Watts looked over at the board propped against

the near wall of the octagonal boat hire office. *Dolphin Smile Coniston Free Swim.*

Dolphin Smile was the name of the commercial swimming set-up that had organized this July race the length of Lake Coniston, the pretty stretch of water at the south end of the Lake District National Park. Since it was a commercial enterprise, the 'free' simply referred to the style of swimming and what Watts jokingly referred to as 'the dress code'. Two-thirds of the fifty or so swimmers gathered at nine this extremely sunny morning for the pre-race briefing were probably going to be swimming as near to *au naturel* as decency would allow. Including Watts and Kate.

But that still left about a third already in wetsuits or in the thigh-length rubber trunks and armless rubber tops that triathletes wore in competition.

A muscular man with a lined, tanned face, a hipster beard and dirty-blonde hair cropped high on his head, was standing near the placard talking to a fine-featured, statuesque woman. Her blonde hair was long enough to reach her waist. Both were well into their fifties, Watts reckoned.

He'd met them briefly at the registration desk: Derek and Rasa Neill, co-owners of Dolphin Smile. The registration fee was £100 per swimmer so the race, one of thirty or so they did each year on rivers and lakes in the UK and abroad, wasn't a bad little earner. The swimmers also had to pay a fee to their boat people of £150 each and Watts guessed Dolphin Smile got a cut from that.

'I'll never do it in three and a half hours,' Kate Simpson said. 'I'll get disqualified.'

'You're not here for the race,' Watts said. 'Which is going to be a bit of a joke anyway with all these people in wetsuits floating along and all the different strokes people will be doing. You're here to swim the distance as part of your training. And if it takes you four hours or even longer that's great too. It will show that you can swim for that length of time.'

Simpson gave a little shiver. 'I'll be all right once I get in.'

'Of course you will,' Watts said. 'I've seen you swim for three hours in the Serpentine and you're going to do six hours in Brighton Bay next week. This is the perfect intermediate distance.'

He pointed across to the car park beside the café. 'And it looks like your kayak man has arrived. Good-looking guy that Liam.'

They both looked across to a tanned, fit-looking young man in dark glasses, who flashed a white-toothed smile as he raised his hand in a lazy wave.

'I only have eyes for Bellamy,' Simpson said. Then she obviously clocked the man's biceps. 'Mind you . . .'

Watts laughed and looked for Eric, his own kayak man, among the vans with roof racks arriving in procession down the narrow road from Coniston town centre.

Watts looked around the other swimmers gathered by the lakeside, some in dappled tree-shade, others in the bright sunlight. Mostly younger than him; mostly fit looking. He glanced down at Kate, her face pink, overheating in her tracksuit.

'You'd better slather yourself with sun lotion before you get in,' he said.

She grinned up at him. 'Yes, Dad.'

Watts smiled back. He thought but didn't say: not dad but uncle. Kate didn't know that her father, William Simpson, was not only Watts' erstwhile friend, he was also Watts's half-brother, since they shared the same promiscuous father. Watts himself had found out only by chance and decided that, on balance, it was a bit late in the day to say anything about it to Kate. However, in consequence, he kept a fond eye on her.

It was sheer coincidence that both of them had made the decision to swim the Channel. Kate was a keen scuba diver, he knew that, but he hadn't quite got to the bottom of why she had decided to aim for the Channel, which was something very different.

He and Kate needed to train hard if they were to stand any chance of making a successful crossing. A Channel swim was going to take somewhere between eleven and twenty hours depending on stroke rate, currents and weather conditions.

Since wetsuits or any other aid to maintaining body temperature were strictly forbidden, it involved getting used to cold water. They had done some cold-water training together a few early mornings in the chilly spring waters of Pells Pool in Lewes, a few miles outside Brighton. They were more or less the same speed. Although Kate was only half his size she had a faster stroke rate than his own long, seemingly lazy, stroke. He'd been finding it quite companionable swimming more or less alongside her.

Bellamy Heap had joined them once. Watts liked the intelligent young man and, insofar as he thought about such things, approved of the match they had made. He thought Heap that rare thing: a person of integrity. Swimming wasn't his forte though and he'd done a painful-looking few lengths of breaststroke, his head held stiffly out of the water, before leaving the pool, shivering and slump-shouldered.

Once the briefing was over, the four of them got in Watts's Saab convertible and he drove them up the west side of the lake to the point where the kayaks had been beached. It was a narrow, winding road, the water glittering through the trees to the left, the sun lancing down through the gaps in the tree canopy above their heads.

The kayakers were laconic men and Kate kept her eyes fixed on the lake. Watts focused on the road and the oncoming camper vans and caravans spreading over into his lane.

Once they arrived, he and Kate stripped to their costumes, handing their clothes to their kayakers to be put in dry bags. They took turns to spray suntan lotion on. Both were doing front crawl so focused particularly on their backs, necks and legs. Then they applied Vaseline to prevent chafing under their arms and at the base of the neck where the edge of the swimming cap might rub. Watts turned away to apply it to himself between his legs where, on a long swim, tight trunks – the only kind allowed – were definitely a chafing problem.

He'd read that Captain Webb had coated himself in porpoise fat to stave off the cold and had assumed Channel swimmers these days still lathered themselves with all kinds of fat or grease.

But, no, that wasn't allowed as insulation although it could be used in spots to prevent chafing. It was messy though, as was lanolin. So most swimmers used Vaseline to stop sores developing.

Aside from that it was just the basic swimming costume, a single thin rubber hat and ear plugs. As Tingley had indicated, Channel swimmers deliberately put on weight to resist the cold.

On the short journey in the light craft across to the starting point Watts and Kate put in their ear plugs and fitted tight swimming caps. Watts didn't much care for ear plugs as they caused a weird acoustic effect inside his head on every breath but they were essential to keep the cold out. He trailed his goggles in the water to clean them, then placed them carefully over his eyes, trying not to smear the lenses with his fingers.

He looked down into the water. It was surprisingly clear and he could see the layers of shale and stone and rock at the bottom. He knew it was much deeper away from the shores, though it was by no means the deepest lake in Cumbria. That honour went to Wastwater, over in the west of the national park, at some eighty metres deep.

He spent a moment putting that into old money – around 260 feet, he reckoned – because although he was the metric generation, the army had worked on feet and inches too during his time with it.

Who knew what bodies had been dumped in the Wastwater depths over the years? One wife-murderer, he knew, had been found out years later when his wife's body was recovered thanks to a shelf of rock sticking out quite some way from the shore on one side of Wastwater lake. Instead of sinking to the bottom of the lake her body had lodged on this ledge in relatively shallow water and a fisherman had snagged her remains.

Watts remembered from his policing days that Coniston itself had been the favoured dumping ground of Manchester drug gangs in the seventies for rivals' dead bodies. He knew too that at some point today he'd be swimming over or near the place where Donald Campbell's Bluebird had crashed and killed him during his fatal attempt on the water speed record back in 1967.

Many years later the boat and Campbell's body had been found and brought to the surface. Watts had read that the boat was in a boatyard somewhere round Newcastle being slowly put back together.

Coniston had no tide or current as it was not a sufficiently large body of water. There was a breeze that ruffled the surface of the water but it came from behind him. He'd been warned that while the water was generally warm there were cold areas where water was entering the lake from the many feeder streams that originated high in the mountains.

Watts pulled his swimming cap down over the top part of the rubber surround of his goggles to secure them and saw Kate in the other boat do the same. Then they both dropped into the water.

The fifty swimmers were starting at noon from a narrow spit of land. Each swimmer was supposed to be two metres from his or her boat but at the starting point it was simply a melee, with boats and swimmers all too close together. Although he and Kate were not swimming as a team both had decided to start strongly to get clear of the crush then settle down into an easy pace.

Neither one was interested in winning; they just wanted to test their mettle in the longest swim either had so far done.

When the whistle blew there was chaos: boats and swimmers jostling for space. After some ten minutes Watts could see ahead that there were around half a dozen swimmers pulling well away from the pack. There was something hypnotic about the sight. All were doing front crawl, as was he, which meant, when he was looking ahead every couple of minutes, all he could see were elbows rising from the water and falling back in with unvarying rhythm.

His own rhythm was the same. Left elbow raised high close to his left ear, long arm stretching and stiff hand sliding down into the water and pushing the water behind him as he raised his right elbow to his ear. He breathed on alternate sides with his face in the water. He came up for air every four or five strokes.

Where he was weak was in scissoring his legs and fluttering his feet. He'd never been able to get a regular rhythm back there, so his legs often trailed in the water. Still, he knew that most of the movement came from shoulders and arms.

Watts couldn't see Kate since her kayak was between them but as it kept level with him and his kayak he assumed she too was keeping pace with him.

The water was warm and calm and he eased

into a steady pace he felt he could keep up all day. He stopped for a quick feed after two hours. Eric reached down from the kayak with the sports flask full of energy drink and Watts downed it in one, bobbing in the water because he'd be disqualified if he steadied himself on – or even touched – the kayak. Kate's kayak was about ten yards behind but was closing in. He handed the flask back to Eric, neither man speaking, and resumed his swim.

He reached the beach at the north end of the lake in just over three and a half hours. He was fifteenth to finish. He looked back but Kate's kayak was still some way out. One of the stewards assured him that her slow progress was not because of the death of another competitor halfway along the lake.

Kate Simpson had been thrown by the opening throng of swimmers so it took her a while to find her rhythm. Then her goggles started leaking so she had to signal to Liam and have him throw her the spares. She didn't know where Bob was as Liam's kayak was between them but she imagined that he was way ahead of her already.

The new goggles didn't leak but nor did they keep the sun from blinding her. Now she couldn't settle because she couldn't see where she was going. She could dimly hear through her ear plugs that Liam was calling to her when she went off course. She was startled when his head suddenly appeared almost next to hers. She stopped swimming and looked at him. He had brought the kayak up close and was leaning over one side to

66

get his face near to hers. He sat straight again as the kayak tipped.

He pointed at her ears and mimed taking her ear plugs out. She fumbled with her ears, irritated at the hold-up.

'It's warm enough that you don't need the plugs,' he shouted. 'And I need you to hear me because you're zigzagging all over the place.'

She nodded and dropped the silicone plugs in his open hand.

'I'm zigzagging because the sun is blinding me – these goggles don't have filters.'

'Just listen to me and watch my signals when you do diverge. You're pulling more powerfully with your right arm – try to even it out more.'

She nodded and glanced at her watch. 'Feed in seventy-five minutes.'

He nodded. 'Get going.'

She set off and established a kind of rhythm. She knew she was a powerful swimmer when she wanted to be and she hoped to make up lost ground. She wasn't interested in beating Bob but she quite liked swimming alongside him on the occasions they had swum together.

She liked to plan and remember and work through things when she swam. She'd come up to Coniston pissed off about Simon, with whom she worked at Southern Shores, Brighton's local radio station. Her powder puff job had changed little after the successful documentary she'd done about the Brighton Trunk Murder. She was still producing and acting as the on-air foil for *Simon Says*, the station's popular but moronic breakfast show.

Simon was a bright guy and very quick-witted but he was irredeemably trivial. That was fine for the breakfast show but she'd tried to get him to do other stuff and he just wasn't interested. It was so frustrating.

She'd pitched an idea for a piece about homophobic gays, specifically gays who were homophobic when it came to camp. She'd heard a very camp TV celebrity say that he got the most homophobic comments from other gays. Simon said no to the piece – although, to be fair, so did the station.

She was in a dilemma. She wanted to do harder news but realistically that meant working for the BBC at a national level. And that raised the possibility people would assume she'd got there through nepotism.

She loathed nepotism. That was why she'd chosen to work for Southern Shores rather than allow her father, former spin doctor William Simpson, to use his influence to get her a job at a national station or on the television.

That wasn't so much of an issue now since his fall from political grace with the change of government several years earlier but he was still seen as some sinister Machiavellian figure.

Which he was. William Simpson, arch-manipulator. He was in international public relations now but his links seemed to be with dodgy regimes that were all about war and suppressing their own citizens. Are you an autocrat and want to gloss over cynically invading some neighbouring state or handing over billion-dollar industries to your cronies? William Simpson is your man.

She avoided seeing him and when she did they argued. It wasn't much better with her mother. She knew that as a daughter she was *supposed* to have issues with her mother but her mother was something else. There was no warmth in her at all. Especially since she had split from Kate's father.

Kate's mother lived in Brighton now, which made things more complicated. It was easy for Kate not to see her father since he was jetting all over the world but she had to make at least a token effort to see her mother. Not that her mother took any interest in anything she did – except how much she was eating.

Perhaps that was why Kate had decided to swim the Channel. She was fed up with being nagged about her weight. Because the unique thing about athletes who signed up to swim the Channel is that they had to put on weight – fat, that is – to be able to achieve this incredible endurance feat in chilly water.

Kate wondered if she should be talking to someone about her utterly conflicted emotions about her parents. Someone other than Bellamy. She'd read enough popular psychology books and articles in trash women's magazines to recognize that bringing Bellamy so quickly into her life was because she had never got the love she needed from her parents. Or maybe it was because he was so sweet.

She looked up and Liam was making the five-minute gesture with his open hand. She looked at her watch. Five minutes to her feed.

The training was also helping her to deal with

something that had happened pretty recently when she had made a pre-work pilgrimage to the part of Brighton cemetery where the remains of the victim of the first Brighton Trunk Murder were buried. This part of the graveyard had been allowed to grow back. The victim was in a grid of unmarked graves under long grass and thistles.

Nearby there were two dogs fornicating, stuck together post-sex, bum to bum. There was what looked horribly like a raven stalking across the graves. And magpies. Lots of magpies.

The male dog uncoupled from the bitch and ran off chasing another, yelping and barking. Kate heard jeering young voices and saw a half a dozen teenagers, boys and girls around fourteen, in a kind of shelter about twenty yards away. They were all smoking.

One of the boys, in a crumpled grey hoodie, grabbed one of the girls by her left breast and squeezed. 'Do you think that bitch was taking it up the arse like you do, the way they were stuck together?'

'Piss off,' the girl said, trying to wriggle free. As she did she saw Kate watching them. 'What's she frigging looking at?'

They all turned and the boy released her breast, spying fresh meat. Kate saw them start towards her. She was frozen to the spot. There was no one else anywhere near her. She took out her phone and speed-dialled the first number that came up.

She held it to her ear and waited for it to ring. Nothing. As the teenagers came close she said into the mouthpiece, 'Hi, is that Detective Inspector Gilchrist at police HQ?'

The boy in the hoodie circled round her. As she half turned the girl he'd assaulted grabbed Kate's shoulder bag. Kate was trying to wrestle it back when she felt a stiff hand go up her skirt from behind and thrust hard between her legs. She heard the boy's jeering laugh. Another boy, who looked about twelve, grabbed at her skirt and pulled it up. Kate tried to hold it down with her free hand.

She could hear the phone start to ring but someone grabbed it from her. The girl had her bag now as Kate reached back to get the boy's wrist and move his hand away. She was conscious she was only wearing a thong as the person who'd taken her phone started to take photos of the hoodie boy's fingers rummaging between her legs.

She tugged herself free but fell as she did so. They stood over her, screeching and yelling, dragging at her clothes and filming her. Two girls were tearing at her blouse and somebody must have had a knife because suddenly the boy in the hoodie was waving her thong in the air and her legs were being forced apart.

She thought they were going to gang rape her and it might have been in their minds but first they were thrusting their camera phones between her legs. And then she heard two men bellowing from the path below.

'You lot – what the hell do you think you're doing?'

And the girl grabbed her purse and address

71

book from her bag then dropped the bag and they all ran off up the hill, whooping and yelling, as the two men came near and she tugged her skirt down for at least some decency.

Kate spluttered and came up for air, swiping her goggles off her head and turning on her back to catch her breath.

'What are you doing? What's wrong?' Liam called.

She waved a vague arm at him. *Nothing*, she thought but probably didn't say. 'Just need a moment,' she called. She gasped for breath and then waved again. Took her time regulating her breathing, ignoring Liam's shouts.

She turned onto her front again. She was back on track. More or less.

Kate's longest swim so far had been three hours but the following weekend she was aiming to do six hours in another Dolphin Smile event in Brighton Bay. The rules of the Channel swimming governing body – the Channel Swimming & Pilot's Federation – required a six-hour swim in water with a maximum temperature of 16°C to qualify for swimming the channel. Relay swimmers had to swim two hours in the same conditions.

Six hours in cold water. Reluctantly she had committed to putting on more weight. One of the experienced swimmers, Dan, had explained it to her as she stood shivering on the beach in Dover.

'The ratio of surface area to volume is crucial. The bigger your body the more heat you retain. But if you have a big frame but are skinny, heat is gained and lost quickly. There is lots of surface area to gain heat but not much volume to retain it.' He pointed at her. 'You're a bit on the short side so you're going to have to put on a bit of weight if hypothermia isn't going to be a massive problem for you.'

Liam was holding out her flask with an anxious expression on his face.

'What?' she said as she took it and peered into it.

'When I opened your big flask to pour into this all the glass inside was broken.'

'But I only bought it yesterday from that mountaineering shop!' Kate held the flask up to the sun, looking for fragments of glass.

'I don't have a sieve or even a thin cloth so I've picked the glass out as best I can.'

Kate took a sip of her energy drink – blackcurrant mixed with Maxim. As it went down she felt something catch at her throat but she didn't know if she was imagining it. She took another cautious sip and held the warm liquid in her mouth, swirling it around, trying to feel any bits of glass. There didn't seem to be any but all the same she spat it out into the lake and handed the flask back to him.

'You didn't bring anything yourself?' she said.

'I'm really sorry,' he said. 'You said you'd provide your own feed. I have some water.'

'I like something warm.' She shook her head. 'OK, I'm going to have to do the whole swim without a feed.'

'You'll be fine,' he said.

'Sure,' she said. But didn't believe it.

She spent the next ten minutes oscillating

between telling herself she could do it without the feed and telling herself she couldn't. She spent a little time blaming Liam for the broken flask, deciding he must have thrown it into the bottom of the kayak and broken it.

Then she thought about what Dan, the experienced distance swimmer in the shop she'd bought the drinks from, had said about energy drinks when he handed over a plastic storage box full of the stuff.

'Maltodrextrin is the important bit of the Maxim. It's a polymer of glucose – glucose is the monomer unit and on its own is rapidly absorbed.'

'Hang on,' Kate said. 'There are a couple of things I don't quite understand in that.'

'Which things?'

'All of it.'

Dan showed his teeth and waved his hand.

'All glucose quickly enters glycolysis which just means it allows quick energy production. That's why glucose is the favourite carbohydrate source for athletes doing intense, short activities. But it is a short-term fix. Long-distance swimmers like you need something else. If you can polymerize glucose it slows everything down – rate of absorption, metabolism – which gives you longer, sustained energy.'

'And that's Maxim?'

'It is and I think it's the best. The molecules of glucose are smaller than in other drinks so dissolve easier in your drink of choice.'

Kate didn't feel she needed to admit she didn't really know what a molecule was. And certainly not 'polymerize'.

'Mixing the complex carbohydrates in Maxim with a sugary fruit drink – which comprises simple carbohydrates – gives you an instant hit from the sugar but then longer energy too. The mixture also helps a swimmer keep the food down. If swimmers can handle nothing but complex carbs in the course of a long swim good for them but if keeping food down is a problem the simple carbohydrate in the mix at least gives fast nutrition so they don't bonk.'

'Bonk?' Kate said, smiling.

'Different meaning,' Dan said. 'Conk out. And you're still going to do it if you miss your feeds but at least it will be later rather than sooner.'

Kate didn't feel she was going to conk out but after another hour she was zigzagging more, if Liam's shouting was anything to go by. She knew that was partly because she was swimming with her eyes closed on account of the sun, partly because when she got tired her strokes got choppy and uneven.

She went through a cold stretch of water that really chilled her so she tried to go faster to keep her body heated. That just tired her even more.

She realized she was focusing on her physical discomfort to the detriment of her progress. She forced herself to think about something else. She'd seen two white-tailed deer that morning in the grounds of the posh house Bob had rented an apartment in for the weekend. A doe and her fawn, the fawn scampering across the grass then skittering back to her mother when rabbits came out to play.

Kate always thought of the lakes in terms of

quaint old cottages and pubs – low wooden beams and log fires and creaky floorboards. Bob had insisted on paying for their accommodation and she had let him, on the grounds he was rolling in it. And instead of a cottage he had chosen an apartment in a converted Georgian house on a hilltop.

'People forget the Lakes have always attracted the wealthy,' he explained. 'It'll make a change to see a bit of that.'

Kate's left shoulder was beginning to ache so she made a conscious effort to straighten her stroke. A swimming coach had advised her that each arm should go out in a straight line in front of her, the left arm being the ten and the right arm the two on a clock. She knew that when she got tired her right arm strayed in front of her head, sending her veering off to the left.

She jerked her foot reflexively as it brushed against something or something brushed against her. She assumed there were carp and other big fish in here but she didn't worry about what might be swimming beneath her. The jellyfish in the Channel worried her though. She knew it was irrational but she couldn't help it.

Dan had tried to reassure her.

'There isn't a real problem with jellyfish,' he said. 'It's rare that a swimmer gets stung. Even if you do get stung it's not going to hurt you. You'll just get a blister. It's more of a psychological worry.'

'What if you're allergic?' Kate said.

'Well, then you might get cramp or be sick or maybe have a heart attack.' He saw her expression. 'But hardly anyone is allergic to them.'

'Isn't there another sort of deadly one in a Sherlock Holmes story?' Kate said.

'You read Sherlock Holmes? You mean the lion's mane jellyfish? Yes. It has very long trailing tentacles – around three metres – and a nasty sting that can cause muscle paralysis. They can be found in the English Channel but I don't know any swimmer who has ever encountered one.'

Kate glanced up at Liam. He was signalling five minutes again with his hand. She squinted ahead through the sun's glare and could make out a narrow beach on the shoreline. A group of people were gathered there.

She hadn't looked at her watch for a while. She didn't intend to until she was on the beach but she figured she had taken almost four hours, which would be her longest swim to date. Since she'd done it without a feed she was pretty pleased with herself. Not too pleased, though, because this was just the start.

'A six-hour swim is your qualifier for the Channel,' Dan had told her. 'But don't think you can stop there. That's just the start, the easy part, when you're actually swimming the Channel. That's going to take you somewhere between twelve and sixteen hours.'

Kate scraped her knee on a rock beneath her. She looked up and around. She could hear scattered applause. It was for her. She got to her feet unevenly, not exactly Venus emerging from the foam, and pulled off her goggles. Liam was sitting in his kayak, beaming at her and applauding. Bob was front and centre on the shore, already in shorts, T-shirt and Crocs.

He stepped forward, her Dryrobe held open for her. She loved the long, towelling-lined, hooded robe for keeping her warm after a cold swim, even though it made her look like a boxer about to step into the ring.

Bob waded into the shallows in his Crocs and put the robe over her shoulders. He put his arm round her and leaned down.

'Three hours fifty-two minutes, Ms Simpson. Well done.'

'Piece of cake,' she said with a shaky laugh.

He looked at her. 'You OK?' he said.

'I haven't had a feed!' she wailed, laughing at the same time. Watts looked across at Liam.

Liam nodded. 'Flask broke,' he said.

'I've got feed – and food – in my bag,' Watts said.

'Jelly Babies?' Kate said, and she and Watts both laughed. Jelly Babies were the great indulgence for Channel swimmers, held out as a lure by tough trainers for a job well done. For reasons of speed and efficiency liquid food was preferred but as a treat a couple of Jelly Babies were the thing as they were relatively easy to ingest. Others preferred half a banana or a mini-roll or a small Milky Way – all with energy drinks, of course.

'The applause sounded a bit half-hearted,' Kate murmured. 'Am I the last?'

'Not at all,' Bob murmured back. 'I think there's an eight-year-old kid doing breaststroke, an eighty-year-old doing backstroke and a dead person.'

She started to laugh but he leaned closer to her.

'That was a dreadful thing to say – there actually is a dead person.'

78

'One of the swimmers?'

Bob nodded. 'Heart attack probably. Occupational hazard of these long swims. A guy called Philip Coates.'

By now they were at Bob's small pile of things. He rummaged in his bag and came up with a feed bottle in one hand. In the palm of his other were two Jelly Babies.

'Well done, Kate,' he said, an unusually fond look on his face. She grinned and gave him a hug, but not before grabbing the Jelly Babies and popping them in her mouth.

Six

There was a bit of ferrying to and fro as Watts drove Liam and Eric back to get their vans so they could put their kayaks on board. Then all four rendezvoused for a celebratory drink in one of the pubs in the centre of Coniston. It was still hot so they sat outside but in the shade of the building.

Liam had a shandy, Eric a pint of local beer, Kate a lime and lemonade and Watts a pint of cider. After the congratulations, conversation was muted.

'The guy who had the heart attack was a friend of Derek and Rasa's,' Liam said. 'Perfectly fit, came out of the blue.'

'They know for certain it was a heart attack?' Watts said.

Kate gave him a look. She turned to Liam.

'Bob used to be a chief constable and now he's a police commissioner – he sees crime everywhere.'

'Hey,' Watts said, 'I didn't mean there was anything suspicious about it. I'm a pen-pusher not an investigator. I just meant: might it have been something else?'

'Heart attack is favourite,' Eric said. 'It happens with mountaineering up here too. Otherwise fit people – often extremely fit to a certain level – put unusual strain on their hearts and suddenly an undiagnosed heart condition kiboshes them. Happens a dozen times a year.'

'It's never happened to me with a swimmer,' Liam said.

'I'm relieved to hear it,' Kate said.

Liam smiled at her and Watts saw her look down. Watts wasn't interested in anyone's sex life – especially his own pretty disastrous one – but he knew that Kate's had been complex. Women and men both. He was pleased about her new connection to Bellamy Heap but he wasn't going to be judgemental if she was drawn to Liam. He imagined most women would be attracted to him.

He was on the back foot when it came to judgements after the way he'd betrayed his wife, Molly, with Sarah Gilchrist. The start of the undoing of what he had complacently assumed was going to be a stellar career.

After half an hour, Liam and Eric went their own ways, each a couple of hundred pounds richer and a couple of drinks heavier. Watts drove Kate back to the apartment he'd rented. It was just outside a village called Scarsland.

It was a warm evening and the breeze that ruffled their hair was pleasing.

'Sure you've got enough glue on the toupee, Bob?' Kate said, a mischievous smile on her face when he glanced across at her.

He tried to give her the finger with his left hand as he steered with it but that went a bit askew, as did the car. She laughed.

'I'm not interested in Liam,' she said a couple of minutes later.

'None of my business,' he said, watching the curves on the road.

'No, it's not,' she said. 'But I'm just saying. Bob, I'm not sure you understand the dynamics of relationships between young people.'

'Undoubtedly true,' Watts said, the thought of his daughter involved with a fundamentalist Christian vicar flashing across his mind.

'I'm with Bellamy and I'm not going to risk messing that up. No, not just that – I'm not remotely interested in anyone else, because I'm with Bellamy, however much someone's biceps flex.'

'OK,' Watts said. 'You don't have to explain.'

'I know,' Kate said. Then, after a moment. 'Great biceps though.'

'Indeed they are,' Watts said as they pulled into the drive of the Georgian house they were staying in. There was a car just ahead of them and two people getting out. Derek and Rasa.

'The Dolphin Smile people,' Watts said as he pulled onto the gravel of their designated parking space.

'Who?' Kate said, distracted by looking for something in her bag.

Derek and Rasa looked across at them as they got out of the Saab. Kate gave a half-wave.

'Sorry to hear the news,' he called.

Rasa turned away but Derek gave a half-grimace, half-smile. 'He was a good friend,' he called. Then both went into the house.

Watts fiddled with the stuff in the boot until he figured Derek and Rasa were inside their apartment. Then he and Kate went in.

Their apartment was on the top floor. Getting up the stairs was taxing for both of them.

'I'm going to have a shower,' Kate said the minute they were through the door.

'Cocktails in twenty?' Watts asked.

'Passed out on the couch in thirty?' Kate said over her shoulder as she went towards her room. 'Actually, I'm going to lie down for an hour or so – drinks later?'

Watts showered and changed then went into the kitchen and got a bottle of Prosecco out of the fridge. He was easing the cork out when the doorbell chimed. Frowning he walked down the corridor, bottle in hand.

Derek Neill was standing in the hallway. 'Didn't mean to be rude earlier,' he said. 'I was wondering if you would like a drink.' He looked at the bottle. 'But it seems you've got that in hand.'

Watts waved the bottle and stepped aside. 'Join

82

me, please.' He looked out into the corridor. 'Rasa?'

Neill shook his head. 'She's taken to her bed. He was more her friend than mine.'

'Heart attack?' Watts said as they walked into the living room.

'I assume,' Neill said, stopping as he saw the view out of the ceiling-to-floor window. 'Shit, this place is far better than ours.'

Watts went over to the kitchen and finished getting the cork out of the bottle. He picked up a glass and tilted it to pour a drink for Neill.

'I'm Bob Watts, by the way,' he said.

'I know,' Neill said, accepting the glass and waiting for Watts to pour one for himself. 'I mean I know not just because you signed up for the swim. I'm a Brighton boy so have followed your career with interest.'

'The rise? Or just the precipitous fall?'

Neill accepted the glass Watts proffered him and raised it.

'Ever tried,' Neill said. 'Ever failed. No matter. Try again. Fail again. Fail better.'

Watts frowned. He hated psychobabble.

'Sounds like a quote,' he said. 'Some New Age thing?'

'You sound judgemental,' Neill said quietly.

Watts spread his hands. 'Got me.'

Neill smiled. He looked tired. He took a sip of his drink. 'You're a copper,' he said thoughtfully.

'Was,' Watts said. 'And not a proper one.'

Neill frowned. 'Meaning?'

'I'm more management than boots on the ground.'

Watts saw Neill lose interest. 'You need a copper, Derek?' he said.

Neill looked out of the window. 'The doe is back,' he said, sounding abstracted.

'Because of what happened in the lake today?' Watts said. 'You said it was a heart attack.'

Neill took more than a sip of his drink this time.

'That's the assumption,' he said. 'But there has been a lot of weird stuff going on . . . Look, I'm going to stand by your window and hope the fawn joins the doe and I'm going to mourn my friend for a couple of minutes. A couple of minutes for now, I mean. Maybe you can make yourself comfortable and after the couple of minutes we can sit down and talk rubbish – well, I can talk rubbish and you can pretend to listen.'

'Sounds like a plan,' Watts said. 'How are you about people snoring?'

'Accustomed to it,' Neill said, flashing him a grin.

Watts busied himself in the kitchen. Then he took his glass of wine over to the long sofa. He looked up at Neill.

'You want to stay for dinner?' he said. 'Rasa too? I'm doing a chicken thing.'

Neill shook his head.

'Thanks, though,' he said. 'I told you Rasa had turned in. I'll get back to her shortly.'

Watts nodded and gestured to the other end of the sofa. 'Maybe you could sit down?'

Neill did so.

'What's your concern about your friend's death?' Watts said.

'Healthy as hell,' Neill said. 'No way that swim was going to kill him.'

'But you know about undiagnosed heart conditions?' Watts said.

'Sure.' Neill finished his drink. Anticipating this, Watts had brought the bottle over. He pushed it towards Neill, gesturing that he should help himself. Neill did and took another long draught. 'But this was not a swim that would have exerted him. It was long but not *that* long. It wasn't cold. How do you feel?'

'I feel fine. How old was this guy?'

'Older than you,' Neill said. 'My age.'

'I thought we were of an age,' Watts said.

Neill showed his teeth. 'You've got to be a woman for that to have an effect on me.'

'I'll work on that,' Watts said. 'Tell me about him.'

'Philip?' Neill said. 'That's a long story. Another time, perhaps.'

'These weird things happening?' Watts said.

'That too,' he said.

Watts frowned.

'I thought you wanted a copper's help.'

Neill shrugged.

'A passing thought. I'm just railing against God for killing my friend. And I don't even believe in God.'

'Well, I'm intrigued,' Watts said.

Neill stood and downed the rest of his drink in one.

'Intrigue is what makes the world go round,' he said. He nodded. 'Until next time.'

Seven

Gilchrist and Heap headed to Lewes to interview Gulliver's ex-wife. She lived on Cliffe High Street at the bottom end of the town. Finding somewhere to park was a bit of a bugger so eventually they abandoned the car on a double-yellow line. One of the perks of the profession.

The narrow doorway between an antiques shop and kitchenware store clicked open when Heap rang the bell. It led down an equally narrow passage that opened out into a large courtyard garden with house, totally hidden from the street.

'Mrs Gulliver?' Gilchrist said, holding out her hand.

'Tamsin Stanhope,' the woman replied, taking Gilchrist's hand gingerly then letting it drop. 'I've reverted to my maiden name. For obvious reasons.'

She ushered them into a narrow living room. She was a short woman, pretty but with a hard, set face. It was clear from her expression she was not the forgiving or forgetting type. Her cheeks were flushed, her mouth a terse line. Everything about this house was narrow, Gilchrist reflected, scanning Stanhope's face.

Gilchrist started to give her condolences but Stanhope put up her hand.

'I'm glad he's dead and I assume you're here

because I must be a prime suspect. And believe me, if I could have killed him, I would have.'

Heap cleared his throat. 'Since you've been so direct, Ms Stanhope,' he said, 'might I ask where you were on the afternoon, evening and night of the murder.'

Her smile was as thin as her lips. 'I was in Paris. All week. Staying with friends in their apartment in St-Germain. They can, of course, confirm that.'

'When did you last see your husband?' Gilchrist said.

'My ex-husband.'

'Are you divorced?'

Again that humourless smile. 'I assume we are now.'

'Ms Stanhope, was it the betrayal or was it the betrayal with a man that hurt you the most?' Heap asked quietly.

'Men,' Stanhope answered him. 'From before we were even engaged. He felt the need to confess to that when he announced he was leaving because he was in love with this paederast.'

'Do you have any knowledge that Mr Gulliver's new partner is a paedophile?' Gilchrist said.

'I didn't say he was,' Stanhope said witheringly. 'Don't you know the difference, detective inspector, between "-erast" and "-ophile"?'

Gilchrist tried not to frown as she wondered what the difference might be. She glanced at Heap. His attention was focused on Stanhope, who twisted her mouth into a horrible grimace.

'The second is attracted to boys; the first sticks his penis up their arses,' she said.

'And you're saying Mr Gulliver's new partner does that with underage boys?' Heap said. 'That's a serious accusation.'

Stanhope shrugged.

'He's queer, isn't he? I assume they all do things with bum-boys – or want to.'

'That's simply not true, Ms Stanhope,' Gilchrist said. 'And I must caution you against making such statements either generally or about specific persons if you have no evidence for the statement.'

'Then I stand corrected. However, I know that Mr Gulliver stuck his penis up the backsides of a range of rent boys and total strangers he met in the dark or in pubs devoted to that express purpose. And it's probable that he then came home and stuck the same penis into me without telling me where it had just been.'

She grimaced.

'I don't know how you would feel about that, detective inspector, but I cannot begin to express my revulsion and disgust.' She looked down. 'One hears often about love turning to hate. I can testify that it can do so and when it does it is a powerful and terrible emotion. It can make you want to wish someone dead.' She looked up. 'But that does not mean I killed him.'

'Did he have enemies?' Heap said.

'Not to my knowledge, but clearly my knowledge of him was entirely partial.'

Gilchrist stood.

'We'll need the contact details of your friends in Paris. And we'd like to take a DNA swab.' She gestured to Heap. 'The detective sergeant here has the kit.'

'You take it from saliva, don't you?'

Gilchrist nodded. Stanhope opened her mouth scarcely at all, as if any wider would be indelicate.

'As long as you leave me enough to spit on his grave.'

Gilchrist and Heap left soon after. They exchanged glances when they saw their car had a parking ticket.

As Heap was putting the car in gear, Gilchrist said:

'I suppose you knew the difference between a paedophile and a paederast, Bellamy.'

'I even know what a *mulierast* is, ma'am.'

'You do?'

'I am one, ma'am.'

Gilchrist looked at Heap sharply.

'Am I prepared for this confession, detective sergeant? It sounds horribly . . . bestial.'

The corner of Heap's mouth twitched.

'It's a joke term, coined by a friend of Oscar Wilde. It's the opposite of *paederast* – it refers to a man who is interested only in women.'

Gilchrist smiled back, then frowned.

'Tamsin Stanhope – a woman scorned, eh?'

'She reminded me of that politician's wife who took revenge on her husband when he left her for a younger woman. You know, she told the newspaper she'd taken his penalty points for a driving offence?'

'And they both ended up in jail,' Gilchrist said as Heap took them out of town. 'Where's your house, by the way, Bellamy?'

'Over the top end – near the prison, ma'am.'

She smiled. 'Can't leave work behind, eh?'

'It would appear not, ma'am. But going back to Ms Stanhope – if you're comparing her to the "hell hath no fury" woman, then you're actually saying she was capable of killing him.'

'Capable but absent when it happened,' Gilchrist said.

'Apparently. A hit man?'

'Would you know how to hire a hit man, Bellamy? I'm not sure I would, even with all my privileged knowledge. How would an ordinary woman know? Especially in Lewes. An extremist animal rights activist capable of any atrocity against humans to protect badgers and toads wouldn't be hard to find. But Stanhope would have to do a damn good spin job to get him or her to kill her husband.'

Heap smiled. 'I'd like to talk some more to Mrs Medavoy. And see what else the phone records come up with. DC Sylvia Wade back in the office is working through those.'

'Fine,' Gilchrist said, a little distracted.

'You have a better idea, ma'am?'

'No, no – I was just thinking that, actually, it wouldn't be entirely implausible for one of the more sociopathic activists to commit a murder if there were the right lever. Perhaps we should do more research on Tamsin Stanhope to see who her known associates past and present are. Get Sylvia to start by seeing if she was part of the anti-fracking demonstrations. Oh, and get her to talk to whoever was supposed to have been on security duty at the lido that night. Find out why he wasn't and more generally if there are any names of regular troublemakers we should be following up.'

She stifled a yawn.

'How are you getting on with tracking down Philip Coates?'

'He's proving unresponsive so far. He works from home so I've left messages on his voicemail, both his landline and mobile.'

'OK – well, let's see what the staff at the David Lloyd centre can tell us.'

Bob Watts was in the outdoor pool at his gym the morning after he brought Kate Simpson back from Coniston. He liked to go during what he called the 'sweet hour', that time after all the eager beavers wanting to do their pre-work exercise had gone and before the pensioners came in and clogged up the lanes.

He did an hour of front crawl and treated himself to ten minutes of back crawl at the end. He took his goggles off for this so he could enjoy the clouds unhindered drifting across the morning sky and the silvery planes from Gatwick leaving vapour trails in their wake.

The water felt uncomfortably warm by the end since his body had begun to adapt to the colder water he'd been swimming in. Even so, after he'd showered he sat in the sauna for five minutes. He wasn't big on saunas. He wasn't patient enough to sit and do nothing. However, his muscles ached from the previous day's long swim so he wanted to soothe them.

He was sitting in the café with a pint of orange juice when he saw Sarah Gilchrist and Bellamy

Heap come into the foyer. He saw them flash their warrant cards at reception then step away. Gilchrist looked around and spotted him. He gave a little wave and Gilchrist leaned down to say something to Heap then both of them walked over.

'Good morning, Bob,' Gilchrist said. 'I forgot this was your gym.'

'My pool, really,' Watts said, nodding at Heap. 'Morning, detective sergeant.'

'Morning, sir. Congratulations on your time yesterday in Coniston.'

Gilchrist looked quizzical.

'Kate and I swam the length of Lake Coniston yesterday,' Watts explained. He turned to Heap. 'Kate did a good job too. Very impressive.'

'She's really stiff this morning,' Heap said. 'And she said somebody died during the swim.'

'Yeah. It can happen – not to Kate, Bellamy. This guy was much older. Friend of the organizers actually so that was a bit of a downer all round. But onwards and upward, eh?'

'Bob,' Gilchrist said, trying not to sound impatient, 'don't suppose you've come across a swimmer called Roland Gulliver in the pool? Maybe doing butterfly?'

'No butterfly swum in the pool at the time I'm there,' he said. 'But Roland Gulliver – don't know the name. What's he look like?'

As Heap described him, Gilchrist glanced back towards the reception desk. A tanned young woman, smartly dressed in a navy-blue fitted suit, was walking towards them, her pony tail swishing.

Watts was shaking his head. 'Doesn't spring to mind. What's he done?'

'Got himself murdered,' Gilchrist said as she turned to the young woman. 'Let's catch up later, Bob.'

Kate had been badly shaken by her horrible encounter with the feral teenagers but it wasn't long before anger replaced the shock. The next day she had begun her research and she had proposed a documentary to Southern Shores Radio about crime committed by delinquent teens in Brighton. To her surprise, they'd gone for it.

Delinquent. It was an old word she'd latched onto because she liked the sound of it but she couldn't quite see how it had come to be used in the first place. She knew it was from the Latin – her parents had at least sent her to a good school, though most of it hadn't taken – but she didn't know why. The literal translation was *to leave completely* which sort of made sense but only sort of. It was almost the same as *to relinquish.*

She noted that the term *juvenile delinquency* was rarely used in these days of ASBOs. Then she smiled at herself as she realized this was all Bellamy. This was the kind of stuff he wondered about and explored and now he'd got her doing it.

There were two main youth gangs in Brighton: Milldean Muscle and the Avengers. They shoplifted, mugged, attacked gays and transgender people, foreign students and asylum seekers. She'd asked her friend, Sarah Gilchrist, about them. Over a glass of wine, naturally.

'We've always had teen gangs of some sort,' Gilchrist said. 'You go back to the teddy boys in the late fifties. Then the mods and rockers. Then the skinheads. And it all comes out of the same thing: poverty. The same housing estates, the same families. Generations of criminals.' She shook her head. 'This town.'

'Yes but not this young,' Kate protested. 'You didn't have twelve-year-old teddy boys.'

'But that's just a reflection of the way kids are growing up quicker these days.'

'I contacted your special task force about what happened to me,' Kate said.

'And?'

'They were sympathetic but not much help. Told me other stories. Yob behaviour on the top deck of buses was the least of it, although their rampaging through a bus could be terrifying. They attacked innocent shoppers in the city centre, goaded commuters in Hove.'

Kate had the name of a gang member. Darrel Jones. She phoned his mother now.

'He don't do nothing wrong,' she squawled. In the background Kate could hear the 16-year-old boy raging. His mother insisted her son didn't cause trouble or commit crimes. Kate insisted he had been identified as one of the ringleaders by the police. His mother swore he was being picked on by the police. Darrel came on the phone.

'You put my name in the paper, you stupid bitch, I'll go fucking mad, you mug. And plus I'm not allowed my name in paper. I'm too young, you silly fucking cow.'

'I work for the radio,' Kate said calmly. Not

94

adding 'you moron', though she wanted to. 'So you're a member of which gang?'

'Gang? Int no gang. Just friends, right? Hang out together. Nuffin wrong with that.'

'Are you Milldean Muscle or the Avengers?'

'Neither – I ain't no fucking bum bandit like those pussies. Wouldn't have nothing to do with them, you cow.'

'Can your mother hear you address another woman like that?'

'Address what? I ain't addressing nothing. What – I'm talking to the Post Office now? Fucking stupid bitch.'

'Could you put your mother back on?'

The line went dead.

Gilchrist and Heap were sitting with Constable Sylvia Wade back at the station. The duty manager of the pool had had little information of use to them. Heap had phoned a couple of days before so that all the staff could be asked about Gulliver's acquaintances and the man in the sauna. Gulliver didn't seem to hang out with anyone in particular there and the description Bilson had given of the man he'd met in the sauna had drawn blanks.

'Security at the Lido that night was supposed to be a man called Terry Dean who called in sick,' Sylvia Wade said to Gilchrist and Heap. 'He works for the council as a lifeguard for his day job, usually down by the West Pier.'

'What was wrong with him?' Gilchrist said.

'Hangover, he said, but probably drunk or still drinking. It had been his day off and he'd been drinking with his mates – someone's

95

birthday – in HA! HA! at lunchtime then they'd gone on a bit of a bar crawl along the boardwalk.'

'Did he have anything of interest to say?'

'Quite a bit actually, though only some of it might actually be useful. He said the deceased banged on a lot about the broken window theory, ma'am. Which I had to look up.'

'I'd be the same, Sylvia,' Gilchrist said. She glanced at Heap. 'Big Brain, on the other hand . . .'

'Before all our times, ma'am, but we did cover it in training and it certainly would have application in somewhere like Milldean. I believe it was used for a while as the basis for a policing policy adopted by the chief constable who preceded Bob Watts.'

'And?'

Heap glanced at Sylvia Wade who nodded for him to continue.

'It has been around since the early 1980s. It's about norm-setting. It looks at the consequences of minor disorder and vandalism on additional crime and anti-social behaviour. If you keep the urban environment in a well-ordered condition, there won't be an escalation into further vandalism or more serious crime.'

'I remember,' Gilchrist said. 'You come down hard on litter-dropping so you don't have knifings?'

'Somewhat crude, if I may say, ma'am, but yes. Fix problems when they are small to stop them getting bigger. Replace the broken windows quickly and vandals won't break more. And, yes, sort that litter every day and it won't accumulate.'

'Gulliver was quite evangelical about it, apparently,' Wade said.

'Yet he had no police background,' Gilchrist mused.

'He was approaching it from the opposite end. He recognized that the police can't do that alone. It requires the participation of the community. According to Dean, he banged on about people feeling a sense of ownership and responsibility towards an area. If a community doesn't care about broken windows and vandalism, if it accepts disorder, then there's little the police can do.'

'That kind of makes sense, and I suppose is the thinking behind the multi-agency approach we've all been stuck with lately,' Gilchrist said. 'But I'm not sure I believe major crimes will be prevented if minor ones are dealt with quickly.'

'There are correlations though, ma'am,' Heap said. 'On the roads, a good percentage of those drivers without insurance are involved in other crime.'

'But for a community to get involved policing itself in some way is a stepping stone to vigilantism,' Gilchrist said.

'Gulliver talked in terms of community watchmen and women,' Wade said.

'Patrolling the streets?' Gilchrist said.

'No, just keeping a lookout. Local businesses, institutions, twenty-four-hour shops give a sense of having "eyes on the street". And, with reference to the lido, keeping a watch on the building.'

'The theory went out of favour as I recall,'

Heap said. 'Local residents often felt that it wasn't their responsibility – they paid their council tax for someone else to do it. We know that people often refuse to go to someone's help not out of selfishness or lack of concern but because they can't think of a plausible reason for accepting personal responsibility. Others, quite understandably, just don't want to put themselves in harm's way. But the main reason it went out of favour was that critics said correlation and causality were not the same and the relationship between minor and major crime was minimal.'

'Was there a specific reason Gulliver organized the security for the lido or was it in response to trouble?' Gilchrist asked Wade.

'Couple of break-ins and graffiti.'

'Local kids?'

'That was the assumption. Or one of the street gangs.'

'Dean has come across them?' Gilchrist said.

'He has and says they are a real pain because, of course, they are under age so normal rules of control don't apply – as we well know, ma'am.'

'Anyone we've been looking at?'

'I'm investigating that,' Wade said.

'Have we still got a police presence at the crime scene?' Gilchrist asked Heap.

'I believe so, ma'am.'

'Find out from whoever has been down there if any kids have been hanging around. Get names and details. Milldean Muscle or the Avengers, for instance?'

'Will do, ma'am.'

She looked around the table.

'Kids and knives, boys and girls, kids and knives.'

Eight

Margaret Lively was sitting on a stool at a high table in a first-floor bar and grill at Victoria when Watts met her again. He still hadn't figured out a way to say something clever about her last name.

The table was beside a long window that looked down on the busy concourse. Watts looked out of the window before kissing her on the cheek.

'Great location,' he said as he took another stool.

'I spied on you as you came across the concourse with your friend,' she said with a smile.

'His name is Jimmy Tingley,' Watts said. 'We travelled up together. He's an old friend.'

'He looked . . . compact,' she said.

Watts laughed. 'That's a very good description of him,' he said. 'Unobtrusive too – that's his stock in trade.' He saw her puzzled look. 'In the kind of work he does.'

'And what kind of work is that?' she said cautiously.

Watts spread his hands. 'I'm sorry. I'm not house-trained. We didn't talk about what I do the other day and I'm sounding horribly cloak-and-dagger and that's just awful.'

She sat back. 'You are sounding a bit suspicious.'

'Well, I'm a police commissioner and my friend Jimmy works a lot with government agencies.'

She looked at him for a long moment.

'I have no idea where to go with that information,' she eventually said.

Watts grinned and ordered a large glass of Malbec. She already had a smaller white wine in front her.

'Sauvignon blanc,' she said when she saw him look.

As the waitress walked away Watts examined Lively's face. He wasn't exactly sure why he was here. She wasn't as young as he'd thought – she was twenty-eight – but even so that made her almost twenty years younger than him. However, they'd had a pleasant breakfast together and she was easy company.

When his wine came they chinked glasses and she began to tell him about a swimming holiday she had booked with Dolphin Smile for a month's time on an island off Thailand.

Watts smiled and nodded but he was distracted by memories of his conversation with Tingley on the train up from Brighton. Tingley too had been talking Thailand.

'Going for a month,' he said as the train passed over the high viaduct spanning the valley at Ardingly. Both men looked down on Ardingly College to their right.

'Work?' Watts said.

'Some but mostly pleasure.'

'You're not still on your journey?' Watts said.

A few months earlier Tingley had been in Vietnam and Cambodia on a kind of remembrance trail for the Cambodian wife of his youth. He had been drawn into a conflict with criminals and artefact smugglers that had ended bloodily.

Tingley shook his head. 'That's all done with. But you know me, Bob, I get restless if there's nothing going on.'

True enough, Watts thought.

'You should come,' Lively was saying now, touching his hand with hers. 'Sounds fantastic.'

Watts shook his head. 'Tempting as it is,' he said, 'swimming in warm water would wreck my training schedule for the Channel. I have to build up resistance to the cold.'

Lively shook her head.

'How can you turn down such an offer?' she said, sounding a little disappointed. He looked at her lovely face. *How indeed?*

Constable Stansfield had been one of two policemen to stumble upon the former director of the Royal Pavilion digging up skeletons in a graveyard on the other side of the Downs a few months earlier. Since then he'd been transferred into the city and had been attached to a small task force dealing with kids spraying graffiti around Salthaven and particularly on Salthaven Lido.

Gilchrist hadn't liked him much when she had first met him some months ago and she saw no reason to change her opinion now. He was lazy and reactive rather than proactive.

'There were four of them who were the most persistent,' Stansfield said now, slouching to attention in Gilchrist's office. 'I have their names but they refused to give me their addresses and as they were children I could not insist, ma'am.'

'Their real names?'

'I doubt it, ma'am. However, there are photographs.'

'CCTV?'

'Not entirely. More of an *aide memoire* for me and my partner.'

'Did you insist on photographing them?'

Stansfield started to smirk then saw Gilchrist's look.

'It was covert surveillance, ma'am.'

'Where are these photographs now?' Heap said.

'On our phones. Want us to email them to you?'

'No,' Gilchrist and Heap said together. Gilchrist wasn't surprised that Heap was as aware as she of the dangers of leaving an email trail. She was about to implicate herself in an illegal activity. The less evidence for it the better.

'What then, ma'am?' Stansfield said. Gilchrist frowned. *What indeed?* She looked to Heap for the answer. He took out his own iPhone and gestured to Stansfield to take out his. Stansfield scrolled to the pictures and Heap photographed the photographs.

When Stansfield had gone, Gilchrist and Heap huddled over the photographs of three tough-looking boys and an even tougher-looking girl.

'Recognize any of them, Bellamy?' Gilchrist said. Heap nodded. 'Darrel Jones,' he said.

'Let's bring him in,' she said. 'With his mother, of course.'

* * *

Darrel Jones was a malnourished, thin-shouldered, bony-faced boy with enormous hands. He was sinewy and Gilchrist guessed would be very strong if he got fired up. He sat in the interview lounge usually used for rape victims, on a sofa with his mother, a buxom, spotty-faced woman on one side and a harassed-looking, straggly-haired woman from child protection services on the other.

'Thanks so much for coming in, Darrel – OK if I call you Darrel?'

Darrel shrugged.

'OK, then, we're hoping you can help us solve a serious crime.'

'My Darrel ain't done no serious crime,' his mother interjected.

'We're not saying he has,' Gilchrist said soothingly, 'but we're hoping he knows something about it.'

'He don't know nothing about one neither,' his mother said.

'Well, we're hoping he knows something he doesn't know he knows,' Gilchrist said, 'if you get my meaning.'

Darrel gave an exaggerated shrug. 'No idea what she's talking about.'

'You mind your lip,' his mother said, then looked belligerently at Gilchrist. 'But what *do* you mean?' she said.

'Well, I know Darrel is a bit of an artist with a spray can—'

'Are you accusing him of graffiti?'

'No, I'm not accusing him of graffiti. We don't mind a bit of graffiti these days. But if I were good with a spray can I'd want to use it on those lovely white walls of the lido . . .'

'Never been near it,' Darrel said, a smirk on his face.

Gilchrist exaggerated her sigh and look of disappointment. 'That's a shame. Especially as there could well be a reward.'

'Reward?' his mother said.

'You never know,' Gilchrist said. 'One hasn't been posted yet, or anything, but it's the kind of case—'

'What kind of case are you talking about?' Darrel's mother said.

'Murder. On the night of the fifteenth.'

She glanced quickly at Darrel. 'Why would he know anything about a murder?'

'A man was stabbed to death,' Gilchrist continued, watching Darrel for any reaction. He gave none, instead just looking sullenly at his feet.

'Why would Darrel know about that? He doesn't carry a knife, do you, Darrel? Do you?'

Darrel shook his head without looking up.

'We thought he might have seen the man with another person around the time Darrel was spray-painting the wall of the lido on the evening of the fifteenth. Did you Darrel? Did you see anything?'

'I didn't see nothing,' Darrel said, still keeping his head down.

Gilchrist smiled to herself. 'What time did you get there?' she said, building on his implicit admission that he'd been at the lido.

'Dunno,' he said.

'Do you remember what time your son came home on the night of the fifteenth, Mrs Jones?'

'I never know what time he comes in. Keeps his own hours does Darrel.'

'So after midnight wouldn't be unusual?'

She glanced her son's way.'

'More like "usual",' she said.

Darrel smirked.

'Were you with anyone else that night, Darrel?'

'Why?' he said. 'Do you split rewards?'

'Well, if there is a reward it would depend on who saw what. You said you didn't see anything, as I recall.'

Darrel was thinking quickly, Gilchrist could tell by the speed with which his eyes were moving from object to object.

'I didn't see no stabbing,' he said.

'Do any of your friends carry knives?'

'Not that night,' Darrel said.

'But usually they would?'

'Not that night,' Darrel repeated.

'Some nights?'

'Yeah, sometimes. It depends on the vibe.'

'And the vibe was good that night.'

'Except for these two geezers having a barney.'

'Physical?'

Darrel shook his head then extended his hand and made a mouth opening and shutting with his fingers and thumb. 'Plenty of that though.'

'Arguing.'

'A lot.'

'Where?'

'On the steps of the baths.'

'What time?'

Darrel glanced at his mother. 'Dunno.'

'What did they look like?'

'Like a couple of poofs.'

'Can you give me a bit more detail than that?'

'Geezer with a beer belly, the other had one of them big beards and his hair cut funny. Didn't have any socks.'

A hipster, Gilchrist thought. *Great*. Only about ten thousand of them in Brighton. That should make an identification parade fun, were one necessary.

'What sort of age are you talking about?' Gilchrist asked.

'I dunno – in their fifties maybe?'

Gilchrist remained impassive. 'Did you hear what they were arguing about?'

Darrel looked ferrety. 'Maybe. How does this reward work exactly?'

'You give us information leading to an arrest and a charge and, if there is a reward, it will go to you.'

'What if my mates saw and heard the same thing?'

'Then they'll just corroborate your story. As I said if one of them knows anything truly significant then that might be taken into account when it comes to handing out the reward. If there is one.'

Gilchrist slid a photograph of Roland Gulliver onto the coffee table. 'Was this one of them?'

Darrel glanced at the photo and shook his head. 'Nothing like.'

Gilchrist turned away to hide her surprise. She had been wondering how Gulliver could have been

106

arguing if the premise about him being near-drowned somewhere else and brought to the steps of the lido was true, but she'd assumed the premise was wrong. Now she didn't know whether this argument had anything to do with anything.

'What time was this?'

'I told you: I dunno.'

Gilchrist made a face. 'Thing is, Darrel, we're going to need a time and if you can't supply it we'll need to talk to your friends. That's important information.'

'About a quarter after midnight,' he said, shooting a quick look at his mum.

Gilchrist gestured to the photo. 'And you didn't see this man anywhere round the lido?'

Darrel shook his head. 'Just those two fairies.'

'And what was there argument about?'

Darrel glanced at his mum. She nodded.

'Some bloke called Lesley,' Darrel said.

'What about him?'

He shrugged. 'Suppose they were both after him.'

'You heard them say that?'

'Not exactly but that was the gist.'

Gilchrist handed him the photograph of Gulliver again.

'Look again. You haven't seen him any other time at the lido? He was there a lot.'

Darrel squinted down at the photo. 'What – some other time? Did I see him some other time?'

'Did you?' Gilchrist said.

'Not there, no. Saw him somewhere else though.'

'Where?'

Darrel looked ferrety again. 'How much is this reward likely to be?'

'Hard to say but people don't usually complain. When did you see him?'

'The day before.'

'Alone?'

'Meeting some geezer. Poncey guy with a beard.'

'The same man you saw arguing the next night?'

'No, different bloke. Same stupid beard though.'

'And what were they doing?'

Darrel had his ferrety look again. 'Kissing and cuddling.'

'Where was this?'

'In Woodvale Cemetery.'

Roland Gulliver's lover, Francis Shaw, came into the police station the next morning. He was taken to an interview room to wait for Gilchrist and Heap. In the lift down to it, Heap told Gilchrist that Shaw had a website for his work.

'What is his work?'

'That's not entirely clear,' Heap said.

'Well, what does it say on his website?'

'*Provocateur.*'

Gilchrist looked at Heap's deadpan face and snorted.

Shaw was a fastidious-looking man in a sharp suit. He had his hair stylishly cropped, short at the sides and combed back on top. He wore a full, brown beard. Gilchrist glanced at Heap.

'You didn't need to come in, Mr Shaw,' Gilchrist said. 'We said we'd come to your home.'

'I was passing and I wanted to get this DNA thing over with,' he said.

'Very well, then, let's get the swab out of the way,' Gilchrist said.

Shaw opened his mouth exaggeratedly wide. Heap took the swab out of its casing.

'Thanks for that,' Gilchrist said when Heap had finished the operation. She gestured to the chair behind Shaw. 'I wondered if we might ask a couple more questions.'

'Of course,' Shaw said. He sat down and pressed his knees together.

Heap sat down on the chair to his left. 'Mr Shaw, we have a witness saying that someone fitting your description was having a row on the steps of the lido earlier in the evening on which Roland Gulliver died.'

Shaw frowned, tugged on his beard and stroked his head. 'My description? Good luck with the line-up.'

'So you weren't on the steps of the lido that evening?'

'Since I have evidence for where I was the answer has to be no.'

'You were abroad?'

Shaw reached into his jacket pocket and pulled out the stub of a boarding pass. '*Voila* – the evidence.'

Heap took it and noted down flight details and booking reference. 'Do you know why Mr Gulliver would have been in Woodvale Cemetery the previous day?'

'Roland in Woodvale Cemetery?' He stroked his beard. 'With whom?'

'Is that somewhere you've been with him?'

'We hardly need to cottage when we've both got perfectly good homes.'

'And you told us Mr Gulliver had never been into that kind of activity,' Gilchrist said.

'That's right,' Shaw said, clasping his hands over his knees.

'I'm sorry to say this at such a time but we have heard stories to the contrary.'

'Stories? I'm sure you've heard stories and I'm sure I know where they're coming from.' He leaned forward over his knees. 'That bitch of a wife.'

'She seemed convinced that he had been quite promiscuous throughout their marriage.'

'I know for a certainty that once he met me there was none of that. And he had assured me there had been none of that before he met me.'

'And you believed him,' Heap said quietly.

Shaw gave him a hostile look.

'Yes. I believed him.'

'What about you, Mr Shaw?' Gilchrist said.

'What about me?' He lifted his chin. 'Oh, you want details of my sex life?'

'You're sure you weren't in Woodvale Cemetery the day before Roland's death? You were in this country then, I believe, so might conceivably have been. And someone broadly matching your description was seen with Mr Gulliver.'

'Do you search for suspects by trawling through sexual stereotypes? How can you be so blundering when I've just lost my partner?'

'I'm sorry if my questions sound crude, Mr Shaw, but I'm sure you're as keen to find your partner's killer as we are. These are routine questions.'

Shaw worked his jaw.

'But wait a minute. You say Roland was seen in Woodvale Cemetery with some queer that you think was me? What were they doing?'

'Was it you?'

'What were they doing?'

'Mr Shaw, can you remember your movements the day before Mr Gulliver's death?'

'They were fucking?' Shaw pressed a fist to his eye. 'The bastard.'

'Your movements, Mr Shaw.'

'I'd need to check my diary,' he finally said. 'The days roll by, you know.'

'If it wasn't you,' Heap said gently, 'can you think of anyone else it might be?'

Shaw looked at him sharply. 'I've no idea.'

Neither Shaw nor Gilchrist said anything. Shaw looked from one to the other then stood.

'Very well – if there's nothing else.'

Gilchrist and Heap stood. Gilchrist shook her head. 'Nope – nothing further for now, sir. Though we will, of course, need to search your house.'

On Saturday morning Watts found Kate among the bustle of people on the Palace Pier preparing for the Dolphin Smile race. Bellamy Heap was sorting her feed. Derek Neill and Rasa were twenty yards or so along the Pier. Neill gave Watts a little wave. Heap caught the wave and studied Neill for a moment.

'Good to go?' Watts said to Kate.

'Six hours?' she said. 'Can hardly wait.'

He smiled. 'Let's just take our time.' He looked into the water. 'No pesky kayaks for us to bump into today.'

'Just other swimmers,' Kate murmured.

They watched as a dozen or so men strode onto the pier, each one wearing Victorian bathing gear and sporting big, black cardboard moustaches held on with elastic bands round the back of their heads.

'I see the Captain Webbs are here,' Watts said. Kate looked puzzled. 'They're all really good swimmers but they turn up at these things dressed as Captain Webb for a laugh.'

'They swim with the moustaches on?' Kate asked.

Watts shook his head.

Kate laughed. 'Bob, I keep meaning to ask,' she said. 'What do you think about when you do a long swim?'

'I plan. I do a lot of planning. Then usually forget what I've planned when I get out of the water. You?'

'Me too,' Kate said. 'And mostly remember. But one of my new swimming buddies said he sang songs to himself, imagining his ear plugs were headphones since he's not allowed to use the real thing according to Channel swimming rules.'

'You fancy doing that?' Watts said.

She shook her head. 'I'd probably want to sing aloud at some point and end up swallowing half the Channel.' She climbed down the ladder to check on her feed.

Neill was suddenly beside Watts and Heap. 'Good to see you again.'

'How're things?' Watts said, shaking his hand.

'The official verdict is that Philip died of a heart attack.'

'Does that give you some closure?' Watts said.

Neill shrugged. 'Doesn't sit well with me but what am I going to do?'

'If you still want to talk through some stuff . . .' Watts tailed off as he saw Neill look beyond him.

'Good God,' Neill said. He squeezed Watts on the arm. 'Enjoy today but excuse me now. I've just seen a ghost.'

Watts watched him as he hurried back along the pier to the promenade but couldn't see who or what he was in pursuit of. Kate rejoined them.

'Who is Philip?' Heap said.

'The man who drowned in Coniston,' Watts said. 'Coates I think his last name was.'

'Philip Coates?' Heap said, or rather almost squeaked. Both Watts and Kate looked at him and Kate began to laugh.

'Sounds like you know him,' Watts said.

'I've been trying to make contact with him for two days.'

'You'll need a Ouija board now, I'm afraid,' Watts said. Heap nodded absently.

There were some fifty or sixty swimmers along the pier, each one with a helper or two. The plan was that all would start from a long deck below the pier, getting there via three steel ladders. In the absence of support boats, bottles of feed were laid out in neat rows, all on long cords, ready for the swimmers' helpers to throw them down to them.

Watts and Kate clambered down.

'See you on the other side,' Watts said as they dropped into the water.

Gilchrist was at her desk early that morning. Sylvia Wade came in about ten and immediately reported that the search of Shaw's house had found nothing significant.

'Bellamy said you were working your way through the calls Gulliver made and received. How are you getting on with that? Are we any nearer finding out who he met the day before in the cemetery and who he was sharing a bottle of wine with on his last day?'

'Nothing yet. The final call he received was from April Medavoy, the Chair of the Save the Lido committee.'

'Time for another chat with her,' Gilchrist said. Her phone rang. Bilson.

'Mr Bilson, a keenly awaited pleasure.'

'Sarah, I know you don't mean that in the way I might hope from the fact we're back to formality.'

'Christian names are only for birthdays and special occasions, Frank. Have you found our killer?'

He chuckled. 'I rather thought that was your job.'

'The widow, Tamsin Stanhope, in the library with a wet towel? Shaw in the cemetery with a stiletto?'

'Mr Shaw is into cross-dressing?'

114

'I don't know about his private habits, but I meant the stiletto knife not the heel.'

'It will cost your department an arm and a leg for us turning round Mr Shaw's DNA test so quickly. Tamsin Stanhope's won't cost much less.'

'But worth it, I hope.'

'If you mean by that you can exclude two people from your enquiries, then yes.'

'Neither of them had any DNA traces either at Gulliver's house or on his person? Not even Shaw?'

'Not even Shaw.'

'Isn't that odd, given they were so close?'

'Odd but not unknown. It depends when they last saw each other.'

She hung up the landline as her mobile started vibrating on her desk. She glanced at her watch. Noon.

'Bellamy. How's Kate doing?'

'Still out there. Two hours to go.'

'What about Bob?'

'The same.'

Heap seemed subdued.

'Something wrong?' Gilchrist said.

'Philip Coates is dead. Drowned in Lake Coniston last weekend.'

'And you've only just found this out?'

'I put tracking him down to one side because I didn't think it a priority.'

'And what do you think now?'

'I think I made a massive mistake that someone else may have paid for.'

'What do you mean by that last bit?'

'Somebody here is missing feared drowned.'

'Jesus, Bellamy. What is going on?'

'I heard a couple of people talking. It's a woman. She didn't turn up for her next feed.'

'But wouldn't someone else see if she was in difficulty?'

'Everybody is pretty much focused on their own thing. And people doing crawl don't see anything anyway.'

'How do they know she's not still out there?'

'The bathing cap. Hers is pretty distinctive apparently. No one can spot it.'

'Shouldn't they be stopping the race?'

'I think it's a "show must go on" scenario. Especially as there would be a lot of unhappy swimmers who haven't yet reached their target if they stopped it now.'

'Do we know who the swimmer is?'

'Someone called Christine Bromley.'

'Poor woman,' Gilchrist murmured. 'And you think it's suspicious, of course.'

'At the moment I'm finding everything suspicious. I've just met a man who fits the description of the man Darrel Jones saw with Gulliver in Woodvale Cemetery.'

'I thought we'd agreed there are hundreds who fit that description in Brighton.'

'Yes, but this one is as involved in the swimming world as Gulliver was. Name of Derek Neill, one of the organizers of this swim and Coniston.'

'Do you want to have a word with him?'

'Now is probably not a good time but once we know more about Christine Bromley.'

'I'm on my way down,' Gilchrist said.

Nine

When Gilchrist arrived, Bellamy Heap was standing on the pavement outside the Palace Pier with Kate and Bob Watts, both swaddled in big, hooded gowns.

'Did you do it?' she asked, addressing them both.

Kate's teeth were chattering.

'We did.'

'Has the woman turned up?'

Watts shook his head. 'Unfortunate coincidence for Dolphin Smile,' he said.

'Is it a health-and-safety thing?' Gilchrist said. 'Is Dolphin Smile being reckless?'

'Not at all. These swimmers all know what they're doing and are given advice. In Coniston the water wasn't cold. Here it was about sixteen centigrade.'

'Doesn't sound very warm,' Gilchrist said.

'In the sea the range in the summer is between fifteen and nineteen centigrade,' Watts said. 'Sixteen centigrade is cold but not dangerous – below ten is dangerous. Very cold water can trigger a heart attack or hypothermia. If you suffer from either in other circumstances you have a good chance of surviving. In water, you're probably going to drown.'

'I'm not really up on hypothermia,' Gilchrist said.

'Heat transfer is always one way – from the hotter to the cooler thing. And heat loss from a human body occurs quickest when the body is totally wet. So swimming in cold water is the quickest way to lose body heat.'

'But some of these Channel swimmers take hours and hours to cross – how do they do it without freezing to death or drowning?'

Watts nodded. 'It's tricky. If you speed up to keep warm you might lose more body heat from increased air and water movement over your body and just from your increased respiration rate.' He gestured to Kate, whose teeth were still chattering. 'Shivering generates heat but you can't do much else while you have the shakes.'

'It's all about metabolism,' Kate said, her voice wavering with her shivering.

'Yes,' Watts agreed. 'Hypothermia varies from person to person, depending on metabolism. It can set in quickly – within two or three minutes of stopping swimming. It can start when you're swimming but you don't realize, except for the fact it takes a lot out of you to swim just a few yards. And then swimming even that distance becomes impossible. If hypothermia set in with this woman and she started to drown she wouldn't even be able to raise her arms to wave for help.'

Gilchrist shook her head. 'Fingers crossed she's OK. Bob, Bellamy mentioned you know Derek Neill, the man behind all this. We're going to need to talk to him if you can point us in the right direction.'

'Sure, though he's hard to miss. Big, muscled

118

hipster type. What is the name of the woman who is missing, by the way?'

'Christine Bromley,' Heap said.

'*The* Christine Bromley?' Watts said.

Gilchrist looked at Heap, who shook his head but reached in his bag for his iPad.

'She runs Bromleys, a Hove-based family company with fingers in many pies,' Watts said. 'Transport – not quite as big as Eddie Stobart but getting there. Aggregate – shipping out of Shoreham. And engineering construction – they tendered for the redevelopment of the Brighton Centre and the West Pier.'

'Big then.'

'Big enough,' Heap said, reading from his iPad. 'Two thousand workforce.'

Gilchrist nodded. 'Yes, yes. She's been in the papers recently, hasn't she, but I can't remember why.'

'She wants to turn the family business into a workers' cooperative,' Watts said.

'Right,' Gilchrist said slowly. 'And the brother doesn't agree?'

Heap was scrolling.

'She intends to give up around £60 million worth of shares,' he said. 'And she's asking her brother and her mother to do the same. They're on record as resisting the idea. Delaying tactics and all that in the hope she'd come to her senses and it would all go away.'

They all exchanged glances. Gilchrist voiced what all were thinking.

'And now she's probably dead.'

*　*　*

Gilchrist and Heap decided against talking to Neill just then about Roland Gulliver or Philip Coates. The other emergency services had arrived and divers were in the water searching for Christine Bromley's body. They left them to it and walked over to a bar on the promenade where Watts and Kate Simpson were going to join them once they'd changed.

'Here we are.' Bellamy scan-read the page he'd brought up about the Bromley family business. 'Two brothers. Bernard from a first marriage and James from the second marriage that also produced Christine.'

'And the mother?'

'I don't think she's on the board but she was still being asked to tip over millions of pounds.'

'Could Christine insist?'

Heap shrugged. 'She was deputy chairman, anointed by her father to succeed him after his death.'

Gilchrist took a sip of her wine. 'Why would someone want to give away £60 million? It makes no sense.'

Heap shrugged again. 'I don't have that information yet. But I hope I won't need it. At the moment, Ms Bromley is merely missing presumed drowned.'

'You're right, of course,' Gilchrist said. 'Let's get back to this potential link between Roland Gulliver and this Derek Neill. Can we get a photograph of Neill and have uniform show it to the delightful Darrel?' She gestured at Heap's iPad. 'What can you find out about Neill?'

Heap fidgeted with his iPad.

'Local boy. Former footballer, former music promoter all along south coast. Set up Dolphin Smile with his business partner, Rasa Lewis, six years ago. Swimming holidays around the world. Tried it out first in Crete with friends and family. That's from the Dolphin Smile website. Nothing on Google; no Wikipedia entry.'

Heap focused on his iPad for a couple of moments.

'Hang on, there's a photo gallery on the website. No sign of Roland Gulliver in it though.'

'What about Philip Coates? Bob said Neill and he were friends. And is there a link between Neill and Ms Sutherland?'

'At the moment we only have one definite murder,' Heap said. 'Coates and – probably – Bromley have simply drowned.'

'Or not so simply.'

Watts and Kate, both looking newly showered and towelled, faces pink and hair wet, came into the bar. As they sat down, Gilchrist pushed her phone across to Kate.

'Kate, I'm going to do something dodgy here, just on the off-chance.'

'Off-chance of what?' Kate said, looking wary.

'The off-chance that you recognize these teenagers I'm about to show you.'

Kate looked, scrolling the pictures along. She nodded. 'All four. That ferret-faced little sod is the one who had his hand up my skirt.'

Gilchrist nodded at Heap. 'Darrel Jones again.'

'He's Darrel Jones?' Kate said. 'I spoke to him on the phone once. And his whiny mum.'

'What's this?' Watts said. 'Hand up your skirt, Kate?'

'It was nothing,' Kate said, glancing at Heap and flushing. 'I only mentioned it in passing to Sarah a few days ago.'

'What kind of nothing,' Heap and Watts said together, concern in their voices.

'I got attacked by some kids.' She flushed some more. 'They just groped me – I think so they could rob me, like that thing in Cologne that New Year?'

'How did you get out of it?' Watts said.

'They ran off. Two men intervened.'

'When was this?' Heap said quietly.

'A few days ago.'

'These men?'

'A big hipster and a nondescript guy.' She stopped.

Heap handed her his iPad. 'Recognize him?'

'People like that all look alike – you know that,' Kate said. She peered most closely. 'But, yes, unusually, he was very tanned.' She looked again. 'Who is it?'

'Derek Neill.'

'The guy who runs Dolphin Smile? I've never actually met him.'

Heap reached over and shifted the screen. 'Was this the other man in the cemetery?'

'Yes, yes – I think so. Who is he?'

Heap showed the screen to Gilchrist.

'Roland Gulliver,' she said.

When Bellamy Heap and Kate Simpson had gone off together, Watts moved around the table to sit beside Sarah Gilchrist. After their florid affair several years ago, he felt they had moved from awkwardness to a kind of relaxed familiarity, based on affection. But what did he know?

Not a lot, he decided, when she seemed to jerk away from him. OK. He recognized he had the sensitivity of a tadpole so, maybe, she had a wholly different view, disguised by her need to make their professional relationship work.

He gave them both more than enough space on the seat.

'How are things?' he said.

At least she looked at him. 'You know what the job is like,' she said.

'Actually, I don't,' he said. 'I never did it properly.'

'I mean from people telling you. Me telling you.'

'This case?'

She looked at him and put her glass down a little too hard.

'There is no "this case". There are a lot of them. But no, not the work. I've just got myself into an odd place emotionally.'

He nodded slowly, wondering what she meant but not knowing how to ask. He wasn't good at the sharing lark and when he tried he thought he came across as some sociopath mimicking human emotions. Even so, he said: 'Want to talk about it?'

Gilchrist looked surprised then smiled at him, fondly, he thought.

'That's kind of you, Bob; but I don't think so. What about you? How are things going?'

'Fine,' he said, feeling awkward.

She nodded. 'Good. Good.'

Watts searched for something to share. 'Kate is my niece,' he blurted out, then almost immediately regretted it.

Gilchrist frowned but didn't say anything for a moment.

'That's nice,' she eventually said slowly.

'No, really. My dad and her grandmother . . .'

'I thought you were talking figuratively. You mean William Simpson is your half-brother? Wow.'

'Wow, indeed.'

'He's been in business with Alice Sutherland, the woman who was trying to develop Salthaven Lido.'

'On that project?'

'No, a West Pier one that lost out to the i360.'

'I thought Simpson was off saving the world for genocidal dictators.'

'I guess that leaves him with spare time on his hands,' Gilchrist said, taking a sip of her drink. 'Kate hasn't mentioned your relationship.'

'Kate doesn't know. I decided not to tell her.'

Gilchrist looked surprised and started to speak but her phone rang.

'DI Gilchrist,' she said in a business-like tone. She listened for a moment. 'OK, thanks.' She turned to Watts. 'They've found Christine Bromley. Bilson will do the post-mortem.'

'After the Coniston death I had a slightly odd conversation with Neill. I think he thought his friend's death was suspicious. He said that strange things had been happening lately. When I asked him he backed off.'

Gilchrist cupped her chin.

'Really? Perhaps I do need to talk to him now.'

Watts started to get up. 'I need to go anyway.'

Gilchrist stood. Watts moved to embrace her but her phone rang again. She glanced down at it.

'Bellamy,' she said, picking it up.

Watts gave her a little wave and stepped away. 'Cheerio, then.'

Gilchrist went back to the station to find Heap and Sylvia Wade deep in conversation. 'Constable Wade here has been to see April Medavoy again since she discovered Gulliver's last call was from her. She's found something interesting.'

'It wasn't the phone call itself,' Sylvia said. 'She said that was just about some paper Gulliver was writing for the committee.'

'You believed her?'

'I pressed her and didn't have any reason to believe she was lying.'

'Go on.'

'I think when she phoned him he was having that glass of wine with somebody. She said she heard him excuse himself to somebody and then she sensed he went into another room to take her call. Even so, he sounded cautious and distracted. Her words.'

'So we know what time he was in his house,' Gilchrist said. 'That's good for the timeline. Did she have any clue about who he was with? Did she assume it was Provocateur?'

Wade smiled at the use of the nickname they'd

given to Francis Shaw because of his pretentious website.

'She didn't mention him at all. But she wondered if it might be this man Derek Neill, from Dolphin Smile.'

Gilchrist and Heap exchanged glances.

'Now why would she think that?' Gilchrist said.

'Apparently he and Gulliver were old friends and had been seeing a lot of each other lately. And Roland had mentioned trying to get sponsorship of some sort out of him for Save Salthaven Lido.'

'Did she say what kind of old friends?'

Wade shook her head.

Gilchrist looked across at the Gulliver murder investigation timeline on the whiteboard on the wall.

'Mr Neill is suddenly proving to be a man of considerable interest. Bellamy, find out where he is and let's go to see him.'

Bob Watts was standing on his balcony looking at the choppy waters of Brighton bay. His six-hour swim had been hard work but not as difficult as he had feared. Now he was surprised to see Derek Neill walk across from the seafront promenade and disappear from sight beneath his building. Was he coming to see him?

When the doorbell didn't ring he leaned out from his balcony but couldn't see Neill on the street. However, he could see Sarah Gilchrist and Bellamy Heap walking in his direction.

He wasn't expecting them but he went over to

his entry phone and on the video monitor saw them climbing the front steps to his building. He pressed his buzzer, and said: 'This is an unexpected pleasure. Come up.'

Gilchrist and Heap looked bemused then into the camera at the entrance.

'We're not here to see you, Bob,' Gilchrist said. 'We're here for a neighbour of yours. Derek Neill.'

Watts frowned. 'I had no idea he lived here. I've just seen him crossing the road.'

'He's out?' Gilchrist said.

'No, no – I think he was coming in.'

'Small world,' Gilchrist said. 'Perhaps we can come up once we're finished with him – assuming nothing arises from our conversation that requires immediate attention.'

'I'll get the cocktail shaker out now,' Watts said.

He walked back over to the balcony, musing on Derek Neill and the enigmatic Rasa. He liked the man and hoped he wasn't caught up in something illegal.

His phone rang and Margaret Lively's name came up on the screen. He let it ring. He wasn't sure what to do about her. Unless he was misreading the signs – and that was a frequent occurrence for him – she was interested in him as a lover. He liked her but she was younger than he felt comfortable with. Had she been Sarah Gilchrist's age that might be different. Had she, indeed, been Sarah Gilchrist.

He had wondered if they might get together after the dust had settled over his divorce and all the shenanigans around the Milldean Massacre but it hadn't happened. Maybe the moment had gone. They'd both had other involvements, both seen them go horribly wrong. Now they were good friends, and he was pleased about that, although from time to time tensions arose.

He had enjoyed his meeting with Margaret Lively. She worked for a venture capitalist, which made him uneasy – as criminals went, bankers and venture capitalists were high on his list of unconvicted ones. But she had made the jokes about her job before he could.

She left no message and when he called her straight back it went to voicemail. He left no message either.

Ten

When Gilchrist and Heap entered Derek Neill's apartment, he was civil and bade them sit. His look intrigued Gilchrist. He was a handsome man, underneath the modish long beard and fastidiously cropped hair. What bits of hair-free face she could see were deeply lined by long exposure to the sun. His tan seemed ingrained in the skin.

He served coffee, then moved over to the window and pulled down thin blinds.

'Can't see for buggery in here at this time of day,' he said. He turned. 'I assume you're here about Christine Bromley. Terrible business.'

'You were seen with Roland Gulliver in

128

Woodvale Cemetery, possibly a couple of times,'
Gilchrist said.

'Not Christine then,' he said with a small smile.
'Roland – yes, that's quite possible.'

'Why were you there?'

'Talking to my friend.'

'Just talking?'

'As I remember.'

'What about the day you interrupted a group
of teenagers attacking a young woman,' Heap
said.

'What about it?'

'When was that?'

'I don't remember. I mean I remember the incident, of course, but I don't remember which day
it was.'

'Did you or Mr Gulliver recognize any of the
youngsters?'

Neill shook his head slowly. 'I don't recall
Roland saying anything. I certainly didn't recognize anyone.'

'You were in the cemetery with him the day
before he died though?'

'We were discussing ways in which Dolphin
Smile might get involved in the Save Salthaven
Lido campaign.'

'And what conclusion did you reach?'

'The discussion was on-going.'

'Someone has said you were, quote, "kissing
and cuddling there".'

'What about it?'

'Were you an item?'

'No.'

'Never?'

'None of your business, but never.'

'How do you explain the kissing and cuddling?'

'I don't. Do I need to?'

Gilchrist sighed. Of course, he didn't. She loathed asking these sorts of questions.

'And you didn't see him the night of his death?' she said.

'As I said.'

'We're going to need a DNA swab.'

Neill just shrugged, clearly pissed off at the intrusive last questions.

Watts answered the door to Sarah Gilchrist. No Bellamy Heap.

'Neill gave us a DNA swab so Bellamy has gone to get it analysed ASAP.'

Watts wanted to ask what was going on but knew better than to do so. Gilchrist would tell him if she chose to. She chose to.

'It's this murder investigation – Roland Gulliver. We heard they were old friends but Neill says Gulliver got in touch to try to get Dolphin Smile to sponsor or in some way help the Save Salthaven Lido campaign. Says he visited Gulliver at home at some point but he wasn't the bloke drinking wine with him on the day Gulliver was waterboarded then stabbed to death.'

'Waterboarded?'

'I've probably said too much – you're not supposed to know about operational matters, are you?'

'As police commissioner, no; but as your friend, maybe.'

'Where are the cocktails then?' she said, then

flushed, perhaps at her forwardness. Watts had always found Gilchrist to be quite shy.

Watts laughed. 'Will you settle for an Australian sauvignon?'

'Done. Anyway, I asked Neill if he thought there was anything odd about Christine Bromley's death – in case he thought it was as dodgy as you say he thought the Coniston death to be – but he didn't open up.'

'You didn't say you'd heard about odd goings-on before Coniston?'

'Didn't want to land you in it and let him know you'd told me.'

'Thank you. Is he a person of interest in the case?'

'Potentially. We have a sighting of a man fitting his description with Gulliver in the cemetery the other day. And Kate, if you recall, seemed to think they were around together on another occasion.'

'Did you bring that up, if you don't mind my asking?'

'He said they were just talking but I have a witness saying something different.'

'Quarrelling?'

'"Kissing and cuddling" – quote.'

'And such a beautiful wife too.'

'He's married?'

'Well, he has a business partner who everyone assumes is also his life partner – is that the right phrase?'

Gilchrist smiled and nodded.

'Rasa. Ice-queen type, mind. And in any case, who is anyone to judge the complexity of the human heart?'

Gilchrist looked thoughtful.

'Who indeed,' she murmured.

When Gilchrist got back to the office Heap was holding her phone away from his ear. He looked relieved when she came in. He mouthed, *Mr Bilson* – Gilchrist was amused by his formality even here – and passed her phone to her with seeming relief.

'Sarah, how lovely to hear your voice – not that it wasn't a delight to converse with young Bellamy. I was explaining to him that it is so nice to have a freshly drowned person to dissect. Floaters, who've been in the water for days, are the worst to do an autopsy on. All those gases bloating the body, all those fish nibbling away at the corpse for days on end.'

'I can imagine, although I'd rather not. Did she drown?'

Bilson ignored the question.

'Are you any nearer to telling me who killed Roland Gulliver?' he said. 'Have you felt someone's collar – do people still say that?'

'I don't know if anyone has ever said that outside of cheap crime fiction. Our investigations are continuing.'

'You're so intoxicating when you play it by the book,' Bilson said.

Gilchrist rolled her eyes. Bilson was pretty certainly breaking a large number of 'harassment in the workplace' rules with his continuing badinage but she wasn't offended and groan-worthy flirtation between equals was hardly the same as what some Hollywood producers got up to.

'So this poor woman who drowned during the swim,' she said. 'Is there anything suspicious about her death?'

'Why do you think that her death might be suspicious?'

'Money. Lots of it.'

'These damn fools swimming in cold water don't know what they're letting themselves in for.'

'I'm not sure I know.'

'Hypothermia. The science of it is fascinating.'

'I'm sure it is to you, Frank. And Bob Watts, as I recall.'

'I consider myself trumped,' Bilson said. 'A word we must use carefully in these mad geopolitical days. But allow me to take a moment to perorate on the wonders of the mammalian body as it accustoms itself to extreme cold.'

'Perorate?'

'If you would allow me.'

'By all means, perorate away in the middle of a murder investigation.'

'Like other mammals it seems that humans can, with sustained exposure to extreme cold, acclimatize in the way small mammals do, through an increased output of noradrenaline and/or thyroxin and the associated activation of free fatty acids.'

'Fascinating.'

'It is, because of a controversial theory that we have both brown and white fat in our bodies. Burning brown fat generates heat thanks to these free fatty acids. And it is this heat production that makes it possible for humans to acclimatize over ten days or so to extreme cold.'

'Frank . . .'

'If the theory is correct, what's intriguing is the possibility of using winter sport as a pleasant method of treating obesity.'

'Frank!'

'Thank you for listening.' Bilson cleared his throat. 'This woman did drown but not as a consequence of a heart attack.'

'You've been quick.'

'And your department will pay the high financial price for that speed.'

'What then, if not heart attack?'

'She was poisoned. Kind of.'

'Come again?'

'I'll know more when I get further information about stomach content. Not that there was much stomach content. I think she'd been throwing up.'

Gilchrist looked across the office at Heap, who had just returned. She put her phone on speaker.

'I'm struggling here, Frank,' she said. 'What did you mean, "kind of"?'

'There were traces of ketamine in her system – horse tranquillizer often used for recreational purposes. Well, she may have taken it herself or she may have taken it unwittingly and, combined with the temperature of the water, it would have made her sluggish and then the hypothermia would have taken over.'

'Taken it unwittingly?'

'Most probably in the feed. The feed is like an intravenous injection – it has immediate impact. The swimmer's body is so pumped it goes straight into the system and goes straight to work. So if you add a poison that is capable

134

of attaching itself to the feed then the body of the swimmer will absorb that without much problem. And it is going to have a massive effect, but not necessarily straight away.' Bilson paused for a moment. 'The swimmer might be throwing up anyway, as she was, so if their body reject the poison nobody is going to think twice. But most probably it gets in their system and absorbed before it can be rejected. It's very interesting science actually . . .'

Gilchrist inhaled impatiently.

'Sorry,' he said.

Gilchrist was still looking at Heap.

'OK, I get the science but you still haven't explained the "kind of"?' she said.

'Well, the poison wouldn't directly kill her. As I said it would have disabled her so that she couldn't help but drown.'

'So we need to find out who put the poison in the feed.'

Heap drew closer when he heard this, tapping away on his laptop as he did so.

'Not so much of the "we",' Bilson said. 'I believe feeds are prepared individually. Should be fairly straightforward to find out who prepared her feed.' He cleared his throat. 'If, of course, she drank her own feed and not somebody else's by mistake.'

Gilchrist and Heap exchanged glances.

'OK, thanks for that last complication, Frank,' Gilchrist said. 'Just what we need.' Heap nodded. 'Now, would you do me a favour with regard to another drowning?'

She gave him the details of Philip Coates's death.

'Contact your equivalent up in the Lakes – not that you could ever have an equivalent, of course.'

Surprisingly, Bilson ignored the compliment. 'You think they're related?'

'It could just be an unlikely coincidence.'

'Do the two corpses have a connection?'

'A direct one is unknown as yet but, yes, there is a link.'

'I was expecting you to have me sitting down looking at CCTV footage from the gym to see if I could recognize the man sitting in the sauna with Roland Gulliver.'

'Believe me, I had you lined up for that. But unfortunately the gym dumps its CCTV footage every five days so that day is gone.'

'As so many days are gone. Where are they now, Sarah, those blue remembered hills?'

'Goodbye, Frank. And thank you.'

'I might have equivalents but no equals,' Bilson said as he hung up. Gilchrist smiled and turned to Heap to tell him what Bilson had said prior to the call being on speakerphone.

'I don't see how nobody saw anything,' she said, 'if she was drowning.'

'What's to see?' Heap said. 'A couple of hundred people doing front crawl; nobody is going to see anything but their own arms and the scissoring legs of the next person in front. They won't exactly be following what's going on unless they bump into it.'

'What do we know about Christine Bromley's support team?'

'I think each swimmer just had one person to

feed them. I was Kate's designated person. Every two hours or so she would pick up a new feed at the Palace Pier from me – I'd throw the bottle into the water attached to a rope so I could haul it out again when she'd drunk it.'

'Who did Bob Watts?' Gilchrist said. 'Just out of interest.'

Heap frowned.

'I don't know.' He tapped on his iPad. 'There's no name on the call sheet. Christine Bromley had a woman called Janet Rule.'

'And what do we know about her?' Gilchrist said.

'If I remember the name in the newspaper accurately, she was to be Bromley's wife.'

Janet Rule lived in Hove. Gilchrist sent Sylvia Wade down to advise her that her fiancée had been murdered, while she called Watts and filled him in.

'Who gave you your feed, by the way?' she asked just before she rang off.

'I tried an experiment as the water wasn't so cold. I didn't have a feed.'

'At all? For six hours? But I thought—'

'It's an army thing,' he said. 'My training was all extreme stuff.'

'And how did you feel after six hours.'

'I felt fine. Now I feel like shit.'

Gilchrist was impatient. She called Heap over to sit with her.

'So what have we got, Bellamy – aside from more lookalike bearded men than we know what to do with. Why haven't you grown a beard?'

'I'm fair-haired, ma'am. The one time I grew a beard, when I was a student, nobody noticed.'

Gilchrist smiled.

'Roland Gulliver is murdered at night,' she said. 'At some point that evening a paunchy man has an altercation on the lido steps with a hipster who probably isn't Derek Neill over somebody called Lesley.'

'And Mr Bilson saw Roland Gulliver in conversation with a paunchy man in the sauna.'

'There's no security at the lido because Terry Dean has drunk too much. At some other point Gulliver is sharing a bottle of wine with a person unknown when Mrs Medavoy phones. At a further point he's waterboarded somewhere, stabbed then dumped.'

'The previous day he's seen in the cemetery with a hipster who, according to Darrel, isn't the same one who was having the argument at the lido,' Heap said. 'In fact this one he's kissing and cuddling, according to Darrel. Neill agrees he was with Gulliver but has no comment about the kissing and cuddling.'

'Kate identifies Derek Neill as one of the two men, along with Roland Gulliver, who rescues her from the aforementioned Darrel on an earlier occasion.'

'So it's possible, ma'am, that Darrel could be making up the kissing and cuddling to get back at Neill. We need to talk to Darrel again. But why are Gulliver and Neill meeting up a couple of times in the cemetery, which has been known to be a cottaging area from time to time?'

'Then there is Christine Bromley,' Gilchrist

said. 'No known connection to Roland Gulliver. Not part of Save Salthaven.'

'In fact, rather, potentially in business with Alice Sutherland over the West Pier, who in turn is a major part of Save Salthaven – as she's the big bad wolf the campaigners are trying to save Salthaven from. And her man, Philip Coates, her boots on the ground, is also drowned.'

'In a swim organized, as is the Brighton one, by Derek Neill.'

'Who has no known business links to either Bromley, other than through the swim, or Sutherland.'

'There,' Gilchrist said, leaning back. 'Clear as mud now.'

She phoned Sylvia Wade and put it on the speaker so Heap could hear.

'Ma'am?' Wade said, her voice a little breathless. 'Is anything wrong? I've just this second finished with Janet Rule.'

'How was she?'

'Devastated. She, of course, vehemently denies tampering with Christine's bottle.'

'Did she tamper with it not-so-vehemently?'

'I think she is denying tampering of any sort.'

'You actually asked her about it?' Gilchrist said.

'Not at all. The second I said, "Ms Bromley may have been murdered," she blurted it out.'

'Did she lose sight of the bottle? Was it swapped?'

'Affirmative to the first. She was watching Ms Bromley. Then she had to go to the loo. She wasn't expecting she'd "need to keep a close eye on a drink bottle". End quote.'

139

'OK but she remains the obvious suspect.'

'If they were about to be married—'

'I know what you're saying, Sylvia – it's only after marriage that you want to kill your partner.'

Heap butted in. 'Actually, there is only her word for it they were going to get married. Find out if there's anyone else to confirm that. And, Constable Wade?'

'Yes, detective sergeant?'

'Can you confirm that you informed her of a possible murder and not of a poisoning?'

'Absolutely certain.'

'I assumed so but which leads to the obvious question about how she knew the bottle was involved,' Heap said.

'I know,' Wade said. 'I thought I would be stepping beyond my remit – and possibly into a procedural quagmire – if I pursued that.'

'Wise of you, Sylvia,' Gilchrist said. 'And well done.'

Gilchrist tapped her teeth with her pen. 'Did Ms Rule have anything else useful to say?'

'Not a thing, aside from accusing Christine's brother of committing the murder.'

'Did she specify which one?'

'She was a bit vague on that one.'

Heap scratched his cheek. 'Supposing this death has nothing to do with Christine Bromley's family. Actually, supposing this death has nothing to do with Christine Bromley. What if she was randomly killed? What if, for kicks or some other sick notion, someone tampered with the first feed bottle they came across?'

Gilchrist shook her head so hard it hurt.

'No, no, no. Trust you to make it complicated, Bellamy. I *like* the idea of it being linked to the family. That's proper. We can do proper police work based on that assumption. Someone killing randomly – that's messy. It doesn't have proper edges. I don't like that at all.'

'Ma'am.'

She sighed. 'Bilson mentioned in passing she might have been given somebody else's feed. Somebody else altogether might have been the target.'

Heap nodded slowly. 'Sylvia, how are we getting along with the timeline for all of the swimmers and their supports?'

'Slowly.'

'We'd better start doing the background checks now on all of them rather than just the ones we thought might be of interest later.'

'Ma'am.'

Gilchrist turned to Heap. 'Any thoughts about where you and I go now?'

'Back to Janet Rule?'

'Is Janet Rule Brighton based, Sylvia?'

'A flat on the marina, ma'am.'

'OK, but let's start with the young brother James Bromley.'

'I've already confirmed he's in the office in Shoreham, ma'am. I'll let them know we're heading that way.'

'Great – then when we go to interview Janet Rule we can go to the pictures afterwards, Bellamy. There's that new Meryl Streep film on.' Gilchrist saw Heap's expression. 'That was a joke, Bellamy.'

'I've already seen it, ma'am. With Kate.'
'Well, touché, detective sergeant. Touché.'

Eleven

The Bromleys HQ was just a little beyond the Ropetackle Arts Centre along the coast road to Worthing. James Bromley's office was on the second floor with a magnificent view of the sea through a ceiling-to-floor window taking up a whole wall. However, he sat behind his desk with his back to the view.

He had a lean and hungry look. The phrase popped into Gilchrist's head and she was pleased with herself that she even knew its source. She had learned something at school.

He was tall and broad-shouldered in a too-tight suit with the currently fashionable too-short jacket. His shoes were long and pointed. His cheekbones were almost sculpted, with hollows below them. He had an intense stare and a five o'clock shadow. He was striking, looking both incredibly ugly and incredibly handsome at the same time. Gilchrist found him utterly disconcerting.

Condolences given and received, they sat in low chairs in front of his desk.

'I'd find it hard to turn my back on that view,' Gilchrist said cheerily.

Bromley gave the smallest of smiles. 'I've learned to turn my back on many things.'

'I'm sorry to ask you invasive questions at such a time, but we need to progress this investigation as quickly as possible,' Gilchrist said.

'Sure, but I don't have any proof it was Janet. I wasn't there.'

'You're accusing Janet Rule of killing your sister?' Gilchrist said.

'She was feeding her, wasn't she? That's what killed her, wasn't it?'

'Such information has not been released. Do you mind telling me what makes you think so?'

Bromley snorted. 'Janet phoned me and accused me of the crime. Told me I'd poisoned my sister's feed. How did she know how my sister had died, do you think?'

'Ms Rule said they were about to be married,' Heap said.

Bromley snorted again. 'She would say that. First I've heard of it.'

'Were you close to your sister?' Gilchrist said.

'On the whole.'

'On the whole, sir?' Heap said.

'My sister was incredibly competitive. I'm somewhere in the middle of the spectrum. That could cause friction. This swimming . . .'

'What about it?' Gilchrist said when Bromley's voice trailed away.

He looked out of the window. 'I run ultramarathons. That's what I do, all over the world.'

Gilchrist tilted her head. 'Ultramarathons?'

'Very long marathons,' Heap murmured.

'There's nothing more exhilarating,' Bromley said. 'My sister couldn't compete with that. So she decided to swim the Channel instead.' He shook his head. 'Take advantage of all that weight she'd put on after the attack.'

Gilchrist and Heap looked at each other.

'You're going to have to unpack that, sir,' Heap said.

'The weight or the attack?'

'Let's focus on the attack,' Gilchrist said.

Bromley sat forward and clasped his hands on the table. His knuckles were blunt and a little battered, his fingers scabbed and scarred. He caught Gilchrist's look.

'I do free climbing too. Ramming your hands into crevices to bear your weight isn't the best form of manicure.' He cleared his throat but it sounded theatrical, not real. 'My sister was raped about a year ago. You people never found who did it. Ever since she's suffered from post-traumatic stress disorder. Which is why she was eating like a pig and acting mad as a bag of snakes.'

'Poor woman,' Gilchrist said, looking levelly at Bromley.

'Oh indeed,' he said, offering the palms of his hands. 'Don't get me wrong – it's a terrible thing to happen to anyone and you feel it even more when it's your sister. But it made her ungovernable.' He looked from one to the other. He had the most intense stare. 'You know about the recent nonsense?'

'The workers' cooperative?' Heap said.

Bromley nodded.

'I mean, the idea was barking. "Hey, James, hey, Bernard, hey, Mum, care to hand over £60 million each to the people who work for us?"'

144

'What was her reasoning?' Heap said.

Bromley flashed him an intense look.

'There was no reasoning,' he snorted. 'That was the point. Janet Rule is full of this left-wing crap and they'd gone off to Argentina and checked out some large cattle cooperative there that's a big success. Christine said it was a great model. And I'm sure it was. But why she has to use it for our family business I didn't quite get.'

He leaned back.

'"Let's each give all our shares to the staff – it's only fair." Well, excuse my language, but fuck fair. My father worked damned hard to build up this business and I'll be damned if we're going to hand it over to others without a fight.'

He caught Gilchrist's look.

'I'm fully aware that gives me a motive to kill my sister but she was, when all is said and done, my sister and that's not what relatives do.'

Gilchrist tried not to raise an eyebrow. In her experience, that's exactly what many relatives did. 'But you were angry with her.'

'Actually, no.' He saw Gilchrist's look. 'Seriously. I was exaggerating for the sake of effect just now. Nobody was upset. All discussion was reasoned and calm from our side. My brother, mother and I had no animosity towards my sister.'

Gilchrist raised an eyebrow. 'I wish I took whatever your family takes to remain calm.'

Bromley clasped his big, knobbly hands again. 'We all recognized that she was ill. As I said, ever since the *incident* Christine had been suffering with PTSD. One consequence, I understand, is that to keep the demons at bay some

145

people work non-stop. Christine was working sixteen-hour days, seven days a week. She burned out. Soon after our father died she had a total collapse.'

'When was that?' Heap said. 'The death of your father, I mean, sir.'

'About a year ago.'

Bromley had an odd expression on his face.

'He was a good age. Eighty-seven. He'd lived a good life.'

'Even so,' Heap said.

'You and your father were close?' Gilchrist said.

Bromley wrinkled his nose in an oddly child-like way.

'Close enough to know that he never, ever discussed our family business becoming a mutual in his entire life,' he said. 'Nor that the family should give up ownership.'

'Might he have said it privately to Christine?' Heap said.

'Christine never claimed that,' Bromley said.

'Were they close?'

Again that odd expression on Bromley's face.

'Oh, yes. He adored her: his only daughter, you know. He'd sometimes talk about the business with her when she was still in the sixth form at school.'

'And with you?' Gilchrist said.

He smiled and shook his head.

'Though in fairness I wasn't interested. Football mad – and Nintendo, of course.' He looked down. 'Anyway, when she was at secondary school she'd work for the business during the school holidays.'

146

'You did the same?' Heap said.

Bromley laughed. He had small pointed teeth, curved inward like a rodent.

'I rather liked having holidays: you know, hanging out with my mates, trying not to get into too much trouble.' He looked from one to the other of them. 'I'm sure you would have been the same.'

'No argument there,' Gilchrist said. 'So she was driven long before the sexual assault.'

'I suppose she was always driven, yes. Anyway, the minute she left university my father made her deputy chairman. It was always understood that she'd succeed him.'

'Was she the eldest?'

'Actually, no. We're the second family. My brother, Bernard, from my father's first marriage, is ten years older.'

'There was no discussion about Bernard taking over the family business?' Heap said.

'Not in my hearing,' Bromley said.

'What did Bernard think about that?' Gilchrist said.

Bromley showed his teeth again. 'You'd have to ask him, Detective Inspector.'

Heap had been scratching his ruddy cheek for a minute or so, each time leaving a white line that would quickly suffuse with blood. 'Do you or your company have any dealings with Alice Sutherland and her Scarborough-based company?' he said now.

'I've heard of her, of course, but that kind of thing would be above my pay grade.' He waved at his large office. 'This is a kind of grace and favour thing. My father and my sister never really trusted me with any kind of real responsibility. Not that I wouldn't be able to handle it – I'm an MBA – but that they wouldn't want me to.'

'Does the same go for Bernard?'

'Of course.'

'Does the name Philip Coates mean anything?'

Bromley shook his head.

'Roland Gulliver?'

'Sorry.' Bromley was starting to look impatient. 'These names are sounding kind of random.'

'They're not,' Gilchrist said. 'Where were you on the morning of the Brighton event?'

'Running on the Downs with three buddies. Just a quickie between Lewes and Wollstenbury Hill. Then we had lunch in the Jack and Jill. Lots of witnesses there.'

'When was the last time you saw your brother?' Heap said.

'Bernard? Couple of weeks ago. We're not close.'

'When did you last see your sister?'

'Oh, in work the other day. Probably Friday.'

'Before we go, would you just clarify what the situation was about the cooperative? With you and your brother opposing, presumably it couldn't go ahead.'

Bromley's eyes glinted as he steepled his hands.

'There are five people on the board, excluding Christine. Three were opposed, two in favour.'

'So including her vote in favour it was a dead-lock?' Gilchrist said.

'She had two votes,' Bromley said. 'Which would be decisive.'

'But she did find other people to favour the scheme,' Heap said. 'Who were those two?'

Bromley grimaced. 'Our finance director and the other union representative.'

'The other union representative?' Heap said.

Bromley looked at him oddly. 'In addition to Christine.'

He saw Gilchrist's frown. 'Didn't you know? Christine was both chairman and union delegate. That's why she got two votes. Her two votes would have carried the scheme.'

'How can the chairman of the company also be its union representative?' Gilchrist said as they walked back to the car.

Heap shook his head. 'Nothing should surprise us with this company, ma'am. But it does seem like a conflict of interest.'

'What did you make of him, Bellamy?'

'Disconcertingly frank.'

'Disconcerting, certainly,' Gilchrist murmured. 'Let's do the mother next, then Bernard, the older brother.'

Heap took a call from Sylvia Wade when they got in the car. 'Janet Rule is home and happy to see us, ma'am.'

'OK, let's fit her in now.'

Rule had a small flat overlooking one of the inner lagoons at the Marina. She was waiting at the lift doors when they opened on her floor.

'Ms Rule, we're sorry for your loss,' Gilchrist said. 'I'm DI Gilchrist and this is DS Heap.' Heap nodded. 'We just need to go over a few things.'

149

'So you can blame it on the queer?' Rule said as she led them down the corridor to her flat.

'We adhere, quite rightly, to a strict code of LGBTQ+ conduct in this force,' Gilchrist said, feeling prim as she said it. 'This isn't about the bottle of feed. It's about your relationship with Ms Bromley.'

Rule shut the door behind them as they entered the flat. She was about the same height as Heap, chunky, with spiky hair to go with her spiky manner. She had a tough look about her. She looked at Heap.

'Is he always red-faced or is it because he's never met a dyke before?'

Both Gilchrist and Heap ignored the remark, though Heap might have blushed a little more.

'If I may say, Ms Rule,' Gilchrist said, 'your hostile attitude is a little surprising since I would have thought we all want the same end – to apprehend the person who murdered Ms Bromley.'

'Actually, I'd rather have her back, but I know that isn't going to happen.'

'How long had you known Ms Bromley?' Heap said.

'Is my answer going to help you apprehend the killer?'

'Please, Ms Rule. We know you're upset . . .'

Janet Rule started to cry and Gilchrist saw beneath the bluster. Heap conjured up a neatly folded wodge of tissues and passed them to her.

'They'll disintegrate if you blow too hard and that could be messy for all of us,' he said.

Rule looked at him in surprise and snorted a

laugh into a tissue. She wiped her nose and gave a couple of tiny blows, her eyes fixed on him.

'We can't be having that, can we?' she said, her voice gentler.

'Preferably not,' Heap said.

'Eighteen months, almost to the day,' Rule said. 'It was love at first sight. We moved in together and I proposed and we were going to be married.'

'We've heard reports that she was a bit all over the place, suffering from post-traumatic stress because of the attack on her. How did you find her?'

Janet Rule blew her nose again.

'Calm, actually. Calm and calming. Full of energy, full of ideas.'

'Like turning the family business into a workers' cooperative.'

'That was just one of them. She wanted to go into politics. She was passionately against fracking, passionately for gender and LGBTQ+ rights.' Rule gave a rueful smile. 'She was passionate about life.'

'Did she say how her family responded to her co-op proposals?'

'She didn't say.' Rule rolled her thick shoulders. 'When we got together she said the one area she wanted to keep private was the family business. It wasn't something she wanted to talk about. Not to exclude me, she said, but because it would get in the way. I didn't really understand but I went along with it. I assume you've talked to the family?'

'We are about to.'

'Bernard?'

'In due course.'

'I heard them having a blazing row a couple of weeks ago. It left Christine pretty shaken but she wouldn't talk about it afterwards.'

'You didn't hear what the row was actually about?' Heap said.

Rule shook her head. 'I saw him on the morning of the swim.'

'Bernard Bromley?'

Rule nodded.

'You've met him then,' Heap said. 'Many times?'

'Just the once. Christine took me to her mother's birthday drinks thing at the family home in East Preston.' She smiled, remembering. 'The family didn't take to me.'

'They were rude?'

'No, no – far too polite for that. James was charm personified. Bernard can't do charm though – his mother's genes, I suppose. He spent the entire couple of hours staring at me. Actually, I saw his stepmother discreetly chide him for it – she had noticed too, so I wasn't imagining it. Let's just say I'm not what they're used to.'

'You saw Bernard on the Palace Pier?'

Rule shook her head.

'On Madeira Drive, near the big wheel. Looking shifty.'

'Yet you seemed a bit vague with my constable about which brother you were accusing of killing her.'

'Well, Bernard doesn't do anything without James's say so.'

'Define "shifty", Ms Rule,' Gilchrist said. 'You said Bernard was looking "shifty".'

'Ratty hat pulled low, head down, trying not to be noticed.'

'What time was this?'

'Around nine a.m.'

'Half an hour before the race started.' Rule nodded.

'Was he heading towards the pier or away from it?' Heap said.

'Neither. He was palely loitering.'

'And you're sure it was him?' Gilchrist said.

'Certain. I never forget an arsehole.'

'You didn't like him because he kept staring at you at this birthday drinks thing?' Heap said.

'I didn't like him because he threatened Christine.'

'She told you this?' Gilchrist said. 'I thought she kept family things private?'

'I heard him.'

'When?'

'During the row I told you about.'

'I thought you said you couldn't make out the words.'

'I couldn't except for the threat.'

Convenient, Gilchrist thought but didn't say. She avoided looking at Heap.

'What did he say?' Heap said.

'He screamed: "Over your dead body."'

'Not over *my* dead body?' Heap said. 'That's the usual formulation.'

Rule shook her head. 'Exactly. It was *your*, definitely.'

Gilchrist frowned. 'And that was it – that was all you heard? You didn't hear anything that preceded it or followed it.'

'Just that,' Rule said. 'It was because he screamed it so loudly.'

'I don't suppose anyone else saw Bernard Bromley "palely loitering" by the big wheel,' Heap said.

'Actually, yes,' Rule said. 'I was with a friend. I pointed him out to her.'

'Did Bernard Bromley see you?' Gilchrist said.

Rule shook her head. 'He was too busy trying to be inconspicuous.'

'We'll need the name of your friend and her contact details,' Heap said.

'Of course.' Rule started rummaging around in her bag. 'She's called Kate Simpson and her phone number is—'

'We have her contact details,' Heap said, flushing as he did so.

'Tell me, Ms Rule, when my colleague DC Wade questioned you, how did you immediately jump to the conclusion Ms Bromley had been poisoned.'

'What other conclusion could there be?'

'Any number.'

'Well, it's been common gossip in swimming circles for years that if you want to commit the perfect crime you do it on a long swim and use the feed.'

'Common gossip?'

'Not in a serious way, just in a shivery sort of way for people who read a lot of crime fiction.'

'And you lost sight of her feed.'

'Everyone lost sight of the feeds at some point.'

'And, in fact, you don't know what subsequently happened to the container.'

'In all the confusion and upset, no, I'm afraid it disappeared. Misplaced somewhere probably.'

'Very well, Ms Rule. We'll probably need to talk to you again. If you think of anything else to tell us, please do get in touch.'

Gilchrist phoned Kate from the car.

'Hi, Kate, this is police business, which is why it's me not Bellamy phoning you.' Gilchrist smiled faintly at her detective sergeant. 'But he's listening on speaker.'

'Hi, Bellamy,' Kate called, then said more quietly, a smile in her voice, 'do I need a lawyer, Sarah?'

'It's about Christine Bromley's murder.'

'Of course,' Simpson said more solemnly. 'How can I help?'

'You're friends with her partner, Janet Rule?'

'I wouldn't say friends, exactly. I've met her a couple of times.'

'Does that mean you knew Christine Bromley too?'

'Actually, no.' Simpson laughed nervously. 'Am I a suspect, now?'

'Don't be daft,' Gilchrist said. 'Janet Rule said she had been with you at about nine a.m. and she pointed out a man to you.'

'Christine's brother. Yes.'

'What happened?'

'We bumped into each other going onto the Palace Pier. Actually, she called my name. I was a bit surprised. I've seen her around the swimming club but we've never really had a conversation. We just know each other to say hello to.'

'Go on, Kate.'

'She was looking over towards the wheel. It was already pretty busy round there, people queuing and stuff. She said something like, "There's that dickhead brother of Christine's. Wonder why he's here."'

'Did you know Bernard Bromley by sight?'

'Is that his name? I don't think so.'

'You don't know?'

'Well, I didn't know who she was pointing at. I was in a hurry to get on the pier. I just said something like "OK, right" and we went onto the pier.'

'So you didn't actually see this person?'

'That's right.'

'Did she say anything more about him?'

'Nothing, but we joined up with another group of swimmers almost straightaway and didn't really speak again, just the two of us.'

Gilchrist thanked Kate and offered the phone to Heap. He flushed and shook his head. She ended the call.

'Interesting,' she said.

'Very,' Heap said. 'The mother next, ma'am?'

Gilchrist nodded.

Twelve

'It was just my daughter being herself,' Mrs Bromley said quietly. They were sitting in a long garden leading down to the beach in West Preston.

Heap had told Gilchrist as they drew up outside it that Mrs Bromley's home was two houses along from where Bernard Rafferty, the Brighton Pavilion director, had been murdered some months ago.

'You weren't angry about the commune idea?' Gilchrist said.

'My daughter has always been difficult but I stopped being angry with her long ago, as it was such a waste of time. And then there was the rape. That terrible thing.'

'She told you about it?'

'Not the detail. Only that it had happened. I don't believe she told anyone the detail, except perhaps her . . . partner.'

'Janet Rule.'

'Just so.'

Kathy Bromley was a shapely woman in her late fifties. She was almost as tall as Gilchrist. She had a confident gaze that at first fooled Gilchrist into thinking she didn't care about her daughter's death. But as their talk progressed she realized that Mrs Bromley had iron self-discipline. She sat not just straight-backed but rigid and her hands were clasped over her knees so tightly her knuckles were white. Heavy make-up couldn't disguise the strain around her eyes.

She was holding herself together in public so that she could grieve in private.

'You were your husband's second wife,' Heap said.

'Anne, his first wife, died in childbirth nearly forty years ago, giving birth to Bernard. They'd had trouble conceiving and had almost given up

157

when she got pregnant in her forties. We married ten years later.' She put her hand up, palm out. 'I know what you're thinking. Yes, there was a big age gap between us. John was sixty and I was in my late twenties when we married. It happens.' She waved her hand around the room. 'As you can see, if I married him for his money we were both most abstemious.'

It was true, thought Gilchrist. Although the house was probably worth a bomb the furnishings were unfussy, worn and comfy looking. There was a lovely grandfather clock in the corner of the room but no other antiques visible. Although the paintings on the wall might be worth a fortune for all she knew.

'In 1945 when he was only 15, he got work in London clearing bombsites then came with a gang of workmen down here to work on the post-war reconstruction in Brighton. They were in competition with the Irish gangs but there was work enough for everyone.'

She looked absently round the room.

'Within ten years he was running his own company. He was a good boss. He made a point of eating with his men in the canteen at least once a week. He paid them fairly and treated them well.' She lifted her hand and tapped a long, lacquered nail on the wooden arm of her chair to punctuate what she said next. 'But he would never have considered handing over the business to them. Never. He was no kind of communist.'

'So you opposed your daughter's proposal to turn the family business into a workers co-op,' Heap said.

She scowled at him. 'Of course. It was madness and, sadly, it came out of some sort of actual madness.' She dropped her head. Gilchrist heard her sigh. 'You know she had a breakdown?'

'We did.'

'She had to leave work for six months. In that time . . .' She shook her head then fixed Gilchrist with her sharp stare. 'Christine has been off the rails. Hyper-active, hyper-driven. She left her husband and moved in with this woman. And she started working on this employee ownership scheme. Sell workers shares at heavily discounted prices – but these would be our shares she was selling to them.'

'Did she have a problem with any of you?' Gilchrist said, making a note to check on this husband of Christine she didn't know about. 'Something she wanted to punish you for?'

'None at all. We all got on extremely well. Even during these discussions there was no falling out, no anger.'

'But you seem angry now,' Gilchrist said.

'Impatient,' Mrs Bromley said. 'And regretful.' Suddenly her face crumpled.

Gilchrist and Heap left five minutes later. They didn't speak until they got in the car.

'This has to be a first,' Gilchrist said. 'Multi-millionaires unconcerned that they are about to lose £180 million. Apparently not even raising their voices in protest or anger.'

'Well, not those losing two-thirds of it.'

Gilchrist frowned at him. He put the car into gear.

'We haven't spoken to the other £60 million

yet,' he said. 'Bernard Bromley might turn out to have been really, really cross.'

'Have you managed to track down Bernard Bromley yet, Sylvia?' Gilchrist asked as she and Bellamy came into the office.

'About five minutes ago,' she said. 'He's somewhere in Thailand. He flew out there from Gatwick on the afternoon of Christine's death.'

'Indeed,' Heap said. 'Can he be contacted?'

'Anyone can be contacted,' Gilchrist said. 'It's whether they respond to the contact.'

'He's not returning calls,' Wade confirmed. 'Or emails or tweets.'

'When is he due back?' Heap said.

'He has an open ticket.'

'Oh, dear,' Gilchrist said. 'I assume we're looking at CCTV footage to see if Janet Rule is telling the truth.'

Wade nodded.

'Nothing so far.'

Heap tugged on his ear. 'He's a person of interest but not a guilty person yet.'

'I'm aware of that, detective sergeant – though his apparent flight doesn't bode well.'

Wade handed Gilchrist a thin folder. 'Here's the rape report, ma'am,' she said, placing the folder on Gilchrist's desk. Gilchrist flipped it open and shuffled the three sheets of paper inside.

'This is it?' Gilchrist said.

'Apparently so,' Wade said.

Gilchrist flicked through again. 'Where are the witness statements. The follow-up?'

160

'Miss Bromley apparently refused to cooperate with any investigation.'

'What?'

'It's there on the front page.'

Gilchrist scanned the page. It was signed by a rape councillor she admired called Cynthia Stokes. Gilchrist looked up at Heap and Wade and frowned.

'Christine Bromley came into the station with a friend claiming she had been raped. She would not give further details. She would not agree to a physical examination. She was clearly distressed. There were signs of bruising on her wrists and neck consistent with being restrained and possibly strangled into submission. She would not allow a closer examination of these marks either.'

She glanced back at the paper.

'Her friend said that he had found her in the street near her home, huddled on the kerb, rocking to and fro. He said she would only repeat that she had been raped. The friend had coaxed her into his car and to the police station.' She looked up. 'And that's it.'

'There was nowhere for the investigation to go, ma'am. Ms Bromley would not say where she had been that evening. There was no CCTV on that particular street but attempts were made to track her on other CCTV in town, without success.'

Gilchrist nodded.

'Curiouser and curiouser. Get me Cynthia Stokes on the phone.'

Heap went back to his desk and five minutes later he nodded as Gilchrist's phone rang.

'Detective Inspector, long time no speak,'
Cynthia Stokes said.

'Sarah, please, Cyn. How are you? And Bobby?'

Stokes was the single mother of an adorable
six-year-old boy. Adorable, that is, when Gilchrist
knew she could leave him at the end of the day.
His existence didn't make her broody.

'Bobby's great. He's eight next week. Come to
his birthday party if you'd like.'

'If I can,' Gilchrist said. Was it that long since
she'd seen her friend? 'Listen, Cyn, I'm sorry to
be abrupt but I'm following up a suspicious
death—'

'And you wanted to know about the rape.'

'You know about Christine Bromley, then?'

'Word gets around. But I'm not sure I can help
you. I assume you've seen the report. That was
pretty much it.'

'No witnesses?'

'She wouldn't tell us where it happened. I
decided to treat it as if she couldn't remember
rather than wouldn't talk. I thought one of our
therapists might open her up but she only agreed
to one session and that was a waste of time.

'We put up incident boards on all the streets
within a quarter-mile radius asking if anyone
had witnessed a woman being attacked. Zilch.
We wanted to circulate her photograph to see if
anyone had seen her that evening but, of course,
she wouldn't allow that.'

'And she never let you examine her?'

'Never.'

'Do you think she was making it up?'

'We never think women are making it up,'

Stokes said, her voice scolding. Gilchrist flushed.

'I know not usually. I just mean in this instance.'

Stokes softened. 'Obviously I wondered. But she was exhibiting all the signs of having suffered a traumatic attack.'

'Would you do me a favour, Cyn? Would you get in touch with her doctor? I know you couldn't when she was alive but now she's dead could you find out if she went to her or him after the rape. Perhaps her doc examined her.'

'Of course,' Stokes said. 'I'll get back to you as soon as I know something.'

'We should have a drink sometime,' Gilchrist said. 'It's been too long.'

'Well, there's raspberry and lemonade in a week's time at Bobby's party.'

Gilchrist laughed. 'I'll let you know. Thanks, Cyn.'

Gilchrist was just putting the phone down when she heard Stokes's voice squawk something.

'What?' she said, putting the phone back to her ear.

'I forgot to say,' Stokes said. 'There was one odd thing. Her friend. I discovered something intriguing much later from some newspaper article or other.'

Gilchrist looked for his name on the front page of the report.

'What about him?'

'He was, I'm sure, a friend, but he was also her husband.'

Gilchrist found the name. Derek Neill.

* * *

When Gilchrist and Heap returned to Derek Neill's apartment he was more cheerful than when they last left him.

'So, has my DNA turned up somewhere it doesn't belong?'

'Not yet,' Gilchrist said. 'We're here about your wife. Christine Bromley.'

'Terrible business. I've heard they recovered her body.'

'Have you heard her death was suspicious?'

He grimaced. 'No.'

'When did you last see her?'

'At the swim.'

Gilchrist looked up from her notes. 'No, before the swim, I mean,' she said.

'Can't remember – weeks, maybe months ago.'

'Odd you didn't mention she was your wife when we were talking about her on our first visit,' Gilchrist said.

'Is it? I suppose I haven't thought about her like that for years – if ever.'

'We know she was living with Janet Rule in the few months before her death.'

He nodded. 'Yes. The modern world is wonderful, isn't it? My wife took a wife. But we'd been living separate lives long before that.'

'You knew about her family and her business?'

'What, how awful the family was and how insanely successful the business was? Yes, almost from the moment we met.'

'You weren't invited to join the firm when you married?' Heap said.

'I had enough trouble getting invited to my

164

own wedding,' he said. 'If her father could have figured out a way for her to get married without her ending up with a husband, he would have. Though in the end he and I rubbed along OK, when he saw I wasn't after anything.'

'Weren't you?' Gilchrist said.

'I've done very nicely following my own path, thank you very much. Beholden to no man – or woman. And that's how I've always liked it.'

'Tell us about access to the feeds.'

'Well, I know that each team made up their own bottles and brought them with them. They were laid out in lines on the pier before the race started then each team was responsible for keeping the bottles filled with feed.'

'Could bottles have been swapped?'

'Well, all the bottles are from two or three suppliers but teams usually put individual markings on them. But, yes, it's possible someone could have swapped.'

'Did you see anyone unfamiliar in the line-up?'

Neill laughed. 'We had one hundred and sixty-five swimmers, each with a team of at least one. Of course there were unfamiliar faces. But why does it need to be unfamiliar? There are enough deadly rivalries in this sport to keep CrimeStoppers – when it was still on, of course – busy for years.'

Heap looked surprised. 'I thought it was collegiate and friendly with everyone helping each other unselfishly.'

Neill let out a loud guffaw. 'I'm afraid it's not so Famous Five. It's like anything – rivalries abound. There is one man who has trademarked

165

the title Ruler of the Channel, claiming he has swum the channel more times than anyone else. It is even beset by rivalries between competing swimming organizations.'

'So is there someone among this group of swimmers who had it in for Ms Bromley?' Gilchrist said.

'I'm not saying that.'

'Was she a particularly talented swimmer? Was she a threat to anyone or to anyone's record or something?'

Neill shook his head. 'I didn't mean that. I was speaking more generally. And I'm not convinced she was the target. It could have been a random attack.'

'We've thought of that,' Gilchrist observed, then regretted being so open.

'Remember that young lad who died doing a parachute jump because somebody had cut the leads on the parachute?' Neill said. 'They never got to the bottom of that, did they? No apparent motive, possibly a random attack. It's the same thing.'

Gilchrist nodded. 'Did Christine Bromley know Roland Gulliver?'

Neill tugged on his beard while he thought about that.

'Yes. Once upon a time. But I'd be surprised if they had kept in touch.'

Heap cleared his throat. 'We're interested in the time you accompanied your wife to the police station to report a rape.'

'Ah. That.' He sat down facing them. 'What do you want to know?'

'Why didn't you identify yourself as her husband then either?' Heap said.

Neill spread his hands. 'I was her husband only in name and, as I said, had been for a long time.'

'Even so . . .' Gilchrist said.

'It didn't seem relevant,' Neill said. He held her look. 'I didn't realize I'd done anything wrong.'

Gilchrist waved it away. 'I'm more interested in what happened to her. The report is a bit hazy.'

'She was raped. I found her in the street near our home and brought her to you guys. You couldn't find who did it.'

'That looks to be because your wife refused to help us in any way.'

Neill pursed his lips but didn't say anything.

'Did she tell you anything she didn't tell the police?'

'Not a thing.'

'Did she allow you to examine her?'

He shook his head swiftly.

'How did she seem when she got home?'

He looked down. 'She didn't come home. We parted that night.'

'She left you for Janet Rule that night?'

'I'm not entirely clear,' he said. 'She certainly didn't stay at the house. Ever again.'

'That night, though, it must have been hard to let her go off on her own, you being so protective to her,' Heap said.

'It was a nightmare but I had to respect her decision. She wasn't hysterical or anything. In fact she was very measured. She said she was going to her mum's and a car was coming to collect her to take her there. And it did.'

'And Philip Coates?' Heap said. 'Did Ms Bromley know him?'

'Oh, yes. They were at university together.'

'They were mates?'

'Christine didn't really have mates. She was too intense and private for that. But they stayed in touch.'

'I believe you were quite cut up about Mr Coates's death,' Gilchrist said.

'I probably ended up being closer to him than Christine was because of Rasa.'

'Rasa?'

'Rasa Lewis, my partner.'

'I know who she is but what was her relationship with Mr Coates?'

'Oh they were an item for years. She was the absolute love of his life.'

'I'd like to come back to that, if I may,' Gilchrist said. 'But may I ask again about your meetings with Roland Gulliver in the cemetery?'

'What about them?'

'An odd place to meet, isn't it? You said earlier you'd been a husband in name only for a long time.'

Neill laughed. It came out as a deep rumble.

'You're back to the kissing and cuddling? I think you're trying to suggest something in a not very subtle way. Why don't you just come out and ask?'

'Were you in a relationship with Roland Gulliver?'

'As I said, I was not. I'm not in the least

offended by the suggestion that we might have been, but that's a lie. Roland Gulliver and I did not – ever – have that kind of relationship.'

'What kind of relationship did you have?' Heap said.

'A long-standing one, almost from when he and Tammy first met. I assume you've met her?' He saw their nods. 'I'm afraid he really knocked the stuffing out of her. She didn't have a clue.'

'Staying with just Roland for a moment: how many times would you say you met Mr Gulliver in the cemetery?' Gilchrist said.

'How many times do people say I met him there?'

'Mr Neill . . .' Bellamy said.

'Well, I'm sorry, but it sounds like you're putting down some kind of snare for me. Treat me fairly and I'll respond fairly.' They waited. 'Maybe four times. I'm a live-in-the-moment guy. I don't keep a calendar of my movements.'

'But why the cemetery?'

Neill walked to his window and lifted the thin blind to look out.

'Somebody we both knew and cared about is buried there.'

'Who?' Heap said.

'Is that relevant? It's ancient history. But I go there regularly.'

'We're investigating two, possibly three, murders so we need to follow all possible lines of enquiry,' Gilchrist said.

'Just an old friend who died tragically young.'

'Did you have a falling out about this person?' Heap said.

169

'No! I told you we both cared. We didn't fall out about anything. It was something about the gravestone.'

'What about the gravestone?'

'An inscription had been added quite recently. I thought he might know who had done it.'

'You mean graffiti?' Heap said.

'No, I mean chiselled. A professional job.'

'So you were just curious about that.'

Neill nodded.

'What is the name of the person, please, Mr Neill?'

'Lesley White.'

'Lesley?' Heap said.

'What did the inscription say?' Gilchrist asked.

'"So we beat on, boats against the current, borne back ceaselessly into the past."'

'What did it mean?'

Neill shrugged.

'That the past can't be forgotten.'

'And you were concerned about this inscription?'

'Curious, I told you.'

'OK, Mr Neill,' Gilchrist said. 'Thank you. Now tell us about your relationship with Rasa Lewis.'

'Why?'

'As before. You are connected to all our victims. You might even be the common thread. I'm trying to get a clear picture of how things are. You said your wife left you for another wife but you seem to be in a relationship with Rasa.' Gilchrist gestured around her. 'Does she live here?'

'She did for a time but no longer.'

'You are no longer in a relationship?'

'That presupposes we ever were.'

'Were you?' Heap said.

Neill grimaced and came over to sit down opposite them. He clasped his hands between his knees.

'Sort of. You know it works out in an odd way for most of us. I've been thinking a lot about the road less travelled although I know that way madness lies.'

'We all have regrets, Mr Neill,' Gilchrist said. 'What is your particular regret?'

'No, I don't mean regrets. I mean the road less travelled with women. I suppose I should say un-travelled. I haven't known many women but I've been thinking about the different lives different women invited me to lead. Women I liked well enough but I had no wish to share the kinds of lives they offered. And then there were the women who didn't offer me a life to lead with them. And inevitably those were the invitations – and the women – I wanted and would have accepted.'

Gilchrist wondered where this was headed.

'Which category did Rasa fall into?' Heap asked.

'Rasa saddened me because there was something in her that moved me, that drew me but I knew she would never make the offer.'

'But you were a couple,' Heap said. 'Are a couple?'

'That doesn't mean she offered to share my life.'

'You're going to have to explain that,' Gilchrist said.

171

Neill looked from Gilchrist to Heap. 'You both look to be very nice people. Steady, reliable. Faithful, no doubt. The people I've always hung around with have been a little . . . freer. Which could lead to some emotional upsets.'

'Rasa was unfaithful to you?' Gilchrist said. 'Or are you referring to Christine Bromley?'

'Unfaithful is not in the vocabulary of people I know. Everyone is free to sleep with everyone else without it having anything to do with fidelity or infidelity.'

Neill was looking at Gilchrist in an intense way that made her feel uncomfortable.

'I'm not sure where this is taking us,' she said.

'You asked about my relationship with Rasa. I was on the move for quite a while. Globetrotting. You know most travellers you meet seem either to be going in search of something or running away. It took me a while to realize that some of us were doing both.'

'What were you running from?'

'I was running towards the future hoping to keep ahead of my past. Which meant I was never in the present. Never in the moment. Rasa showed me how to stay in the moment.'

'What in your past was causing you such distress?'

He looked from one to the other of them. 'Well, that's the million-dollar question, isn't it?'

'Are you going to answer it?' Gilchrist said.

'If I knew the answer, I would. If I ever figure it out, I'll let you know.'

The air in the room suddenly seemed heavy.

'Fair enough,' Gilchrist said. 'Mr Neill, can I

ask you about Philip Coates. Bob Watts mentioned that you thought there might be something suspicious about it even before the coroner had reached any conclusions.'

Neill tilted his head. 'He did, did he?'

'He didn't know you were his neighbour, by the way.'

'Nor me his.'

'Your suspicions?' Heap said.

Neill shrugged. 'A passing fancy.'

'What were your grounds for them? Had anything strange been happening?'

Neill gave his long beard a little tug. 'Philip and Rasa were very close. Rasa had been having some problems and Philip went in to bat for her.' Neill started to pace. 'The danger is giving these things oxygen by drawing attention to them.'

'Murders?'

'No, no. Trolling.'

Gilchrist looked blank. Heap said: 'Internet or tweets or both?'

'Everything.'

'What had Rasa done to invite trolls?' Heap said.

'It was a Diana Nyad thing.'

'Diana Nyad?' Gilchrist said. Heap started tapping on his iPad.

'Nyad, age sixty-four, swims one hundred and ten miles from Cuba to Florida through shark and jellyfish infested waters without a shark cage,' Neill said. 'One hundred and ten miles non-stop. Remarkable achievement. Remarkable woman – you can get her Ted Talk online. She'd already swum round Manhattan and from the

Bahamas to Florida. Her first attempt at swimming from Havana to Key West had failed.'

'She does sound remarkable,' Gilchrist said, feeling even more unfit than usual.

'I believe she is. But doubters quickly pitched in. She seemed to get through some stages of the swim very quickly. There is video for some but not all of the swim so they claimed she had got in the boat for a few miles. Satellite tracking lost her for a few hours. But if they can lose a plane in the Indian Ocean they can lose a swimmer, right? Also, her doctor said she had swum for seven and a half hours without a feed which doubters said was impossible.'

'Bob Watts just did six without nourishment,' Gilchrist said.

'Exactly. But the online Cold Water Swimming Forum had people demanding to see the data. The rumours that she hadn't done it became a torrent of abuse.'

'And the same thing has happened with Rasa?'

'It's pretty stupid to cheat with so many eyes on you. In fact it's impossible to get away with it. And it's not as if Rasa is claiming to be a Queen of the Channel.'

'Is that an official title?' Gilchrist said.

'It is. It's a Channel Swimming Association title for women who have swum the channel the most times. In one hundred and thirty-five years of Channel swimming only five swimmers have been awarded it. The first was Gertrude Ederle – she was the first woman to swim the Channel so she got it even though she only did it once.'

'*Only* once,' Gilchrist murmured.

Neill smiled. 'I know. But these days, many people swim the channel every year for up to twenty years. Cindy Nicholas was the first to swim it both ways – in fact she swam it both ways on five occasions.'

'How long a gap before she headed back on the return legs?' Gilchrist said.

'About ten minutes.'

'Ten minutes! You're saying she swam the Channel, had a ten-minute breather then got in and swam all the way back. That's impossible.'

'Clearly not. And she did it on five occasions. The thing is, you're not allowed to hang about on the French beach anyway because you haven't gone through Customs so, essentially, you're on French soil illegally.'

'Do many people swim just the one way from France to England?' Heap said.

'Not anymore. The French authorities discourage it and the channel swimming bodies here don't accept it for some reason. Anyway, Cindy has been eclipsed by Alison Streeter. She has swum the Channel forty-three times, more than anyone in the world. So far she's the quickest female – eight hours, forty-eight minutes – and the only one to swim the Channel *three* ways non-stop – in thirty-four hours, forty minutes.'

'Now she's just taking the Michael,' Gilchrist said, finding herself unwillingly drawn into this. She sat up straighter to fool herself into thinking it made her fitter. 'But getting back to Rasa – what was she accused of?'

'Getting in the boat for part of the crossing,' Heap said, reading from his iPad.

'Some creep called Sting Ray – the name is a bit of a giveaway – began saying mean things on various forums, Wild Water Taming especially. Then others joined in.'

'And what did Philip do?'

'Got into an online altercation with Sting Ray. Threats were made.'

'Can you access all that, Bellamy?' Gilchrist said.

'Not right now but with the right links.'

'Rasa will be able to help you with that. She has all the stuff.'

'What does Rasa think?'

His face took on an odd expression. 'And you'd better ask her what she thinks. I'll give you her address when you leave.'

'Won't be much longer, Mr Neill. Just saying hypothetically that as Mr Coates's death is suspicious, is there a link between him and Roland Gulliver? Aside from you that is?'

Neill seemed to ponder for a moment. 'Not that I can think of.'

'And – again hypothetically – do you know if Gulliver or Bromley had dealings with Sting Ray? Did they intervene in the trolling? Or dealings in any other way?'

Neill shook his head. 'Not that I know.'

'Then we're done,' Gilchrist said, standing. 'For now.'

Thirteen

Heap brought Gilchrist's glass of wine and his own half of shandy back from the bar. They were in the Colonies, the quirky little Victorian pub beside the Theatre Royal, where Watts would be joining them shortly.

'Well, now, Bellamy, we have a lot of information to process and my brain is tired.'

'Cheers, ma'am,' Heap said, raising his glass.

'Chin-chin,' she said, then wondered why, as it was not an expression she'd ever used before. 'Do you think our chat with Neill shifts the focus for Bromley's death away from the family dispute?'

'I think it embeds it more, although it suggests another dimension. Certainly, I think we can forget the random attack idea.'

'Do you think Derek Neill is part of this?' Gilchrist said.

'I think I'm looking forward to getting the DNA comparisons. I also think he's being quite cagey but I can't put my finger on how.' He took a minute sip of his drink. 'I was also thinking that this cross-Channel swimming thing would be a great cover for smuggling – goods and humans.'

'Humans?'

'Certainly, ma'am. You know how many thousands of refugees were crammed into Calais hoping to get across to the UK? Well, a drop in the ocean, so to speak, but they are still around northern France somewhere. No reason why these pilots couldn't add a couple to the roster on the return journey from France.'

'That would involve a lot of people looking the other way, Bellamy, for quite meagre returns.'

'They'd be looking the other way, anyway – everyone on board looking over one side as their swimmer heads for French sand. Couple of refugees hop on from the other side and stow away.'

'As I said, meagre returns, but, yes, something to consider. Do you think Neill was telling the truth about his relationship with Gulliver?'

'That they weren't kissing and cuddling?' Heap said. 'I think so. But let's not forget Bernard Bromley, unresponsive in Thailand.'

'Who is unresponsive in Thailand?' Bob Watts said, sliding into the seat beside Gilchrist. 'Jimmy Tingley?'

'What are you, a ghost?' Gilchrist said. 'Jimmy Tingley is in Thailand?'

Watts nodded. Gilchrist looked at Heap. Heap gave the slightest of nods.

'Do you think he might locate somebody for us on the quiet?' Gilchrist said. 'Have a word with him? A nice word?'

'Don't maim him, you mean.'

'That kind of thing,' Gilchrist said.

Watts fished out his phone.

'Shall I call him?'

Gilchrist looked at Heap.

'Do we have the details?'

Heap lifted his iPad from the seat beside him. 'All human life is here,' he said.

Watts grunted. 'And how sad is that?'

Watts copied down the details and excused himself. He went outside, dialling as he crossed the bar.

Heap put his device on the table between him and Gilchrist. 'You can find anybody on the internet,' Heap said. Gilchrist looked at the page. 'Sting Ray?'

Heap nodded. Gilchrist started reading the first blog post.

'Why do people expose themselves in this way?'

'Well, his being a nutter could have something to do with it in this instance,' Heap said.

Gilchrist frowned at him.

'It's not like you to call somebody a nutter, Bellamy.'

'Read on, ma'am. Start at the bottom.'

There was a message on Wild Water Taming on a Monday morning in May. The subject heading was: 'Rita Goodis swam around Jersey on the weekend.'

Rita decided to swim around Jersey on Sunday, and made it in eleven hours and twenty minutes. Quite the achievement given the water temperatures! Is this the earliest it's ever been done? Well done, Rita.

'Then Sting Ray commented.' Heap read aloud:

Awesome, Ms Goodis! WOW.

Rasa Lewis added her congratulations:

Fabulous Rita! You did it on my birthday. We had a little swim and beach party in Brighton knowing you were doing all the hard work for us – although I'm next! :-)

'Then what?' asked Gilchrist
'Well, this is where he, it, kicks off.' Heap read out Sting Ray's response:

No offense, Rasa, but just because Rita did it, don't fool yourself into believing that you can do it too. I don't even know you, and I already know you won't succeed. Or get even close.

'Hmm. Weird stuff.'
'Exactly,' Heap said. 'And Rasa is cheesed off by this out-of-the-blue remark.'
Gilchrist read Rasa's reply in which she pointed out she was the next person booked to do the Jersey swim and that Rita would be part of her crew. She had piloted around thirty swims, including two by Rita, her friend, in the last year alone.
She went on, now reading from Heap's iPad:

Sting Ray – ridiculous name – there is no room in this fantastic sport for such nasty comments so whoever you are, I suggest that you issue an apology.

'Fair enough,' Gilchrist said.

Sting Ray had replied within minutes:

Lighten up, Ms Lewis. Can't you take a bit of light-hearted ribbing and tongue-in-cheek humour? Why so serious all the time? I'm not a Channel swimmer and don't intend to be one if everyone is so solemn. Try to enjoy your Jersey swim – and, Jesus, life in general.

'Tongue-in-cheek humour. Right,' Gilchrist said. Rasa Lewis was back:

Dare I ask why you are even on this group? After all it is for Channel swimmers.

Gilchrist scanned Sting Ray's reply. 'Oops,' she said. 'Lots of capital letters.'
She read it aloud.

No, I am not one of your exalted Channel swimmers, just like you are not one who has run fifty marathons, ten ultramara-thons, competed in six Ironman or any of the other 'lesser' accomplishments I have achieved as an athlete.

She looked at Heap. 'James Bromley runs these ultramarathons.'
'Yes, ma'am.'
'Is this him?'
'I'm wondering, but I need to make some calls to get the name behind the comments.'
Gilchrist looked back at Sting Ray's comment.

You are also right that it is not my intention to attempt a Channel crossing, as I think that it MAY be beyond me. Apparently that means I am not welcome on this HOLY SITE, reserved for the Super Elite Club of Superhumans you so righteously belong to so I will return to my lowly existence as a mere human, with flaws and shortcomings, along with dreams and aspirations. I am sorry that I have offended you so, who chooses to treat fellow humans with nastiness and unfounded snobbery. In closing, in spite of the ugliness and nastiness of your writing, I wish you nothing but the best, not only in your future swim attempts, but with life in general.

Humbly.

'Is it me or did that get intense really quickly?' Gilchrist asked.

Heap nodded. 'Can't hold it in. Then someone else joins the conversation.'

Gilchrist nodded. 'I see it. Jessica.' She read out:

Don't sweat this Sting Ray, Rasa. Ultra-runners in the States are so wrapped around distances they don't get the swimming concept at all.

'That isn't going to go down well,' she said.

Sting Ray replied within minutes.

*I see that, like the pious Ms Lewis, you
too are nasty, psychologically ugly, vicious
and insecure. I am not 'wrapped around'
any of the insignificant activities of my
insignificant life. I am replying to you
because as a fellow human you deserve
the respect and decency you have signally
failed to accord me. I also want to show
to the other members of the group what
a bitter, nasty and pathetic human you
seem to be.*

Gilchrist laughed. 'I love the way he signs off
after that tirade: "lovingly yours".'

Heap smiled. 'That's good from such a
solipsist.'

'Careful, Bellamy, I've been able to keep up
with you so far. Don't be throwing big words
at me.'

'Ma'am.' He looked back at the screen. 'It took
Jessica an hour or so to respond. She was clearly
googling this man because when she came back
she said this to Rasa.' Heap read out:

*Oh my God!! Sting Ray lives in the United
Kingdom!! I am so disappointed and
embarrassed. Oh, well, anyone can live
here, including serial killers.*

'Ha!' Gilchrist said. 'I like Jessica coming to her
friend's aid but she shouldn't poke the bear.' She
looked at Heap. 'You know where she found him?'
He nodded. 'You found him too?' He nodded again.

She carried on reading. Sting Ray had replied quickly to Jessica:

> *You are attempting to humiliate me in front of a rather large audience. I can't allow that. I am not a serial killer. However, I would be wary of being in the same room with you (or Ms Lewis, for that matter) if you had a handgun in your possession. How many more nasty, insecure, bitter, angry and vicious people am I going to meet in this group? Maybe it's from spending too much time in cold water. With much love and warmth to everyone.*

Then Philip Coates pitched in about half an hour later.

> *A word of well-meaning advice, Sting Ray. We have a saying in England: when you've dug yourself into a hole, stop digging.*

'It's late now,' said Heap. 'When Sting Ray wakes he writes to Philip.'

> *Thanks for the unasked for advice. Why don't you take it and place it where the sun doesn't shine. There is a saying in America: Get a life. I have chosen to disassociate myself from your thin-skinned and intolerant group. I wish you and your cohorts nothing but blessings as I get on with My Life.*

Finally, Rita Goodis, the woman who had long ago been congratulated, pitched in. She thanked everybody for the congratulations then asked that the thread end.

I have not previously been exposed to this in my swimming career. Please stop.

This brought the inevitable reply from Sting Ray in the form of a self-serving apology.

I need to issue a formal apology to ALL members of 'The Group' for my involvement in that horrid thread of yesterday.

'For starting the horrible thread, maybe?' Gilchrist said.
'He's not going to admit blame, is he?'
Sting Ray went on:

In my daily living, I try to practice the principles of unconditional love for all fellow living beings. However, I am a weak person with many serious flaws and I responded to perceived attacks on my character. I should have maintained silence and humility but I lashed out and said deliberately hurtful things. I am sorry for every word I uttered. You won't hear from this pitiful creature again.

Gilchrist blew out breath. 'OK, so the guy has problems. He can't admit that he started the nastiness, for instance, but has he done more?'

'He's written more, yes: once she does her Jersey swim he casts doubt on it. And the Channel swim. She posted about getting across.' He pointed at the screen. 'There it is.'

Rasa had written:

I did it! I set off in darkness at 1am and the first few hours were fine until the middle of the swim when some oil in the water I swallowed or the fumes from the support boat made me violently sick. This slowed me down considerably and as a result the tide took me far off course. Then right at the end, when I was weakest, I was swept down the coast of France and it took me several hours to land.

In spite of everything that happened earlier, it was the most challenging part of the swim. I was physically exhausted and France looked tantalizingly close yet I just couldn't reach it. But eventually I did and when my feet touched the sand, it was the most profound and incredible experience I've ever had. I can now proudly say I am a Channel Swimmer.

Heap nodded. 'He started dissing her after that.'

'Dissing her, Bellamy?'

Heap flushed. 'I believe that is the correct terminology,' he said.

'I suspect not for the past decade,' Gilchrist said.

'Ma'am. Now look in that file called *Pumping Legs*. It's a running blog. Seven entries from before and after Christmas. The last one dated fifteenth of January.'

'This is Sting Ray in his running guise?'

Heap nodded.

'So he stopped writing this *Pumping Legs* blog months ago.'

'And then not long after that he turns up on the swimming website. But by then he's unable to run. In his last post on *Pumping Legs* he said he was borrowing a friend's motorbike to go up into the mountains to chop wood for him. When he first pops up on the swimming website he says at one point that he had a bad motorcycle accident and broke both his legs.'

'On his friend's motorbike,' Gilchrist said.

'I would think. Anyway, ma'am, it isn't going to take long to track him down.'

She read on:

Twenty-one December. I wish Christmas did not exist. We should be kind to each other EVERY day, not just some arbitrary day in December every year. Need to kick up the running mileage. Did nine yesterday morning then fourteen down to my girlfriend's last night at close to race pace, nine home this morning. Feeling stronger and faster every day. Ordered 25-lb weight vest yesterday. I intend to run in it every day. That should make things somewhat unpleasant! LOL.

She looked at Heap. 'He has a girlfriend?'

'His girlfriend has her own blog site called

Mad Cow. He talks about her in the next blog.'

'Aha.' She read on. 'Sting Ray talks about running twenty-four miles with his lovely and beautiful girlfriend riding her bike alongside. Then he spent the night with her and her cat. According to this, Bellamy, he was able to give more fully of himself, addressing his girlfriend's physical and emotional needs, since his were essentially taken care of – at least for the time being.'

Heap said, 'You'll see that he thinks she is too good for him and someday she'll realize it. But until then, he's going to keep on enjoying her company and soaking up her love and caring.'

'I feel nauseous,' said Gilchrist.

The next blog was addressed to a 'Mr Krupicka'.

'He doesn't like this Krupicka guy. Who is he?'

'According to Wikipedia he's the ultimate ultra-runner. The best in the business. So I guess Sting Ray – excuse me, Pumping Legs – is seething at that.'

'Hmm. He thinks Krupicka is boring because all he writes about is running. He calls him a simple-minded soul and a single-minded moron.' Heap read out:

> *Is twenty-two miles at eight minutes per mile what people really want to hear? Isn't there more to life – how about cleaning a kitchen to perfection?*

'Cleaning a kitchen to perfection . . .' Gilchrist repeated.

188

'I don't think he realized how odd that last comment might sound to most people,' Heap said.

'So he's obsessive compulsive. Oh look, he intends to tidy a forest.' Gilchrist read out loud again.

Taking my friend's motorcycle up to the mountains for a week of gathering wood, splitting wood, stacking wood, arranging wood, burning wood. Plan is to rise early, run twelve miles, labour for seven to eight hours, then run twelve again. Then sleep 8 until 6. When I'm done the woods will be completely cleaned out of dead and fallen trees, wood neatly stacked, kindling arranged in a bucket, order restored. My friend will want to pay me, but this time I'm not accepting any money (and he can whine all he wants). He's doing me a favour giving me solitude, hard work and good runs.

'That's when he had the accident, I assume,' Gilchrist said. 'I hope on the way up there so at least the forest was saved from his obsessive-compulsive craziness.' She sat back. 'OK, I'm seeing a weirdo but that doesn't make him a killer.'

'He's quick to anger,' Heap said. 'And all the traits he sees in others are just his own that he's projecting onto them.'

'But that's a big step into killing.'

'Not so big, ma'am.'

She returned to the screen. Pumping Legs writes:

I'm fucking sick of this. I just want peace in my life. And because I care so much for others, I want peace in their lives too. Some runs bring me the peace I long for. But endorphin highs are not reality. The emotional comedown soon occurs and I'm back in the real world. Maybe I'm not running hard enough. Do I need to run at a fucking six minutes a mile pace to find peace? Or will the problems still resurface, the depression come back. If so, why do it in the first place? I want PEACE. Leave me alone, LIFE.

Gilchrist and Heap were contemplating this when Watts came back to the table. He put drinks down and said: 'Jimmy is on it. No maiming. You didn't say anything about kidnapping though.' He took a sip of his beer. 'That's a joke.' Another sip. 'I think.'

Fourteen

Gilchrist hated waiting around so thought she and Heap should go down to Dover to explore his hypothesis about people or drug smuggling. Heap made an appointment with the coast guard while Gilchrist cleared it with the Dover police.

The drive to Dover was a bit of a pain, up to the M25 then along and back down the M20, but it gave Gilchrist time to think.

The coastguard service was housed on the high cliffs just east of Dover harbour at a place called Langdon Battery. The coast guard officer who greeted them was a woman who looked familiar.

'Welcome to Langdon Battery, I'm Kathleen Harrison,' she said, holding out her hand.

'Hang on,' Gilchrist said as they shook hands. 'I know you, don't I?'

The woman tilted her head and scanned Gilchrist's face. 'You came to Shoreham a few months ago asking about smuggled artefacts from Asia.'

'And you were the harbour master,' Gilchrist said. She remembered now how impressed she'd been by the woman and how she thought they might have been friends. Before Gilchrist went into her mad slump.

'I found that job a bit restricting,' Harrison said. She held her hand out to Heap.

'DS Bellamy Heap,' Gilchrist said. 'And I'm DI Sarah Gilchrist.'

'So how can I help?'

'Great view,' Gilchrist said, looking over the sea spread before her.

'You should see the office of CROSS – the French coastguard service – at Cap Gris Nez. Their view is absolutely spectacular.'

'As I understand it, this is a busy part of the sea, but between you and the French coastguard, you track every boat.'

'Correct. With radar and VHF we watch this whole area and liaise with every vessel using the Channel. We broadcast navigation bulletins every half hour and log vessels using the lanes to

191

coordinate their movements and monitor safety. And, yes, the English Channel is one of the busiest shipping lanes in the world. Up to six hundred ships pass through the Dover Strait each day.'

'Moving stuff all over the place,' Gilchrist said.

'Clothing, electrical goods, cars, molasses, oil, armaments, nuclear fuel. Then there are a hundred ferries a day, fifty to seventy local yachts and holiday makers, coastal protection vessels, naval vessels, cruise liners, fishermen, charter boats for anglers. All going at different speeds, from eight to forty-five knots.'

'And then you have the cross-Channel swimmers crossing the paths of all these vessels,' Gilchrist said.

'Yes, God bless them, we do.'

'How do you track them?'

'We track the pilot boat alongside them. Every swimmer has one. Do you mind my asking why you're asking – perhaps I can give more focused answers if I know what you're looking for.'

'We're wondering if there might be some smuggling going on behind the swimming,' Heap said.

'Smuggling how? I thought the men were just budgie smugglers. Not much money to be made from that.'

Gilchrist smiled. 'We're thinking the pilot boats.'

Harrison frowned. 'As I understand it, most of the pilots have been doing it for years. They are pretty well regarded. I'd be surprised if that were happening. And I'd tread very carefully there.'

'They might not even know it,' Gilchrist said,

192

peering at different coloured boats pulsing on a big screen.

Harrison chewed the inside of her lip as she thought about it.

'It's pretty chaotic when someone reaches the other side. Everyone is focused on the swimmer. It's conceivable someone could offload some cargo into the sea, near one of the warning buoys, to be picked up later. Or pick up something. What kind of cargo are we talking about?'

'Drugs, presumably. Diamonds, conceivably.'

'We were wondering about low-level but regular human trafficking,' Heap said.

'Picking up refugees when the pilot boat reaches France? It's possible, I suppose.'

'Perhaps bringing over a whole boat load from France when someone tries to swim from there to here.'

'Nobody starts from there,' Harrison said. 'The French don't allow it. So you're talking about one, maybe two, people per trip but that would mean the collusion of the swimmer and the swimmer's support team. These people's focus for months and months is solely on that swim. I'm sorry, but I just can't see it.'

Gilchrist was inclined to agree. Heap looked a little abashed as he stared at the pulsating dots on the monitor.

'Look,' Harrison said. 'One of the pilots is popping in to see me in a moment. Phil Kettner. Pilots the *Argos*. Why don't you talk to him – unofficially? But, as I said, please tread carefully.'

The pilot had a weather-beaten, raw-red face and

193

a gap-toothed smile. He was medium height and chunky.

Introductions made, Gilchrist said: 'We've got an investigation underway that involves in some way – we don't know how yet – cross-Channel swimming.'

Kettner just listened.

'How fast do swimmers go?' Heap said.

'At any given time you have maybe five Channel swimmers moving at 1.5 knots per hour. And they're cutting across all the shipping lanes. There are so many international vessels passing through the Strait that shipping lanes are essential and ships must stick to their own lane. On the English side, the south-west lane is for vessels heading down Channel to the Atlantic. The north-east lane, on the French side, is for vessels up to North Sea ports. Then there are local inshore zones on both coasts.'

'And the route of the swimmers cuts across these zones?'

'Exactly. Swimmers usually start from Shakespeare Beach here in Dover so they immediately join the English inshore traffic zone. That's about five nautical miles wide. Then they cross the south-west lane – that is four nautical miles wide. Mid-Channel they cross the one-mile-wide Separation Zone into French waters and the north-east lane. That's five nautical miles wide. The French inshore traffic zone is at least three nautical miles wide, depending on where the swimmer is in relation to the French beaches.'

'And your job is to ensure the swimmer can just do her or his job safely,' Heap said.

'More and more women doing it – and, yes, that's a lot of my job. Some of these vessels are big – a thousand feet long, with hundred-foot-deep draft – and weighing over three hundred thousand tonnes. If you're in the way, who do you think is going to come off worse?'

'We've been hearing about accusations against a Rasa Lewis about her swim.'

Kettner nodded.

'The man who started it calls himself "Sting Ray". That twat – excuse my language – he's done some Iron Man competitions so he thinks he's tough. But crossing the Channel requires a different sort of tough.' He tapped his head. 'It's all in here, you know.'

'So I understand,' Gilchrist said. 'So what Rasa is accused of isn't possible?'

'Is it possible Ms Lewis didn't do her whole swim?' he said gruffly. 'No.'

Heap nodded. 'Could you say a little more?'

'We're tracked for the entire crossing by these coastguards here. And though I hate to give praise, even where it's due, Harrison and her team are bloody brilliant. Bloody brilliant.'

'Why, Phil, that's the nicest thing I've ever heard you say,' Harrison called across the room.

'Aye, well make the most of it,' he called back. 'You won't be hearing it again.'

Harrison grinned.

'We report to the coastguard as the swim begins,' Kettner continued. 'Check in with them as we enter each of the shipping lanes and then again as the swim finishes. The coastguard advise shipping of the presence of our pilot boats as they cross the shipping lanes and keep a watchful eye on our progress.'

'That's the boat. What about the swimmer?'

'Well, I'm tracking her. Are you suggesting Rasa's pilot lied? That he colluded with her in making a false claim?'

'Is that possible?'

The pilot shook his head wearily. 'I've been doing this for thirty years and nobody has ever accused me of that. Why would I do that now?'

'I'm talking hypothetically, not about you or Rasa's pilot,' Gilchrist said.

Kettner gave her a long, fierce look. Gilchrist held it.

'I thought you realized. I *am* Rasa's pilot. Look. People think swimming the Channel is a solo effort. It's not. It's a team effort. Every swimmer is supported by a team. Family, friends and colleagues. The team on my escort boat, the observer, me and my crew. Are you suggesting all of us colluded in this fraud?'

'So what happened?'

'She swam the channel.'

'So where have these rumours come from?'

'People are vicious. You think you're part of a big supportive club and on the whole you are, but Channel swimmers have the same character flaws as anyone else. Maybe more because the determination that's required is a kind of ruthlessness and brings with it a focus on yourself that excludes thoughts and feelings about anyone else. That means, if some of the people in this community see the merest hint of weakness or doubt, they pounce.'

'So we're discovering,' Gilchrist said.

'And anyway, the twat who started the fuss isn't even a swimmer. Ultramarathon runner?' Kettner snorted. 'I've shat 'em.'

'Sorry to waste our time again, ma'am,' Heap said on the drive back to Brighton.

'Not wasted at all, Bellamy. I learned a lot. Knowledge is power, isn't it?'

'They say, ma'am.'

Gilchrist's phone rang. *Bilson*, she mouthed.

'Which bit of exciting news are you going to impart first, Mr Bilson,' she said cheerily.

'Derek Neill's DNA.'

'Matches with . . .?'

'Nothing. Nada.'

'That's distinctly unexciting,' Gilchrist said. 'What about Provocateur.'

'Well, he's splashed all over Gulliver's apartment but not on that other wine glass.'

'Do you have any exciting news at all?' Gilchrist said.

'Always save the best until last, Sarah. That's a motto you might consider as you get older with regard to us older men.'

'I'll bear that in mind,' she said. 'Now I've got Bellamy here waiting with bated breath.'

'Tell the Boy Wonder he may abate that breath momentarily. Or do I mean unabate?'

'Bilson!'

'Philip Coates also had ketamine in his system.'

'Great!' Gilchrist exclaimed. 'I mean . . .'

'I know what you mean, Sarah,' Bilson said. 'Nothing so wonderful as establishing a thesis bit by bit. Even if it does involve real people and their suffering.'

'There wasn't poison in Roland Gulliver as well, was there?'

Bilson chuckled.

'You do like icing on your cake, don't you? What, you mean he was not only drowned and stabbed to death he was also poisoned? There would be a killer who took absolutely no chances. Well, I'm sorry I can't tie it up all neatly with a bow, to mix metaphors, but no: toxicology came back with no indicators for poison in him.'

'You've been great, as always. Do we have anything outstanding, professionally speaking, I mean?' Gilchrist said.

'I think I've given you everything I've got. Professionally speaking. I'm sorry we can't do more with that man I saw Roland in the sauna with. I'm sure he's crucial.'

Gilchrist thought for a moment. Bilson was right. He always was in his area of expertise but he was right about this. She chided herself for not paying more attention to him.

'If there's CCTV footage of him to watch then I'll harass you about it.'

'I look forward to your harassment.'

Gilchrist turned to Heap. 'Even though the gym doesn't have CCTV footage we should have checked who the day members were the day Bilson saw Gulliver in the sauna with this guy.'

'The deaths started coming thick and fast for us just around then,' Heap said.

'I know. But let's make it a priority, shall we?

And what have we concluded about that fraudulent petition?'

'It's just sitting there,' Heap said.

Jimmy Tingley always felt like the ugly American when he was in south-east Asia, even though he wasn't American nor particularly ugly. Nondescript is the way he tried to be and in decades of undercover work he felt he had succeeded. But in the novel and films the diplomat described as the ugly American did more harm than good, despite his best intentions, because of his woeful ignorance of the actual situation. That's how Tingley felt.

He'd just got back to Bangkok when Watts phoned him to ask him to help out. Find a guy? His life's work. Were it not so humid he wouldn't even break a sweat but as it happened, lying in his cheap room under a wobbly wooden fan beside one of Bangkok's many canals, he was already in a sweat. The ice-filled glass of vodka on his forehead helped.

He heard a ping and glanced at the laptop beside him. Bob Watts with further details. He read through the email, took a swig of the vodka and reached for his phone.

Gilchrist had been using her flat like a hostel for days. She'd been sleeping on the sofa, avoiding the bedroom and what she regarded as her polluted bed. The place she'd always regarded as her haven and refuge was soiled by her invitation to a stranger to share that bed. She wasn't into self-examination but she knew something had changed for her the morning Bellamy had summoned her so early.

She made a pot of coffee and stripped her clothes off, leaving them where they fell on her bedroom floor. After she'd showered and put on her bulky dressing gown she stripped the bed too and threw the sheets and pillowcases not in the washing machine but in the bin.

She sat looking out on her balcony. How to make sense of all this? Finance was not her strong point, so the big business stuff baffled her, but people were her strength. She got people. However, figuring out their motivations, that was the tricky bit.

Her phone rang. Kate Simpson.

'Kate, how are you doing?'

'I'm trying to stay focused. What is going on?'

'Best not to ask if you need to focus.'

'Well, I'm just about to start going to Dover every week to do my regular six-hour swims then a ten-hour. I've got my date for my Channel swim. It's in a month!'

Gilchrist realized that was all Kate was interested in. Anything else was a distraction. She wondered how Bellamy Heap felt about that. Probably fine – he was so bloody perfect.

'I wondered if you'd come with me,' Kate said, possibly for the second time.

'Yeah, right – I'd get about two hundred yards.'

'Not swimming, you chump. In the pilot boat. I can take half a dozen people with me as my team. It would be great if you were one of them. Bob is coming. And Bellamy, of course.'

'But I wouldn't be any use.'

'You're a policewoman; you could arrest any jellyfish that come for me.'

'OK then. Glad I can be of some use. Is Bellamy there?'

'Er, I'm not sure. I'm afraid I've been neglecting him rather. Hang on a second.'

Gilchrist got up and put her jacket on. Kate came back on the line.

'He's out.'

'OK. Thanks, Kate – and thanks for asking. I need to find what I can charge them with.'

'What?'

'The jellyfish.'

Gilchrist phoned Heap.

'You're still working.'

'I was just about to call,' Heap said. 'Rasa Lewis is around now if we want to see her.'

'Well, we do. We definitely do.'

Gilchrist loathed Rasa Lewis on sight. As Lewis gestured with long elegant hands for them to enter her hidden, hippy house at the bottom end of Lewes High Street and follow her, her long blonde hair swayed above her perfect bum. She was long-legged, big-breasted and slender with a tiny oval face and perfect features.

Gilchrist wasn't into psychoanalysing herself or others but she had always assumed that very long hair was something for little girls to look cute with but that any woman who wore very long hair over the age of about thirty was a self-absorbed narcissist who thought herself a fairy-tale princess. Just a theory.

Lewis offered them the sofa and, once they were

seated, lowered herself into an ample armchair, bringing her feet and legs up into the cross-legged Lotus position. *Trust her to do the look-at-me sitting posture*, Gilchrist thought, wondering if she had actually just ground her teeth.

'We're here to ask about your relationship with various people,' Heap said, introductions over. 'Can we start with Roland Gulliver?'

'I've known him and Tammy for years, though I wouldn't regard them as friends. Just in the same loose circle.'

'What did you think about their parting?' Gilchrist said.

'I didn't think anything about it. These things happen. I'm not judgemental about what people get up to in their relationships.'

'What about your relationship with Derek Neill?' Gilchrist said.

'What about it?' Lewis said, running her long fingers through her long hair.

'Are you together or not?'

'Yes.'

'Together?'

'Or not. Neither of us feels the need to define our relationship, for in defining it we limit it. I've always tried to make my relationships as fluid as possible.' She looked at Heap. 'With no boundaries.'

'When did you last see Roland Gulliver?' Heap said.

'It must be a couple of years. As I said, we weren't close. And I can't remember the last time I saw Tammy. I might have bumped into her in town but I don't recall.'

'But Derek has been seeing quite a lot of him,' Gilchrist said.

'You'd have to ask Derek about that.'

'He didn't say anything to you about those meetings?'

'Isn't that hearsay evidence or something?' Rasa said. 'I'm afraid I don't do gossip.'

'What about Christine Bromley?'

'Obviously, I've known her for years. Though, again, we were never close.'

'Do you have close girlfriends?' Gilchrist said, imagining this perfect woman cutting a swathe through all the men she met, her long hair swaying as she strode over them. *Steady, Sarah, steady.*

'I don't have close anybodies,' Lewis said, smoothing her hair again. 'I learned early in life to be self-sufficient. Very early.'

'What about Phil Coates? You were close to him, weren't you?'

Lewis seemed to search for the most appropriate facial expression until it settled into sadness.

'Philip could always be relied on. I will miss him.'

'Can you think of anyone who might wish him harm?'

'Harm? He had a heart attack and drowned, didn't he?'

'He was poisoned and he drowned as a consequence. His death is being treated as a murder.'

It seemed to take a moment for that to sink in. A single frown line appeared on Lewis's flawless forehead.

'I didn't know his working life well enough to

know if that would create enemies – although capitalism is essentially divisive. He lived up in York but I'd seen him a little recently because he was working on a project in Salthaven.'

'The lido,' Heap said.

'Yes. But I don't think anything came of it.'

'You weren't part of the Save Salthaven Lido opposition to his company's plans then?'

'I don't do protests. I focus in my life on living properly. If everyone did the same the world would be a better place, don't you think?'

'I'll need to think about that,' Gilchrist said.

'Do,' Lewis said simply. Gilchrist tried not to bridle at Lewis's patronizing tone. She caught Heap glancing at her. Clearly she wasn't succeeding.

'You have been the target of online trolling by someone calling himself Sting Ray,' Heap said. 'Philip Coates tried to defend you.'

'He was always gallant. But both of us decided to rise above such pettiness. What? Do you think Sting Ray could have harmed Philip? I thought trolls were so horrible because they're too pathetic to engage in any real-world activity.'

'That's generally true,' Heap said. 'So there is nothing for you to worry about. But has anything been happening out of the ordinary in your life.'

'Aside from people dying all around me, you mean?'

'Yes, aside from that. Any interruption to your routine? Odd meetings or incidents? Anything at all.'

'Not that I can think of,' Lewis said, standing.

'But if I think of anything I'll be sure to let you know.'

Gilchrist would ordinarily have resisted being so summarily dismissed, but instead she laughed.

'Just one final question, please Ms Lewis,' she said, as she too stood. 'A man in his late forties, early fifties. Paunchy, but strong-looking arms. Not gym-workout pretend strength, but properly exercised. Tanned. Dark hair, neatly cut. Ring any bells?'

'Not the tiniest one,' Lewis said. 'Sorry.'

Back out in the street Gilchrist and Heap exchanged looks.

'You don't get many of those to the pound where I come from, ma'am,' Heap said.

'I don't know where you come from and I don't really know what you mean but your analysis sounds about right,' Gilchrist replied.

Fifteen

Tingley doing what he did best: tracking a man down. With the help of a few contacts it didn't take him long. Bernard Bromley's timeline was laid out before him. Ticket to Thailand booked the day he flew but it was a regular trip for him anyway. Made three trips a year for the past three years. Always stayed on the same island, in the same hotel. Not apparently a paedophile with either girls or boys but enjoyed his grown-up adventures, both paid for and consensual. Except this year. This year he had scarcely left his room on the beach.

Perhaps that was because it looked from the CCTV footage that he left England a little bruised and battered around the face.

Tingley booked a ferry for later that day. He packed his snorkelling gear. The waters off the island were renowned for their reefs and exotic marine creatures. All work and no play and all that.

Sylvia Wade was just putting her phone down when Gilchrist and Heap came into the office. She stood, as she always did when addressing Gilchrist.

'Ma'am, the desk sergeant just phoned through. A drink driver was asking for you. Said you knew her.' Gilchrist frowned. 'She doesn't want to spend a night in the cells and hopes you'll let her go home. Says you'll vouch that she's been under a lot of pressure.'

'Who is it?'

Wade looked down at her pad.

'An April Medavoy.'

'Mrs Medavoy,' Gilchrist murmured.

Heap shrugged: 'It's always the quiet ones you have to watch.'

'That's what I keep telling people about you,' Gilchrist said. 'But Kate clearly took no notice.'

Gilchrist dialled down to the desk and put her phone on speaker.

'She's being quite cantankerous, ma'am,' the desk sergeant said. 'Won't let us swab her and is insistent she be allowed to take a taxi home.'

'How pissed is she?'

'Three times over the limit.'

'Perfect time to interview her again,' Heap said. Gilchrist gave him a look. 'Only joking, ma'am. I know we absolutely can't.'

'A friend of hers just got murdered,' Gilchrist said on the phone. 'How did we get her?'

'Driving erratically on King's Road.'

The road along the seafront.

'Has she said anything about why she's drunk. Has she just come from somewhere?'

'A friend's house.'

'You've already booked her, of course.'

'Oh yes.'

'OK, tell her that if she cooperates with you she can go home in a taxi, if that's OK with you. But first she has to tell us who the friend is – and she must have the swab. Explain that she has been arrested and everyone who has been arrested must be swabbed. Sorry, I realize I'm telling my granny how to suck eggs – it's been a long day.'

'I've never really fancied sucking eggs. Will do, ma'am. Leave it with me. Sorry you've been bothered.'

Gilchrist turned to Heap. 'I think the dodgy petition is a side-story, don't you, Bellamy?'

'I do. Especially as our techies have got the goods on Sting Ray so we can focus on him.'

'Is it James Bromley?'

'Wouldn't that be neat? Alas, no. A new name for us. Raymond – see what he did there? – Newell. Currently, according to his Wi-Fi connection, sitting in the café of the new art-house cinema in Lewes.'

'Isn't that naughty, us knowing that.'

'It's out there, ma'am, for anyone to pick up.'

'Lewes has a cinema now?'

'Very nice. The Depot. Down near the station. I'll get the locals to pick him up.'

'Do we have a picture of him?'

'Should have soon.'

'Then let's get back to Lewes.'

At Lewes nick, after the usual official pleasantries about cooperation, Gilchrist and Heap were shown into a brightly lit, glossily painted interview room while Newell was sent for. Gilchrist was hoping for a tanned, paunchy guy with strong arms in his late forties. What she got was a tall, stringy man with not an ounce of fat on him, in well-worn trainers, singlet and shorts. He had a scrubby beard. His face was deeply lined. He looked agonized.

'Thank you for coming in, Mr Newell.'

'I wasn't aware I had a choice.'

'What have you been doing today?'

'I spent two and a half hours cleaning a house at the top end of town. I don't have a car so I rode my bike to get there.'

'Healthy.

'I prefer riding my bike, frankly.'

'You cleaned a whole house?'

'Just the kitchen. I was only there two and a half hours.'

Gilchrist tried not to look at Heap. 'Two and a half hours on a kitchen. How much did you get for that?'

'They gave me £50 but I gave them £20 back.'

'You hadn't done a good job?'

'I did an exemplary job. But I'm not sure they appreciated it so I was unable to take the full amount.'

'Tell us about your running regime.'

'Pre-accident?'

'Unless you've been running with two broken feet.'

'I used to run for results or to show off or to attract attention. But now I'm running for myself. To examine myself. To embrace the solitude.'

'How was that going before your accident? Was the accident when you were going to, or heading from, the wood by the way?'

Newell looked at her intently. 'On the way there. It's a Buddhist thing. I wouldn't expect you to understand. It's lifelong. I want it to be a moving meditation, meditating on me and on humanity, on the questions we all must face in the West. Maybe I'll get a few answers, or at least a better understanding of the questions.'

'So how far do you run?'

'I was averaging thirty-six miles a week but I was aiming for hundred miles a week running, one hundred fifty cycling. I was sixty lbs overweight.'

Gilchrist looked at the skinny man in front of him.

'But you got rid of that.'

'Thirty of it.'

Gilchrist nodded slowly.

'Why run so much?'

'Only way to get strong, mentally and physically.'

He really had intense eyes. In fact, everything about him was intense.

'What kind of thing are you looking for in Buddhism?' Heap said.

'Look, when I first visited Brighton some years ago I spent six hours alone on the beach, counting the waves, allowing them to exist, listening to what they had to say.'

'Allowing them to exist?' Gilchrist said.

'Did they have much to say?' Heap said.

Newell scowled. 'We have become a mindless lot, consumed by numbers and accomplishments. Wouldn't it be more telling to say that you had tea with your daughter and that later she told you she loved you? You don't even realize how sweet a kiss can be, or a stroke of the neck, or sweeping up the street just so things can look nice. You could do better.'

Gilchrist ignored his peroration. (She'd decided she liked that word.)

'Do you have a thing about cleaning? Kitchens in particular?'

'There's something Zen about all labour,' he said.

'Tell us about your daughter,' Heap said.

'My daughter?'

'You said you had tea with your daughter and she told you she loved you.'

'I wasn't referring to me. I was just saying wouldn't that be something?'

'There are always choices in life,' Heap said, 'but you made a good one by coming here and telling us about your meds.'

'My meds?' Newell said, looking off-balance.

'When did you stop taking them?'

'My meds?'

'The lithium you take for your paranoid schizophrenia.'

'I don't have paranoid schizophrenia.'

'Sorry – I'm using an old-fashioned term. I mean for your bipolar disorder.'

'I'm not bipolar. Who says I'm bipolar?'

Heap picked up a sheet of paper. 'According to Brighton hospital you've been admitted twice in the past three years for psychotic episodes. The police have been called to restrain you four times over the same period.'

'I've got anger issues, I don't mind admitting that,' Newell said, chewing on the edge of his moustache. 'Paranoid schizophrenia is defined in the *Diagnostic and Statistical Manual of Mental Disorders*, fourth edition. But it's not in the fifth edition. It was dropped. You know why? Because nobody can figure out what it is. The American Psychological Association eliminated subtypes because they had limited diagnostic ability, low reliability and poor validity.'

'You know a lot about it for someone who only has anger issues,' Heap said. 'We've seen your medical reports from the hospital. You have serious paranoid thoughts.'

'Is that why I'm here? My thoughts? You're the thought police?'

'We're here to ask you about the deaths of three people.'

'Three among so many.'

'What do you mean – there are more?'

'I mean that as we've been speaking who knows

how many thousands of people have died. And you're concerned with three. You can't see the wood for the trees.'

'We see the wood is made of individual trees,' Heap said. 'And we value each and every one of those trees and how each grows in its own unfettered way. Whereas, if I understand you right, you like order in a wood – not a tree out of place and certainly none that have fallen down. In fact, in your life too – those streets you want to clean, those kitchens you want to make spotless.'

'I knew somebody once who couldn't make a meal until he'd cleaned the kitchen from top to bottom,' Gilchrist said. 'He invited me round for a romantic dinner but it wasn't romantic at all since by the time he'd finished the kitchen stank of bleach, it was nearly midnight and it was time for me to go home.'

'Life has no meaning the moment you lose the illusion of being eternal,' Newell said.

'I'll need to ponder that,' Gilchrist said. 'When did you first meet Rasa Lewis?'

'Who?'

'The woman you were taunting about her Jersey swim.'

'I've never met her.'

'This man?' Heap said showing him a photograph of Roland Gulliver.

'Don't know him.'

Photos of Christine Bromley and Philip Coates drew the same response.

'Who are these people? What do they have in common? Why am I supposed to know them?'

'Well, you know Rasa Lewis and Philip Coates

virtually because you made threats to them in online fora,' Heap said.

'Forums to you,' Gilchrist said, doubting that this man was up on Latin declensions.

'I don't notice the names of people attacking me on those things. And that other stuff you were saying about me tidying woods and shit. Where'd you get that from?'

'Your own words,' Heap said. 'On one of your blogs.'

Newell gave her his intense stare again.

'Is there something you want to accuse me of?' Newell said.

'We're building up to it,' Gilchrist said. 'Now we have the right to hold you for forty-eight hours without charge and we intend to exercise that right while we're checking the things you're about to tell us. That would be your whereabouts on certain dates and other boring but essential meat-and-potatoes stuff. But the sooner you furnish us with those details the sooner you can be out of here. If the facts check out, that is. If they don't, well then it will get interesting for you.'

The next morning Watts was in the Serpentine before the changing rooms had even opened. By the time he had done an hour, the changing room was crowded. Margaret Lively was there, already in her costume and swim hat.

'How's the algae?' she said.

'Flourishing,' he said. 'How are you?'

'Busy.'

'Me too.'

'Working with a friend of yours, actually. He said to say hi.'

'Who's that?'

'William Simpson.'

'Really.'

She smiled and leaned in. 'I can't tell from your tone what that "really" means. Listen, I have an invite to a book launch at Foyles early this evening. It's a book about wild-water swimming. If you're still up town would you like to come? Maybe supper afterwards?'

'I'd like that,' Watts said.

'Which part?'

'All of it.'

'Let's meet in Polpo at Cambridge Circus at six and go on from there,' Margaret said, leaning further in to kiss him on the cheek. 'I'd better go now and brave the briny deep.'

Watts watched her go, her athletic body looking pretty sensational in her swimming costume. A beautiful young woman but he was thinking how cynical he was to agree to a date mostly to find out more about her connection to his erstwhile friend and more recent enemy, William Simpson.

Gilchrist was woken from a heavy sleep by her phone ringing. Nothing new there. She was groggy. She and Heap had questioned Newell until after midnight.

It was Lewes nick.

'Hello, Gilchrist here.'

'Sorry to disturb you so early, Detective Inspector.'

Gilchrist focused on her bedside clock. Eight a.m. Not so early.

'Has something happened to Newell?' she said, her voice a little croaky.

'Newell? Oh – no, no. But I believe a Ms Rasa Lewis – different spelling to the town – is a person of interest to your investigation.'

Gilchrist was sitting up now.

'She has been found dead in suspicious circumstances, ma'am. DI Mountain is in charge of the investigation and wonders if you would like to attend the scene of the crime.'

'I certainly would, with my colleague DS Bellamy Heap accompanying me. Where is the scene of the crime?'

'Her home address at—'

'We have it. We were with her last night.'

'Indeed, ma'am. Then DI Mountain will be particularly pleased to see you.'

Tingley took a water taxi to Bernard Bromley's hotel. Reception was by the jetty.

'You're here for Mr Bromley?' the tiny woman at reception said. Tingley slipped a wad of money across the desk and she fluttered it instantly out of sight. 'Fourth Cabin along the beach. Jacaranda. He has not been seen yet today.'

Tingley hoisted his bag over his shoulder and stepped down onto the sand. He walked along the waterline, the warm water lapping his bare feet. The sea was flat, shimmering, opalescent. He saw the sign for Jacaranda hanging from the branch of that very tree outside the beach hut. He walked up to the entrance.

'Hello,' he called through the door. 'Mr Bromley. Bernard Bromley. Sorry to disturb you, sir, but I'm here to get a witness statement from you.'

No response. He tapped on the wood.

'Mr Bromley?' Nothing. 'Mr Bromley, I'm coming in.'

He turned the crude handle. He expected the door to be locked but it started to open. He put his face to the crack. 'Mr Bromley? Then he smelled it. That unmistakeable iron tang of spilled blood. He pushed the door wide and stood in the doorway, his eyes adjusting to the gloom within. Silhouetted like that he was an easy target for anyone in the room with evil intent but he rather thought evil intent had been and gone.

For there was Bernard Bromley, flat on his back on the bed, gouts of blood down his chin and the front of his shirt, with any chance of a witness statement as dead as the air around his lifeless body.

DI Mountain was a short, peevish-looking woman who was professionally friendly but clearly didn't much like Gilchrist towering over her, in any sense.

'I hear you were at this house last night,' she said, addressing Heap, who was more her size. 'That might be a first: the police contaminate a crime scene before a crime has even been committed.'

Gilchrist acknowledged the comment with a smile.

'How did she die?' she said.

216

'Brutally.'

'Do you know when yet?' Heap said.

'Before midnight. What time did you leave?'
Gilchrist looked at Heap.

'At 10.58,' Heap said.

'So the killer might have been watching and
waiting for you to go.'

'Bloody cheek,' Gilchrist said. 'Method of
death?'

'Beaten to death with some heavy implement
laid across the side of her head. Then this weird,
presumably post-mortem, thing. Her mouth has
been stuffed with Jelly Babies. There were a load
more scattered over the floor. Don't know what
that's about.'

'She's a distance swimmer,' Heap said. 'Jelly
Babies are a treat in the water because they taste
nice, they're easy to swallow so they don't slow
you down and they give you a sugar rush of
energy.'

Mountain looked at Gilchrist. 'He's handy to
have around. I've heard about you two – Little
and Large.' She reached out a placatory hand
before Gilchrist could respond. 'You should try
being my height with a name like Mountain.' She
gestured to the police and SOCO around them.
'They think I don't hear they call me Ain't No.'
Gilchrist frowned. 'As in "Ain't No Mountain
High Enough"?'

'"Ain't no valley low enough,"' Gilchrist
murmured. Maybe this woman wasn't so peevish
after all.

'So Ms Lewis figured in your current investigation as a witness.'

'And now she's part of it. Have you contacted any friends or family yet?'

'We can't find her phone to get contacts,' Mountain said. 'You got any?'

'Derek Neill. They are business partners and more. He's slap in the middle of our investigation too.'

'Do you want to . . .?'

'No, no. You need to talk to him about this. Bellamy here can fill you in on what we've got then we can liaise afterwards.'

'You're off?' Mountain said.

'Don't think I can give you added value here until we know a bit more.' She turned to Heap. 'Brief DI Mountain, please, Bellamy. I'm going to see how DC Wade is getting on with Ray Newell's various alibis.'

Sixteen

Jimmy Tingley called Bob Watts while Watts was splashing out on breakfast in Balthazar, the pretend turn-of-the-century French brasserie out of New York, which had opened in Covent Garden a few years earlier.

Watts wouldn't normally be so flashy as to eat here but they did a particularly nice herb omelette and endless refills of great coffee, and now he was going to be in London all day he could take time for a leisurely breakfast.

'He's dead,' Tingley said.

'Murdered?'

'Not sure. It could go either way. No immediate sign of death except a lot of blood. Probably haemorrhaged but it needs the post-mortem to figure out why.'

'Are you in the investigation?'

'Inevitably.'

'Fuck.'

'I know. But maybe not so bad. I'm not going to tell anybody I was doing something for the Brighton police.'

'But it won't take long to connect the dots. And this family are wealthy.'

'You'll have solved stuff at your end by then.'

'You think?'

'I think that I've got maybe a two-hour swim back to my starting point and I've got my snorkelling gear. So I'd best get going.'

'Jimmy?'

But Jimmy Tingley was gone.

'What have you got, Sylvia?' Gilchrist said from the police station in Lewes.

'This gentleman is definitely weird in his movements but they are his movements. He could not have committed these crimes.'

'I was guessing that, since he was in prison when Rasa Lewis was murdered last night.'

'I heard, ma'am, I'm sorry,' Wade said. 'Where now?'

'Have we heard from Cynthia Stokes, the rape councillor?'

'She phoned yesterday – I left you a message.'

'Busy times. You spoke to her?'

219

'She left a number.'

Gilchrist sat in her car and dialled Stokes.

'Cyn, hope I'm not disturbing any mother-and-child stuff but I've only just got your message.'

'I'm at work already. I spoke to Christine Bromley's doctor.'

'Was he willing to talk?'

'Very much so. I've known him for years. He's the family doctor for the entire Bromley family. Christine had visited him but not to talk about a rape. He didn't know if it was just very violent consensual sex. She wouldn't say. But she had injuries consistent with forceful sex.'

'Forceful sex. So if it was rape, why wouldn't she take it further?'

'Well, answering that kind of question is your area of expertise, Sarah. From my experience, a common reason is because the victim is close to the person who raped her.'

Gilchrist thanked her and rang off, thinking about Cynthia's remark. Her phone immediately rang.

'Confusing news,' Bob Watts said.

'It's proving to be that sort of day.'

'I'm sorry to tell you that Bernard Bromley is dead.'

Gilchrist's heart fell. 'Tingley?'

'Actually, no. He arrived too late.'

'How did Bromley die?'

'Tingley isn't sure whether it was accident, self-inflicted or he is a murder victim. It's going to need the autopsy.'

'Another one.'

220

'Bit of a stretch to think whoever is killing people here has that kind of reach.'

'Bob, you know better than that. If this is all about money, and a lot of it is swilling around, then getting to somebody on the other side of the world isn't going to be difficult.'

'You mean the Bromley money? Killing Christine so she doesn't give it away makes sense. Killing Bernard doesn't.'

'So you're inclined to think his death is unrelated?'

'If it's self-inflicted then it's related to something, but perhaps not what you expect.'

'But is Tingley's unofficial presence going to come back and bite me?' Gilchrist said.

'Tingley is a ghost. He's gone off the grid. If ever anybody makes any kind of link it will be way after you've solved this.'

'I'm touched by your faith in me.'

'Don't be, it's based on experience with you.'

She wanted to smile into the phone but she said: 'Rasa Lewis was murdered last night.'

Watts sighed. 'Somebody is on a rampage. Have you found a link between Rasa Lewis and the Bromley fortune?'

'Nothing immediately stands out.'

'Suspects? That mad blogger?'

'Not him. In detention at the time.'

'Derek Neill?'

'He's in the mix, for sure.'

'The paunchy guy in the spa?'

'We have so little to work on with him.'

'Look, I'm a regular there and I can't place him,' Watts said. 'But then we just might never

221

have coincided. You've checked the day-pass people, I'm guessing.'

'We've got a list of a dozen people over a three-day period sure. But they don't give their addresses.'

'They probably pay by credit card so you can track them.'

'We're doing that with most but some paid by cash.'

'How many?'

'Three. Who just signed in, each one with indecipherable names.'

'And no CCTV.'

'That's right. All wiped.'

'The cameras on the road won't have been wiped.'

'I know that but he might have come over the Downs from Rottingdean,' Gilchrist said. 'No cameras there.'

'He might. In which case you're stuffed. But the football club has some pretty impressive technology around its stadium and I bet there will be some overspill onto other bits of that area. And the road both ways – from Lewes and Brighton – has advanced vehicle registration number recognition technology in place.'

'But we haven't pursued that avenue as we don't know what car we're looking for.'

'Sure you do, within a certain margin of error yet to be determined. Remember when you were a member of that gym?'

'Sure, I had to give them my vehicle registration so they knew I wasn't some student ligging a free parking space in its car park.'

'Same still applies.'

'Still leaves a long, old list cross-referencing every car going down that very busy road with every car that pulled into the gym car park?'

'You let the computers do all the heavy lifting. There's a speed camera with the right technology just before the turn-off to the university and the gym, in the Brighton to Lewes direction. Focus on that one for now and see if God is smiling at you.'

'God rarely smiles at me at the moment,' Gilchrist said, then cursed herself for being so mawkish.

'Well, a lot of people who care about you are smiling at you – all the time,' Watts said, hanging up the phone. Gilchrist stared at her own phone and swallowed. She walked to the window and looked down on the slow slop of the sea and the people on the promenade drifting along in their different ways. She looked back at Sylvia Wade, hunched over her computer.

She wondered when Bellamy Heap would get back, recognizing how much she depended on him. She wondered about Kate and Bellamy and how Kate's obsession with her swim might be affecting their new relationship. But mostly she wondered how the hell she was ever going to solve this case she didn't really understand.

She was saved from further introspection, as always, by the bell of her phone ringing. Her landline.

'A Mrs Jones on the line,' the operator said apologetically. 'About her son Darrel?'

'Put her through,' Heap said.

'When is he going to get his reward money?' Mrs Jones said, the moment she was put through.

'Well, the investigation is ongoing, Mrs Jones. A lot of "i"s to dot and "t"s to cross first.'

'And a lot of fucking groceries to buy too. He's given you what you want now give him what he's earned.'

'Well, he hasn't fully earned it yet, Mrs Jones.' Gilchrist had a thought. 'Is he around now?'

'In his bed sleeping off whatever he got up to last night.'

'How do you two feel about a trip to Woodvale Cemetery this morning? I'll send a car to pick you up in half an hour?'

'Don't want no rozzer's car turning up here, thank you very much. This is a respectable address.'

'So you'll make your own way there? I'll meet you outside the cemetery office. You know, the entrance is just off the Lewes Road – the Sainsbury's is over on the other side of that big road junction?'

'What – you think I wasn't born here?'

'Half an hour, then.'

It felt odd having Sylvia Wade drive her, but Gilchrist didn't feel Bellamy should be part of this, given Darrel Jones's attack on Kate.

Darrel was the same ferrety little creep he'd been the last time she'd seen him and his mother was the same mess. Wade got them in the back seat of the police car and they drove slowly up towards the chapels in the centre of the cemetery.

'Darrel, I think you said you'd seen those two men on more than one occasion in the cemetery. I wondered if you could show me exactly where?'

'Wherever they could get a snog,' he said, sniggering.

'It would be helpful to our inquiry – and you'd be helping yourself with regard to that reward money – if you could be more specific. I mean do you have a regular hangout when you're here. Where were they in relation to that?'

His mother cuffed him and hissed something to him. It seemed to do the trick.

'They were hanging out over there,' Darrel said. 'Above where all those kid's graves are.'

Sylvia Wade went over and started looking for the grave of Lesley White. Gilchrist stood a few yards away from Darrel and his mother. She looked up the hill to where Kate had once taken her to see the unmarked grave of the Brighton Trunk Murder victim. The woman had never been identified so the crime had never been solved.

Wade came back.

'All done?' Gilchrist said.

Wade nodded.

'OK then,' Gilchrist called to Darrel. 'Anything else useful to tell us?'

'When do I get my money?'

Gilchrist put on a fake smile.

'Well now, someone is keeping it for you. Remember that day when those two men interrupted all their kissing and cuddling to come over to stop you and your gang assaulting and stealing from a woman just about here? Well, she has your money.'

'What's she talking about, Darrel?' his mother said, not sure who to glare at first.

'How the fuck should I know? Bitch is fucking barmy.'

His mother cuffed him. 'What have I told you? Don't say the F-word.' She squared up to Gilchrist. 'What's all this about?'

'It's about your son being a lying, vicious little creep,' Gilchrist said. 'Those men were never kissing and cuddling. They came to the help of a woman your son and his feral friends were viciously attacking. They scared off the cowardly little creeps and now your stupid son thinks he can get his own back.' Gilchrist pointed vaguely up into the trees. 'Except we have it all on CCTV.' Darrel looked up and around. 'That's right, Darrel. You wouldn't expect to find security cameras in a graveyard, would you? Well, it's because of people like you.' She looked at Mrs Jones. 'We'll be in touch with charges in due course.'

'He's underage,' Mrs Jones said sharply.

'We'll be back with underage charges.' Gilchrist indicated the open door into the back of the police car. 'Do you want to hop in or would you rather walk?'

'Cyn, it's Sarah Gilchrist again. The Bromley family doctor. I wonder if you might ask him about Bernard Bromley.'

'I feel very uncomfortable about this. I'm feeling a bit used.'

'Only for the common good.'

'You say. What is it you want to know?'

'State of mind, physical problems etc. He's

226

dead in Thailand and there's some confusion about whether it was an accident, natural causes, he killed himself or was murdered. The locals over there don't seem to care either way so long as they can ship the body out of the country.'

'So can't it wait for a post-mortem over here?'

'With all that we've got going on it would be nice to get a bit of a move on. Please, Cyn.'

Stokes sighed. 'I'll see what I can do.'

Stokes phoned back twenty minutes later.

'OK, the doc was happy to talk. In fact he was eager.'

'I'm relieved to hear it.'

'Bernard has been on some happy-clappy pill for years to stop him getting depressed. Sometimes it takes him the other way and he needs calming down. Pretty healthy generally although has needed to visit the STD clinic at the hospital a couple of times following his trips to Thailand.'

'Nice.'

'But here was the thing the doctor was dying to share. It has obviously been preying on his mind for ages but he couldn't tell anyone.'

Gilchrist tried not to show her excitement. 'Go on.'

'Bernard suffers from Peyronie's disease.'

Gilchrist had no idea what that was.

'You're going to translate, I hope,' she said.

'Peyronie's disease is a knot of scar tissue on the ligament in the penis that causes it to bend or rather prevents it becoming fully erect as the blood can't flow all the way along the penis. It can be excruciatingly painful for the man when he does get an erection.'

'Ouch,' Gilchrist said, but she was still at a loss.

Stokes obviously sensed Gilchrist's bafflement. 'He first went to the doctor about it around a year ago. Shortly after his sister had been about her genital and anal injuries.'

'How do you get this Peyronie thing?' Gilchrist said, letting out her breath slowly.

'By accident when the penis is erect. The man thrusts into or against something that doesn't give so the penis violently bends – fractures if you will.'

'Ouch,' Gilchrist repeated quietly. 'The kind of thing that might happen during a violent rape, then?'

'Exactly that kind of thing,' Stokes said.

Bellamy Heap walked into the office as Gilchrist was contemplating what to do about the information she'd just been given that might mean Bernard had raped his half-sister. That would provide a plausible explanation why she would not help the police with their investigation. But did it make Bernard Bromley her murderer? And why would he murder Philip Coates? Perhaps, Christine had confided in Coates? Had she confided in Derek Neill too?

And how did all that tie in with Roland Gulliver?

Supposing Bernard Bromley had gone on this murderous rampage, he was in Thailand at the time of Rasa Lewis's death. And how to explain his own death? Remorseful suicide or vengeful friend of the three dead people who had figured out Bromley's guilt?

'Bellamy, I'm going bananas here. The more information we're given, the more muddled this case gets.'

'Well, I have information which might make it worse or better, depending on your point of view,' Heap said. 'From Bilson.'

Gilchrist tilted her head.

'He couldn't get through to you and I guess he was bursting to tell somebody so he called me.'

'Quite properly. With what news?'

'A breakthrough on the DNA on the wine glass.'

'A match!'

'Not a match from the existing database but from somebody who only added to it a couple of days ago.'

'Whose DNA?'

'The DNA of April Medavoy.'

Sylvia Wade was a cautious driver so it took twenty minutes or so to get to April Medavoy's Victorian terrace house in Salthaven. It felt odd for Gilchrist to be sitting in the back of the car with Heap but they used the time to catch up.

'Mrs Medavoy, Mass Murderer?' Gilchrist said. 'I can't see it, can you, Bellamy?'

'The idea of her getting hold of ketamine from somewhere is enough to punch a hole in that, I agree,' Heap said. 'So perhaps we're back to regarding these crimes as unconnected.'

'Or two connected and two not. I'm guessing Bilson is not going to find any ketamine in Rasa Lewis. Unless we slipped it to her. You didn't did you, Bellamy?'

'Not that I recall, ma'am.'

'And I didn't. Has Derek Neill been informed, by the way?'

'He has.'

'If I may, ma'am,' Sylvia Wade said from the driving seat.

'You may,' Gilchrist said.

'I emailed the photo of the inscription to you both.'

Heap read from his iPad: '"So we beat on, boats against the current, born back ceaselessly into the past."'

'Is it from the Bible, Big Brain?' Gilchrist said to Heap. He frowned, considering she supposed, but before he could respond, Wade chimed in.

'It's the last line of *The Great Gatsby*, ma'am.'

Wade saw Gilchrist and Heap both staring at her in the rear-view mirror. She flushed. 'I'm in a pub quiz team. It comes up a lot.'

'You'd better be looking to your laurels, Bellamy. Looks like you've got competition in the office.'

'Ma'am,' Heap said as Wade flushed some more.

'It's quite beautiful, actually,' Gilchrist said. 'Read it again, Bellamy.'

When Heap had done so, Wade said: 'I checked with the cemetery office who commissioned it. According to their records it was paid for in cash. By Derek Neill. But it wasn't him – I showed them his photo.'

'Our paunchy man again?' Gilchrist said.

'Quite possibly, ma'am.'

'Well done, DC Wade,' Heap said.

'Very well done, Sylvia,' Gilchrist added,

noting that now Wade was blushing almost as much as Heap usually did.

Seventeen

April Medavoy didn't seem surprised to see them. In fact she seemed resigned. She ushered them into the kitchen and put the kettle on.

'You haven't been honest with us, Mrs Medavoy,' Heap said.

'April, please,' she said weakly. 'Tea or coffee?'

'Neither, thank you,' Gilchrist said as Heap and Wade both shook their heads.

'I'll have a coffee if you don't mind,' Mrs Medavoy said. 'I need the energy.'

'Why did you make up that story about telephoning Roland Gulliver when he was with someone else?'

'Well, I did telephone him, just as I said.'

'When you were actually with him?' Heap said.

She nodded as the kettle boiled. 'From his bathroom.'

'Why?' Heap said.

'To give myself an alibi. I read a lot of Peter James so I know how these things work.'

'An alibi for what, Mrs Medavoy?' Heap continued.

'April,' Medavoy whispered. 'I wasn't sure for what but I thought I might need one.'

'You thought you might do him harm?'

'I didn't know what I was going to do.'

231

'Mrs Medavoy, we're a bit in the dark here,' Gilchrist said. 'Was it because of the petition?'

She put a spoonful of instant coffee into a flowered mug and poured the hot water in. She sat down at the table and started stirring her coffee.

'The petition?' she said blankly. 'Why the petition?'

'What then? Why might you do Roland Gulliver harm?'

Medavoy continued stirring, the spoon scraping around the inside of the mug, the coffee starting to slop over. Wade reached out a hand and covered hers to stop her. She looked down at Wade's big hand and smiled a wide, cheerless smile.

'Hell hath no fury, Detective Inspector, hell hath no fury.'

'Roland Gulliver scorned you?' Gilchrist said, watching Wade's hand as she withdrew it. Medavoy let go of the spoon and laid her hand on the table.

'He said he was going to leave that stupid wife for me and then he tells me he's in love but not with me. How humiliated do you think I felt?'

'Very, I would imagine,' Gilchrist said, totally sideswiped by this news. 'How long had you and he . . .'

'Since we first met. I got him involved, with Save Salthaven Lido so we had an excuse to be together.'

'And you had no idea about him and—'

'He said they were just friends!'

'And you and he . . . .?'

'Often.'

Gilchrist sat back. She didn't dare look at Heap.

'So what happened on the evening you went round?'

'I brought the bottle of wine. I wanted it to be civilized although I wasn't sure if I was going to smash it over his head before we were finished.'

'Hence the alibi,' Heap said.

She ignored that.

'We talked and drank and the next thing I knew I was back at my house.'

'You seemed to have jumped quite a lot there, Mrs Medavoy,' Heap said.

'I know. But that's how I remember it. One minute I'm sitting at the table with him, the next I'm lying on my sofa in my sitting room.'

'Alone?'

'Yes.'

'Where was your car?'

'In my drive. I had walked to his house.'

'You didn't phone him to find out what had happened?'

'I was bewildered. And scared. Had I blacked out and done something terrible? So when you came and told me he had been murdered it was quite a shock, I can tell you.'

'Did you really think you might have murdered him?'

'I had no idea. But when you told me where he had been found I knew it couldn't have been me.'

'We'll have to do a forensic search of your house.'

'To be sure he wasn't here? But I've told you.'

'You look panicked, Mrs Medavoy.'

'Well, of course there will be his fingerprints and DNA all over the house from his visits.'

'What about your husband, Mrs Medavoy?'

'I don't have one. I say I'm married just to keep nosey-parkers away from my business.'

'Is there nothing else you remember about that night?'

'Only the towels, of course.'

'Towels?' Gilchrist said sharply.

'When I went into the bathroom here there were two of my towels in the bathtub, both soaking wet. I don't know how they got there. The only thing I could think is that I'd been sick when I got home and used them to clean up the bathroom.'

Heap nodded to Wade and she left the room. Gilchrist heard her summoning SOCO as a matter of urgency.

'Do you have somewhere you can stay for the next couple of days, Mrs Medavoy? Friends?'

'Not really. Why?'

'I'm afraid your home is now a crime scene.'

'What crime? You said Roland had been found on the steps of the lido.'

'He was found on the lido steps but he was murdered elsewhere,' Gilchrist said. 'And it looks like that elsewhere might have been your bathroom.'

Bob Watts opened the door to Derek Neill.

'Mind if I come in, sport?' Neill said.

'Not at all. I'm working on a bottle of Malbec if you want to give me some help.'

Neill walked over to the window, turned back. 'Pretty much the same configuration as mine. Coppers must earn well.'

'So must swimming tour people,' Watts said, handing him a glass of wine. 'Mine was an inheritance. My dad. Big name crime writer back in the day.'

'I'm not much of a reader,' Neill said. 'But I've always been good at business. Not cutthroat, just charging a fair price for what I provide.'

'I've heard about Rasa. I'm sorry. You're in the thick of it.'

Neill smiled sadly.

'So we beat on, boats against the current, borne back ceaselessly into the past.'

'Is that where we're headed now?'

Neill nodded. 'In a while, perhaps, when we've got through your bottle.'

'Am I the one you should be sharing things with?'

'Oh, it's not a confession. More an explanation. And I was hoping you might invite your friend Sarah Gilchrist and that alert young man, Bellamy Heap, over to hear it with you.' He held up his free hand. 'I *am* in the middle of it. And no doubt a major suspect. I just want to make a few things clear.'

Watts raised his glass in a toast. 'Let me make the call.'

Gilchrist and Heap found Neill and Bob Watts sitting companionably on a long sofa, an empty wine bottle on the low table in front of them. Watts went to the kitchen to get another bottle.

Neill stood and smiled wanly at Gilchrist, nodded to Heap.

'Should I be cautioning you?' Gilchrist said.

'Well, I'm not confessing to killing any of my friends and loved ones, if that's what you mean. But I realize that I've been holding information back and by doing so I might have got Rasa killed. And I guess I'm responsible for the deaths of the others. Which is something I have to live with.'

'That is starting to sound like a confession,' Gilchrist said. She continued: 'The argument you had with Roland Gulliver. It was over Lesley White who is buried in Woodvale with that lovely inscription on the gravestone?'

'"So we beat on",' said Heap, '"boats against the current, borne back ceaselessly into the past."'

Watts looked up sharply at that as he was pouring the wine.

'Lesley loved *The Great Gatsby* but to put that on her gravestone was a desecration,' Neill said.

'The man who paid cash for it to be done claimed he was you,' Gilchrist said. 'A paunchy man. Do you know who that might be?'

'Nobody immediately springs to mind but if it was someone from my past, people can put on weight.'

'Lesley was a "she"?' Heap said.

'Yes. Oh, I see, you thought Roland and I were arguing over a man – more of that gay stuff you've been imagining.'

'Why a desecration?'

'It was a warning to me, I realize now. The past can't be forgiven or forgotten.'

236

Watts handed out glasses as Gilchrist and Heap sat down in the chairs facing the sofa. Watts resumed his seat. All three looked at Neill. He took a swig of the wine, set the glass down and took a deep breath.

'Let's begin then, shall we? Christine and I got together on a yoga retreat about eight years ago. Rasa was running it. That's how I met them both. Christine was there to relax. She was already driven by her focus on the family company. I didn't know what a big deal the company was and she didn't say – made it sound like some ma-and-pa grocery store or something.

'I'd been making good money organizing rock and roll tours along the south coast for a few years. I'd been quietly salting it away and putting it into property. But I saw a big opportunity with this yoga lark. Everywhere I looked, yoga was booming. Rasa had a good following but she was rubbish at the business. So I proposed we go into business together. And that worked out for both of us.

'I was looking at related possibilities and we messed about a bit with free diving because of the breath being at the core of both that and yoga. Then it was just a hop and a skip into wild-water swimming. About six years ago, we started working on Dolphin Smile.

'I had the idea for a swimming centre some-where warm and then special trips to different parts of the world for swimming holidays. By then, Christine was going off in her own direction, although I don't think even she knew what that direction was.

'We'd never talked about commitment or fidelity. Rasa was a no-commitments kind of woman too, although she had some kind of thing with Christine's old school friend, Philip Coates. At the time he was a senior planner for the council, which makes him sound more boring than he ever was.

'Dolphin Smile was going to need some big upfront costs. Rasa and I both had money but not nearly enough. Christine and I never talked money and I never dreamed of asking her for backing, although by then I'd realized what a big deal the company was.

'I found a site in Crete that might work – beautiful little bay with an abandoned taverna with a few rooms and a proper taverna just down the track a couple of hundred yards. I put together a small party of friends and acquaintances to go and check it out with me and do some swimming and to see if they might be potential investors.

'Aside from me they included Rasa, Christine, Rasa's pal Philip Coates, Roland Gulliver and Tamsin Stanhope. Lesley White was there too, with her then partner, David Blue.'

'The Lesley White buried in Woodvale Cemetery.'

Neill nodded. 'Remember I talked about the roads un-travelled and the women I would have travelled with had they invited me? Well, she was the one, before Christine came along. In fact, without in any way speaking ill of the dead, Christine was a rebound for me, as I think I was for her. That had become obvious long before this trip to Crete.'

'Can I just interrupt there,' Gilchrist said. 'Did Christine never confide in you who raped her?'

'Never. I told you, we were living separate lives long before then.'

'What about her relationship with her brother, Bernard?'

'What about it?' Neill said.

Neill looked from one to the other of them.

'Bernard's dead, you know,' Heap said. 'In Thailand.'

'Is he?' He gave a little shake of his head. 'Is he?'

'Dolphin Smile does a swimming retreat on one of the Thai islands,' Heap said. 'The same island Bernard died on. In the same hotel you block book actually.'

'It's about the only hotel on the island,' Neill said, his face impassive.

'Apparently, he turned up for his flight from Gatwick looking the worse for wear.'

Neill nodded. 'Bernard liked a drink.'

'As if he'd been beaten up.'

'Really.' Neill took a glug of his wine.

'Indications are that when he was found dead his face and body showed bruising a couple of days old from such a beating. The Thai authorities did some kind of half-hearted autopsy and decided cause of death was internal bleeding. He'd ruptured something inside. He'd been haemorrhaging blood into his stomach for those couple of days. Coughed up a lot too, at the end.'

'So he suffered,' Neill said.

'Oh yes,' Heap said. 'A lot.'

Neill sat quietly, looking from one to the other of them.

'Carry on with your story, Mr Neill,' Gilchrist said.

'Well, things were pretty open on that trip. There were others there who came and went for odd days while we were there. Friends of friends kind of stuff. There was a gay friend of Christine's who turned out not to be quite so gay after all. David Blue kind of stuck out as being more conventional but the rest of us were pretty free.'

'And this David Blue was with Lesley – the woman you had really liked?'

'Yeah, he was with Lesley. But by then I realized it was Rasa I wanted. OK, look, I was a bit of an emotional mess at the time. Maybe I always am. Christine and I were on the downside of our marriage and she wasn't exactly faithful to me there. Lesley I'd adored and still thought I loved, until it dawned on me that it was Rasa I wanted.' He caught Gilchrist's look. 'I know, I know but behind all that front she has there is somebody else. Was somebody else. Anyway, the whole time there got pretty emotional all round and then it turned very bad.'

'How emotional?' Gilchrist said.

'How bad?' Heap said.

'What happened?' Watts said.

Neill smiled.

'Well, the emotion, short version. It was like *Le Ronde*.'

That passed Gilchrist by but Heap gave a small smile. He would.

'Roland lusted for Christine's gay friend – I

can't for the life of me remember his name –
who in fact wasn't gay but gender fluid or
gender curious or whatever the modern expression is. That guy pined for Christine, who was
oblivious to that as I think she had always
hankered for Philip, who was happy with Rasa
who I was infatuated with. I was ignoring
Lesley, who was now realizing she should have
stuck with me but instead she was miserable
with David Blue, who was obsessed with her
but also abused her. And I was using Tamsin
for sex because I couldn't have Rasa.'

'I'm glad I asked,' Gilchrist said.

'What happened?' Watts repeated.

'Headline or long version?'

'Why bury your lead?' Heap said.

'Lesley died.'

Neill stood and started pacing. 'The jellyfish
arrived in the night. Thousands of them blown
in by strong winds on fierce tides. Jellyfish are
see-through but none are totally colourless, you
know. In their pink and their purple and their
turquoise tints they actually are quite beautiful.
But, as with many beautiful things, they are
deadly.'

He stopped pacing and stood by the window.

'I remember it all so vividly. When I came
down, it was not yet seven in the morning but
already the sun was burning brightly in a clear
blue sky. The storm had blown itself out and now
the bay was calm. I was about to swim when I
looked into the water and saw them. It was only
in daylight you could see these translucent discs,
big as hubcaps, closely packed on the surface of

the water and beneath them the iridescent ones, dangling and hanging in the water with their long beads.

'David Blue came down to the beach raving. It must still have been dark when Lesley had slipped from the room she'd been sharing unhappily with David and gone for an early morning swim. He always went crazy when he didn't know where Lesley was. He went crazy when he did. It turned out later that the previous night he'd slapped her around.'

Neill came and sat back down.

'We found her in a grotto in the rocks at the near end of the beach. It was almost a tunnel, hollowed out over the millennia by the action of the sea. It went in to a depth of some twenty yards and at its furthest extreme there was a sandy shelf, some twelve yards across by five yards deep. Rasa liked to do her yoga there. Light splashed down on this hidden beach through a funnel in the rock above it.

'The acoustics were such that when the wind blew you heard groans and strange noises. I'd read that the Delphic oracle had been nothing more than an odd acoustic effect from a curious rock formation.

'Anyway, I ducked down to get into the cave and led the way, shuffling forward along a three-foot-wide walkway beside the lagoon. It was cool in the grotto and I was relieved to get out of the sun. It was beautiful in there. The turquoise water slapped idly against the walls, sucked at the sand at the far end of the cave.

'Sunlight streamed down the funnel almost like

a spotlight onto the sand bar. And what it illu-minated was Lesley's body lying still, arms and legs akimbo.

'She was covered in huge wheals and welts and rashes, her face and limbs swollen. She was groaning.

'David Blue came in, rushing so much he almost brained himself on the low ceiling. He grabbed at my arm. "Do something!"

'It took twenty minutes to get her out of the grotto and across the beach, David dashing around us getting more and more agitated. "She's in anaphylactic shock," I said. "Haven't you got something for it in your medicine chest?" he said. Of course I didn't, back in those days. "There is nothing for it you can buy over the counter," I explained.

'But he wouldn't accept that. He got up close. "Why haven't you got stuff that would help?" I stared him out. Truth is, I wanted to punch him for treating Lesley badly. "Because I'm not a doctor and only a doctor can use this stuff."

'He backed off then and dropped down beside Lesley. "Jesus," he said. "Lesley, stay with me, stay with me." Lesley was panting now. Her eyes were rolled up into their sockets. If she could hear, she didn't respond.

'Well, we drove her to the nearest clinic but it was a two-hour drive. All the time David screeching at me to do something. "Like what? I'm driving as fast as I can." But he wouldn't let it go. "What kind of shit medical chest was that?"'

Neill swirled the wine round in his glass.

'She died an hour away from the hospital. Rasa

knew she had died but didn't say anything. David realized when we got her out of the van. Shoulders slumped, head down, his eyes rolled up in his head so that he could glare at me, a look of utter hatred on his face. I affected not to notice but I did.'

'So Lesley died of anaphylactic shock,' Gilchrist said. 'She swam into an armada of jellyfish. She got stung dozens of times and had an allergic reaction.'

Neill sighed. 'Yes. And David Blue looked as if he wanted to kill me. He thought it was my fault. According to him I should have warned her about the jellyfish even though they arrived in the night and she went for a swim at dawn before I even knew they were there. Then he thought I should have had all the paraphernalia of stuff on hand to deal with the anaphylaxis.'

'But you didn't,' Gilchrist murmured.

'As I said, nobody did in those days except in hospitals.'

There was silence for a moment.

'So you're saying all these deaths could be David Blue's doing,' Heap said. 'Out for revenge for something that happened six years ago.'

'I'm just filling you in on a background that may be significant because it links all the people who have been killed.'

'Why did he wait so long?' Gilchrist said.

Neill shrugged. 'That's for you to find out, isn't it?'

'Who else was on that trip?' Watts asked. 'You said friends of friends came and went.'

Neill rubbed his eye for a moment. 'I don't

really remember. Somebody called Genevra? She only stayed a couple of days. We met her in the other tavern. She did a moonlight flit with her boyfriend. I don't remember his name. I remember he was stuck up. We took the piss out of him a lot.'

'But you'll have records?' Watts said.

'Not from that trip – that was a kind of test run.'

'When was the last time you saw David Blue?' Heap said.

'Lesley's funeral. But he didn't let it go. He tried to sue me for negligence but everyone had signed waivers and what happened to Lesley was kind of an act of God.' He looked away. 'Which doesn't mean I don't blame myself.'

Eighteen

'We might have been focusing too much on the Bromley family squabbles as motive,' Gilchrist said to Heap when they were back in the car.

Heap nodded. 'It does seem to be shifting to this stuff in Crete. Are we assuming Derek Neill beat up Bernard Bromley?'

Gilchrist didn't speak for a moment. 'I think we are – because he found out that Bernard raped his half-sister? But I think that is off at a tangent now too.'

Heap nodded again. 'I agree, ma'am. What do you think about this David Blue and his blaming

Neill for the death of his girlfriend? Is that enough to go on a killing spree? And, if so, why now? What took him so long?'

'Living abroad?' Gilchrist said. 'In prison? In a mental institution?'

Back at the station Heap had the answer within ten minutes, courtesy of the research he could do so adroitly on his laptop.

'Prison. Released two months ago.'

'Around the time the threats to Neill started,' Gilchrist said. 'What was he in for?'

'Manslaughter. Hit-and-run, though he handed himself in twenty-four hours later. May have been drunk though no way of being certain by then.'

'Who did he kill?'

'Woman in her fifties. On a zebra crossing.'

Gilchrist nodded. 'Sounds like this was just after Lesley died. If Neill was accurate about David Blue's feelings, then Blue would have been in a pretty bad way. Do we know where he is?'

'Edinburgh,' Heap said. 'Morningside.'

'That's a posh bit, isn't it?'

'It used to be. Not sure about these days.'

'Are we going to see him?'

'I've spoken to Police Scotland,' Heap said.

'It's easier than it would have been if Scotland had voted for independence, but we still need to be politeness personified up there. They can be a prickly lot.'

Heap nodded.

'Is Blue working?' Gilchrist said.

'That I don't know.'

They flew from Gatwick and were descending pretty much the minute they ascended. Gilchrist was half expecting there to be an official car waiting but there was no apparent sign. They had a choice of tram, bus or taxi at Edinburgh airport. They opted for the taxi.

'Nobody with any sense takes the tram,' the driver, a chunky man in a thick jumper said in a soft burr of an accent. 'It's more expensive and slower than the bus.'

'It's been a long time coming, hasn't it?' Heap said.

'Too long – it's a national disgrace.'

'Has it affected your business?' Heap said.

'Not one iota,' the cabbie said as he pulled up on a side road in Morningside. 'Simple reason: they don't go anywhere anybody wants to go. Or if they do, people can get there cheaper and more efficiently by other means.'

All Gilchrist knew about Morningside was that Miss Jean Brodie lived there in the novel she'd studied at GCSE. It was a pleasant enough part of the city and Blue lived on an attractive terrace.

There was a policeman at the front door.

'DI Gilchrist and DS Bellamy, I take it?' he said affably. 'Constable Jardine. The chief suggested we ensure Mr Blue was home for you.'

'He's inside?'

Jardine, a slender man with a crinkly grin, said: 'We haven't chained him up or anything, but he is expecting you.' He turned and rapped on the door. 'Mr Blue? Your visitors.'

Blue came to the door, a cigarette in the corner of his mouth. Music blared and a phone was ringing.

'Mr Blue?' Gilchrist said. 'A word if you would.'

Blue closed the door behind them and started to shoot a bolt.

'Don't do that, please, sir.'

There were four heavy locks on the door. He saw them looking. 'I was burgled and I hate the neighbours. They spy on me with binoculars and they burgle me.'

'I think you're quite safe for the moment, sir,' Heap said.

Blue led them up a narrow flight of stairs made narrower by piles of yellowing newspapers and magazines down one side. He led the way into a cramped, crowded room and leaned down to turn the volume of the music down. Gilchrist and Heap exchanged glances. He had no paunch.

The curtains were closed but a bare light bulb provided garish illumination.

'I don't like net curtains so I keep the curtains closed all the time.'

There were no ornaments in the clutter; nothing on the walls except photos of celebrities torn out of magazines.

'Monica, can you get the phone,' he shouted. 'I'll get back to them later.' He turned to Gilchrist and Heap. 'Monica is lying down in the bedroom in the dark. She has a bad back.'

Gilchrist didn't know who Monica was or why a bad back would require dark, but simply waited for the phone to stop ringing, which it eventually did.

She looked round the room. It was chaos. Piles everywhere. A couple of dozen boxes were stacked in tottering towers. A huge photocopier stood in front of the window, which was curtained off.

Blue saw her look.

'Sorry for the state. I hate this place. Haven't had time to make it my own since I got out.' He indicated the sofa. 'My dad gave me that sofa. Please, sit.'

Heap was looking at a three-foot-high pile of copies of a tabloid. Blue saw his look.

'I get a bit compulsive about buying magazines and newspapers,' he said sheepishly.

'Do you read them?' Heap said.

Blue thrust his hands into the back pockets of his jeans. 'I flick through.' He looked pained. 'I must get into reading.'

'Since you got out,' Gilchrist said. 'When was that?'

'Couple of months ago,' Blue said.

'Have you been in touch with Derek Neill since you got out?'

'That killer? I never want to be in touch with him ever again.'

'What about Roland Gulliver or Christine Bromley or Philip Coates?'

'Just names to me, man.'

'Do you use recreational drugs, Mr Blue?' Heap said.

'I'm going to tell a policeman the answer to that?'

'You'd be wise to,' Gilchrist said.

'A little dope every now and then but who doesn't?'

'Ketamine?'

'Don't know what that is, so I'm going to say no.'

'Have you been to Brighton lately?'

'Couple of months ago. Is this about Lesley's grave?'

'What about it?'

'That inscription – the Gatsby quote.'

'You arranged for that to be inscribed?'

'No, but I wish I'd thought of it. I assumed it was Neill out of guilt. I see it as a permanent reminder to him of how he killed the woman I loved.'

'It was surely an accident?'

'Neill was responsible. He'd been shagging her the night before.'

Gilchrist waited a moment as she digested that. 'That may well be so,' she said cautiously. 'But how does that make him responsible?'

Blue looked at his clasped hands. 'That night, I'd gone to the telephone box by the other taverna. Warm night. Still. Wood smoke just hanging in the air. Like fog. When I came back I saw her with a man standing outside a blue door. Lesley held the man's hand.' Blue sniffed. 'My stomach churned. The man opened the door and moved aside to let her pass. She had a little smile at the corners of her mouth.'

'This was Neill?' Gilchrist said.

'I couldn't see his face but he looked about the same size.'

'You could see a little smile at the corners of her mouth but not this man's face?' Heap said.

Blue's knuckles were white. 'Maybe I didn't want to see his face. When they went in I moved

250

across to the window but they closed the shutters just as I got there. I peered through the gap between the shutters. I could see a small sliver of the room.

'The man excused himself and went into the bathroom. I saw my wife take off her cardigan and shoes. She had on a blouse, a red skirt. She wasn't wearing her bra. She crossed her arms over her breasts and waited until the man came back into the room. He put his nose near her hair and inhaled. She walked over to the bed, sat on its edge, looked up at him. He went and sat next to her. She leaned in and whispered in his ear. He moved his head to kiss her on her mouth and she put her arms round him and drew him back onto the bed.'

'Mr Blue, I'm not sure we need to hear all this,' Gilchrist said, feeling increasingly uncomfortable. 'Perhaps you can move on to what happened next.'

'What do you think bloody happened?'

'I mean over the next few hours.'

He grimaced. 'All I know is that's why I hit her. And that's why we slept apart that night and that's why I didn't know she'd gone out early in the morning.'

Gilchrist and Heap glanced at each other.

'You hit her,' Gilchrist said.

'Boyfriend and girlfriend stuff. Just a cuff. She'd just been screwing someone else for Christ's sake.'

'And that man was Derek Neill?'

'I assumed so.'

'Did you actually see his face?'

251

'Not really but it had to be him.'

'Did she come straight back to your room after that someone else?' Gilchrist said.

'I don't know. I went off for a wander. When I came back to our room she was sitting on the rug by the fire. Staring into it, her wet hair clinging to her shoulders. "I saw you with him," I said. She must not have heard me come in because she started. She looked up but not at me. Somewhere to the side of me. Her voice was low and toneless and at first I didn't realize she was speaking as her lips didn't seem to move. "I'm wondering why I don't want you like I used to. And wishing I did." I started to touch her cheek but she flinched. I started to cry. Not noisily but my face contorted and I felt the tears gush. She still wasn't looking at me but she must have realized because she looked back at the fire, chewing her lip. "Don't you think you've overplayed that one a bit lately," she said harshly.

'I was disconnected from the open hand that hit her across the face. Disconnected from the person who started to punch her, raining blows on her as she cowered then crumpled. I could hear someone bellowing incoherently but didn't realize until afterwards that the voice was mine.'

Blue looked off to one side then directly at Gilchrist.

'It took three of them to get me off her,' he said.

'Who were the three?'

'I have no idea.'

'How was Lesley?'

'Not as bad as she should have been. Although

I was punching her and I pulled half her hair out trying to drag her across the floor. I didn't know how to punch so I'd mostly been hitting bone. I broke two knuckles on the back of her head and my big toe from kicking her barefoot.'

Blue rubbed his chin. Gilchrist couldn't help but look at the two knuckles that were misaligned.

'And that was your last night together,' Gilchrist said.

'The last time I saw her until I saw her dead.'

'Where did she stay that night? With Neill?'

'I have no idea. Somebody stayed with me but I have no idea who that was either. I wasn't in very good shape.'

Gilchrist and Heap exchanged a look.

'Did you decide to take revenge on everyone involved with that trip?' Heap said.

'What do you mean?' Blue looked puzzled.

'Roland Gulliver, Philip Coates, Rasa Lewis and Christine Bromley are all dead.'

'Who?'

'Other people on that trip,' Heap said quietly.

'Don't recall the other people. But you mentioned revenge. Early on I was all about revenge, especially when I couldn't get anywhere suing Neill. Not that it was about the money – it was about making him accountable. That period is a bit of a blur for me.' He gestured to the bedroom next door. 'If Monica hadn't come along I don't know what I'd be like . . .'

'May we have a word with Monica?' Gilchrist said.

'Why?' Blue said, something shifting in his expression.

'See if she can shed any light on what's been going on.'

'She can't,' Blue said flatly. 'She doesn't know any of these people.'

'Maybe she took a call when you weren't around.'

'I'm always around,' Blue said shortly. He had a smile on his face but it was as if he was struggling to keep it there, as if it was going to slide away at any moment. His eyes were burning.

'Perhaps if she could confirm that?' Gilchrist said.

'Well, as I said, she's resting right now . . .'

'You were saying about wanting revenge,' Heap said.

'Yes, but not killing-people kind of revenge. I'm just an ordinary Joe.'

'Who beats up women,' Gilchrist said. 'Have you and Derek Neill been in contact after you added the inscription to headstone?'

'I told you that I never added that inscription. I wish I had. I wouldn't know how to get in touch with him and he certainly has no idea where I am.'

'And you maintain you have never been to Brighton or Coniston in the past two months?' Gilchrist said.

'Coniston?'

'You have?'

'No, of course not. Why would I go to Coniston, nice as I'm sure it is? If I wanted to see a lake, you may have heard there's the odd loch here in Scotland.'

'And you have someone to confirm your

254

whereabouts on certain specific days,' Heap said. 'Monica perhaps?'

Heap took a step towards a closed door.

'There's nothing in there,' Blue said quickly.

'Not Monica?'

'She's in the bedroom, lying down. That's just a cupboard.'

'May I see?' Heap said.

'It's locked and I don't have the key. I guess the landlord keeps some stuff in there.'

Gilchrist watched him. Heap stepped forward and held out a card.

'Get her to call me when she's up and about. It will only take a couple of minutes.'

Blue looked blankly at Heap for a moment then took the card and nodded.

'Absolutely, sir. Later today, I expect.' He tucked the card carefully into his shirt pocket then looked from Heap to Gilchrist. That odd fire had gone out of his eyes. 'Is there anything else? Only I have a lot to do.'

Heap glanced at Gilchrist.

'That's all for now, thank you, sir,' he said. 'Once we've done a DNA swab.'

'What do you think, Bellamy?' Gilchrist said as Jardine drove them back out to the airport.

'I think we're still not much nearer finding our killer or killers.'

'But at least we're whittling down our suspects.'

'Blue not your man, then, ma'am?' Jardine called from the front seat.

'Unlikely,' Gilchrist said. 'Though you might want to get someone around to check on his girlfriend, Monica. She might be suffering a bit of domestic.'

'Despite the clichés about the Scots, you might be pleasantly surprised to know we're hot on that stuff these days. The days of our Greatest Living Tax Exile, Big Tam, saying that sometimes women need a slap are long gone.' Jardine made the call.

'Glad to hear it. Whatever happened to him?'

'Retired, ma'am,' Jardine said. 'As did Gene Hackman.'

'Is that so,' Gilchrist said.

'I was thinking about Big Tam the other day when the wife and I watched on some cable channel a remake of the *Murder on the Orient Express*. That Kenneth Branagh with a ridiculous moustache. Big Tam was in the first, of course.' Jardine chuckled. 'Always thought it was a bit of a cheat, that story – Agatha Christie having everyone committing the crime. Usually, with books like hers, you expect the guilty person to be the least likely person.'

Gilchrist nodded and the rest of the journey went off mostly in silence and general chit-chat. Jardine dropped them off and as they watched the car pull away Gilchrist and Heap, simultaneously thinking of least likely suspects, said: 'Tamsin Stanhope.'

Tamsin Stanhope was looking haggard when Heap and Gilchrist arrived.

'I've not been sleeping,' she said. 'It's getting worse rather than better.'

'There is a lot going on,' Gilchrist agreed. Heap

had been to the local coffee shop and bought three take-outs. He handed one to Stanhope and put milk and sugar on the table.

'That's thoughtful,' Stanhope said reluctantly.

'We wanted to ask you about something that happened six years ago. In Crete.'

'I wondered when you'd get to that,' Stanhope said, putting the coffee down on the table.

'Well, you could have helped us get to it earlier,' Gilchrist said mildly.

'I see crime stuff on the telly. The police work in mysterious ways.'

'What do you remember about the trip?'

'How long have you got?'

'Did you see any acts of violence?'

'Of course. There were a couple of people wound way too tight.'

'A couple of people? David Blue and . . .?'

'Harry somebody.'

'We don't know about any Harry,' Gilchrist said.

'He didn't last long. Had some kind of break-down. He was creepy. Always trying to grope you. He was a watcher. You'd suddenly see him peering in through your bedroom window.'

'Harry who?'

'I don't remember.'

'Was he a friend of Derek Neill?'

'I don't remember.'

'What about the death of Lesley White?' Heap said.

'She drowned.'

'Surely not quite that,' Gilchrist said.

'What do you mean?' Stanhope said.

'Wasn't she stung horribly by jellyfish? She died before you could reach help?' Heap said.

'I thought you were talking about Lesley White.'

'We are,' Gilchrist said, hoping if she took a sip of coffee Stanhope would follow suit and get her brain in gear.

'The one with the headstone up in Woodvale?' Stanhope continued.

'Yes,' Gilchrist said warily.

'She drowned,' Stanhope said. 'Body never recovered as far as I'm aware.'

'I think you might be mistaken, Ms Stanhope,' Heap said.

'Well, there are no certainties, it's true,' Stanhope said, finally taking a sip of her coffee. 'As I now know only too well. Everything is fluid, even gender. But I've always assumed that grave was either empty or maybe had Genevra Flynn in it.'

Derek Neill had mentioned a Genevra.

'Who is Genevra Flynn?' Gilchrist said, feeling a kind of free-falling sensation.

'She's the one who brought Harry along. She was on the rebound from her husband, Tim. He abandoned her. But he had always treated her like shit and really took away her confidence.'

'You were friends?'

'Acquaintances. Tim Flynn taught at Sussex – something obscure – and she worked in admin there.'

'Had you met Harry before?'

'Never. I knew she'd been with him a few

months but our paths hadn't crossed. She was still in a bad way though.'

'What makes you say that?' Heap said.

'Well, she was pretty much the trip's bike for a couple of days.'

'Excuse me?' Gilchrist said.

'Anyone could ride her,' Stanhope said, her mouth turning down. 'And most of the men did.'

'Is that why Harry got angry?' Heap said.

'Wouldn't you?' Stanhope said.

'Why would she be in Lesley White's coffin?' Gilchrist said.

'Because she was the one stung to death by jellyfish.'

Nineteen

When they had continued to question Stanhope it had transpired she had not seen Lesley White's body when Derek Neill and Rasa Lewis rushed off to hospital with it. Nor had she witnessed Genevra Flynn drowning – or seen any evidence of it.

'So how can you be so sure?' Gilchrist had said.

Stanhope looked puzzled.

'I-I don't know. With all that has happened my mind is very muddy.' She looked at the ceiling. 'I think Harry told me.'

'Harry told you?' Gilchrist said. 'When?'

'At the time. I think.'

'We're going to need more detail than that, Ms Stanhope,' Gilchrist said.

'I've a vague memory of bumping into Harry on the quayside in Hania. I'd gone there for a night because it was all getting too much for me at the swimming retreat. I asked him where Genevra was and he said she'd been stung to death by jellyfish.'

'When was this?' Gilchrist said.

Stanhope waved her hands.

'Then,' she said vaguely.

'When exactly then?'

'I think it was the day after the death.' She flung her hands up. 'I'm sorry I can't be precise. Everything was such a muddle then and is even more of a muddle now.'

With that the pair left Tamsin Stanhope and, on Gilchrist's instructions, Heap parked on the promenade near the West Pier. Gilchrist looked out at the wildly churning sea. The wind buffeted the car.

'I just needed a moment to discuss this with you, Bellamy. Our investigation seems to be careering out of control.'

'Not out of control, ma'am, but we are getting a lot of new information in all at once. A very good idea to pause a moment and see where we are.'

'What do you think about Stanhope saying Lesley White drowned and that it was this Genevra who was stung to death?'

'Well, it doesn't match anything David Blue said. And she couldn't offer any kind of chapter or verse.'

'I think this Harry has become a person of great interest, ma'am,' Heap said, as rain began to pelt the windscreen.

'And I think we need to speak to Derek Neill again,' Gilchrist said, tapping his number into her mobile.

The rain began to fall more heavily, rattling on the roof of the car, sluicing down the windscreen.

'Who is Genevra Flynn, Mr Neill?' Gilchrist almost shouted down the phone. 'And Harry?'

'Flynn – yes, that was the last name of the Genevra I told you about. Harry must have been her boyfriend. I think he was a kind of rebound for her from a marriage gone wrong. They were a couple who were just with us briefly.'

'Just briefly because Genevra Flynn got stung to death by jellyfish?'

'What? No! That was Lesley.'

'We've been told Lesley drowned and her body was never recovered. That Genevra Flynn was the woman stung by jellyfish.'

'Told by whom?'

Gilchrist wondered whether to say. She didn't need to.

'Wait, let me guess. Tammy Stanhope, right? Jesus, that woman.'

'She seemed very certain.'

'Tammy only does certainties. Things are either black or white. She doesn't do grey.'

'So are you saying she's mistaken or that there are shades of grey here?'

'I'm saying her brain is one big shade of grey, though she's too far gone to realize it.'

'She seemed to be pretty lucid when we spoke to her,' Gilchrist said.

'Except for any detail to support her mad suppositions, I'll bet.'

Gilchrist didn't respond. Then: 'Why were Genevra and Harry only there a couple of days?' she said.

'Harry had a kind of meltdown and they both left.'

'Just like that?'

'Pretty much. Middle of the night stuff. They didn't pay for their room.'

'When was this in the itinerary of the stay?'

'The night of the day Lesley was injured.'

'Why is Tamsin Stanhope convinced that Lesley drowned and Genevra was stung to death?'

'She's confused. She was high most of the time she was there. She wasn't even with us when Lesley was stung. She'd gone somewhere for a couple of days because it was all a bit much for her – I think it was the drugs that were really too much for her. She went to Hania, I think.'

'When was the last time you saw Genevra?'

'How can I be expected to remember that now? Give me a minute.' Gilchrist watched the rain thumping on the promenade, sluicing onto the road. 'Not on the day of Lesley's death, I'm pretty sure of that,' Neill said. 'It was pretty full on. That's when Genevra and Harry slipped away.'

'Ms Stanhope said most of the men slept with Genevra.'

'Ha! What do you call that thing? Projection? Tamsin was fucking anything that moved. She was pretty hot in those days, in every sense.'

'You had personal experience of that?'

'I've already told you I did. And she got jealous when she heard I'd fucked Genevra. Thinking about it, that may have been why she went away for a bit.'

'I thought you were married to Christine and had a thing about Rasa?'

'So? We're just talking about sex here. No biggie, right, DI Gilchrist?'

Gilchrist felt herself flushing.

'And Roland Gulliver knew what Tammy was up to?'

'I don't know if he knew but I know he wouldn't have cared. He had a crush on Christine's gay friend and I think he was having a thing with one of the Greek guys at the taverna. You know what the ancient Greek attitude to homosexuality was? If you're the one doing it, it's manly; if you're on the receiving end, you're a poof. I'm guessing Roland was the poof in that relationship.'

'And Harry?'

'OK, so you know what? I took Genevra into the shared bathroom for a bit of privacy – it was one of the few places in the taverna with a lock on it. I threw a towel on the bathroom floor to protect her arse but it was rubbed raw anyway by the time we'd finished.'

'This is too much information, Mr Neill,' Gilchrist said.

'Not like a police officer to say that, DI Gilchrist. But what I'm saying has a point. What I didn't know was that Harry, who was in their room right next door to the bathroom, could hear noises and voices, quiet as we tried to be and whispering as we were, coming through the wall while Genevra and me were at it.

'Except, it turned out, he didn't know they were coming from next door, he thought he was hearing voices or hallucinating voices coming out of the walls below his aural threshold and it drove him nuts, which he was worried he was anyway and this just seemed to confirm it. And it did tip him over the edge.'

'What happened to him?'

'We sedated him with Tamsin's sleeping pills and locked him in one of the rooms. We didn't know what else to do.'

'And then?'

'And then he and Genevra did that moonlight flit. End of story.'

'Did you keep in touch?'

'Not likely.'

'Never heard from either of them again?'

'Nothing.'

'So why does Ms Stanhope think Genevra was the one stung to death by jellyfish?'

'Search me. But she's one hundred per cent mistaken, I can assure you.'

'I don't suppose you can remember the last name of this Harry?' Gilchrist said.

'As we've been talking it has come to me. Mogford. I'm pretty sure he was called Harry Mogford.'

Heap phoned Sylvia Wade to ask about the cars at the gym.

'Has a Harry Mogford come up in the cross-check, DC Wade?'

After a moment she said: 'He has. Is he of significance, sir? Do you want his licence photo?'

'Send it through. Where's he living?'

'Well, his licence is registered to an address in London but that might not be up to date.'

'Let's start with that. Contact the Home Office to see if she came back into this country. And somebody needs to check with the Greek embassy whether they keep immigration records of people coming in and out of that country. We know Genevra Flynn arrived in Crete. I hope for her sake that she also left.'

Twenty

Harry Mogford sat in the Bull in Ditchling, contemplating the log fire and what he might do next. A famous actress was sitting with her back to the room on the other side of the fireplace. He'd heard she lived nearby. She was flanked by a couple of young men who giggled a lot. She glanced over to Mogford from time to time.

Maybe his next project would be to make her his lover. Actresses, he knew from previous conquests, were pretty flaky. That vulnerable mix of ego and lack of self-esteem. He knew how to manipulate that.

He'd always known how to manipulate. Except for that time in Crete, six years ago, when he'd totally lost it. Cocaine just didn't suit him, as he'd discovered too late.

The details either side of his breakdown on the island of Crete were crystal clear. When that bitch had been stung by jellyfish and everyone had rushed her off to get help, he had a detailed memory of leaving the bay in a borrowed boat with Genevra.

He had a detailed memory of where he landed alone in Hania. He'd intended to stay there a few days – he'd heard it was really nice. But then he'd bumped into that hot Tammy bitch he'd been sneaking looks at – great tits – on the quayside. He'd given her some jive about where Genevra was – he couldn't even remember what he'd said – but then thought he'd better get out of Crete.

But he'd never forgotten that bunch of creeps. He blamed them all for what had happened to Genevra. His involvement was merely incidental. She'd jumped out of the frigging boat when he was just trying to have a discussion with her. She was high but, even so, what was that about? He hadn't put his hands on her, not really, even though she was driving him mad and he was so pissed off with her that she'd been sleeping with most, if not all, of the men.

He was a patient man. These last six years he'd been making a good living in America. Real estate. Can't go wrong with that. But he had this axiom. *Never forget; never forgive.*

He sipped his beer. The movie star was getting up to leave. She cast one last glance his way. He grinned and she turned away. She was a shapely woman in her forties, very sexy. He watched her exit the pub and inhaled the sweet, smoky smell

266

of whatever wood had just been put on the fire. Apple, perhaps. He went out to the car park. He would drive into Brighton over the Ditchling Beacon. It was time to finish the job.

'I've found Harry Mogford, ma'am,' Sylvia Wade said to Gilchrist. 'He doesn't still live at the address on his driving licence but we've traced him to an address in Brighton just off the Ditchling Road.'

'Send someone to invite him in for questioning.'

When a couple of constables delivered him, they reported to Gilchrist that Mogford hadn't seemed unduly surprised and had come willingly to the station. He had strong arms and a paunch and fitted the description, such as it was, that Bilson had given of the man in the sauna with Roland Gulliver.

In the interview room Mogford seemed very confident. He pointed at Barnaby.

'Don't let anyone give you any shit about being short,' he said to him. 'It was the tall men who died first in prisoner-of-war camps. You know why? The guards were usually shorter than them and liked humiliating them – they treated them worse. Plus they had less fat on them so they starved quicker.' He shrugged. 'Mind you, not that you've got much spare flesh on you.' He pointed at Gilchrist. 'Not like you darling. Mind, I'd still give you one, hefty as you are.'

'We want to ask you about Genevra Flynn,' Heap said. Gilchrist looked across at Heap. Interesting angle to go in on. Of course, she should have asked the first question but she understood why Heap had leapt in, bless him. She sucked in her stomach.

'Who?' Mogford said.

'Your girlfriend who drowned in Crete on the swimming holiday you were on several years ago. You left abruptly.'

Mogford scratched his head. He'd definitely been working on his biceps. 'Is this a request from the Greek police? Because otherwise I can't quite see what jurisdiction you're in or why you have a right to ask such a question.'

'Do you know a Genevra Flynn?' Heap persisted.

'I'd have to give you the same reply,' Mogford said. He looked at Gilchrist.

'What about Christine Bromley?' Heap said.

'I think I might have given her one but that period of my life is a bit hazy.'

'Roland Gulliver?' Gilchrist said.

'A bloke? I know I live in Brighton but I definitely wouldn't have given him one. I don't mind the odd bit of anal but it's definitely with the opposite sex.'

'We're talking about their deaths,' Gilchrist said. 'And those of Philip Coates and Rasa Lewis.'

'These are all linked?' Mogford said. 'Somebody has been a busy bee, haven't they?'

'We have evidence you have had encounters with each of these people recently.'

'Encounters of the Third Kind?' Mogford asked.

Gilchrist didn't immediately get the reference but Heap clearly did.

'Those encounters were benign as I recall, Mr Mogford. These are more murderous.'

'I'm a businessman, not a murderer.'

'What kind of business are you in, Mr Mogford?'

'Refurbishment.'

'Swimming pools and such?' Gilchrist said.

'More the "and such",' he said. 'I relocated down here originally to get involved with re-developing the West Pier. That didn't work out when the council went for the i360 but I thought I would stay.'

'Were you part of a conglomerate?' Heap said.

'Well, I wasn't going to do it all on my bloody ownsome, was I?'

'With William Simpson?' Heap said equably.

'Among others,' Mogford said.

'Have you known William Simpson long?'

'A little while,' Mogford said, wary for the first time.

'Derek Neill?' Heap said.

'I think I went on one of his beach holidays once. One out of your jurisdiction.'

'You seem enormously concerned about juris-dictions,' Gilchrist said.

'I used to be a copyright lawyer in America. Jurisdiction is everything in that business.'

'And now?'

'Entrepreneur.'

'Were you surprised to see Roland Gulliver in the sauna at the Sussex Health Club?' Gilchrist said.

'Who says I did?'

'An unimpeachable witness,' she said, adding the lie, 'backed up by CCTV images.'

269

'I knew I knew him but I couldn't place him,' Mogford said.

'But then you did place him,' Heap said.

'From the Save Salthaven Lido Campaign, yes.'

'Not before?'

'Not that I'm aware of,' Mogford said.

'Not from that beach holiday you went on?'

'Was he on that?'

'Was that your first visit to the health club?' Gilchrist said.

'It was. First and last.'

'Why did you go?'

'Check it out. I wasn't impressed so I didn't go back.'

'You didn't go specifically to see Mr Gulliver?' Heap said.

'Why would I want to do that?'

'You tell us, Mr Mogford.'

'Well, since it's your proposition not mine that I went specifically to see Mr Gulliver, I think you should answer that. Why would I want to see him?'

'Perhaps you were asked to have a meeting with him?' Gilchrist said.

'I don't know about you but I'm not in the habit of conducting meetings in Jacuzzis.' He leered. 'Not business ones anyway.'

Gilchrist was having trouble matching the cocksure man slouched in a man-sprawl in front of her with the voyeur who had a breakdown in Crete.

The custody room door opened and Sylvia Wade, blushing, put her head in the room. Gilchrist turned and shooed her away. The door closed but

270

Wade's face was still visible in the viewing rectangle at head height, peering in.

Gilchrist turned back as Heap said: 'Mr Mogford, we're hoping to solve these crimes today. With your help, sir.'

'Solving things. That's the human neurosis, right there: the need to find a solution. Sometimes, you know, there just isn't one.'

'Not in our line of work, Mr Mogford,' Gilchrist said.

'Well, no. In your line of work, if I understand the statistics correctly, it's more that crimes aren't solved rather than that they are not soluble. I understand your clear-up rate is pretty abysmal here in Sussex.'

'I can't comment on that,' Gilchrist said. 'But I can guarantee we are going to clear up these particular crimes.'

'Well, that's good news, Detective Inspector – I've got your rank correct, I hope? Very good news.'

'But, as DS Heap mentioned, for that we require your help.'

'Happy to be of service,' Mogford said.

'Excellent, Mr Mogford,' Gilchrist said. 'So we need to keep you here longer for a formal interview—'

Sylvia Wade tapped on the window. Gilchrist turned and glared at her. When she turned back Mogford showed his teeth.

'This seems pretty formal,' he said.

'Mr Mogford,' Gilchrist continued. 'We're concerned that you are implicated in – may indeed be the perpetrator of – four linked deaths, excluding the disappearance of Genevra Flynn.'

'You say there have been four linked deaths?' Mogford said. He shook his head then gestured to Sylvia Wade's face at the window. 'You can get that, you know.'

'Yes, four linked deaths, Mr Mogford,' Gilchrist said, indicating to Heap to go and see why Wade was so keen to interrupt their interrogation.

'You lot can't get anything right, can you?'

'Excuse me?' Gilchrist said, then turned when Heap came back in, a frown on his face. Mogford gave that chilly smile again.

'I think you've just discovered it's five linked deaths.'

Bob Watts found Derek Neill sprawled on the sofa of his apartment. Watts had been phoning him without success then decided to nip downstairs to knock on his door. The door was ajar. Watts pushed it half open and peered in. The window was open, the curtain billowing. He could see an empty bottle of wine and two glasses on the coffee table by the sofa. He saw Neill sprawled on his couch, a fogged-up clear plastic bag over his head, taped around his neck. If that was the cause of death, he'd been suffocated.

Watts stepped into the room and surveyed the scene. He'd seen death before but it was always a sobering thing to see someone you knew suddenly inanimate. He called for an ambulance then dialled Gilchrist. He was diverted to Sylvia Wade. He left a message with her then stood by the body.

The ambulance and the police came at pretty much the same time. Watts didn't recognize the policemen but it seemed they recognized him. He gave them what information he had, suggested they too called Gilchrist. Then he went back to his own apartment to await developments.

Twenty-One

Gilchrist couldn't figure out Harry Mogford. Why did he alert them to the death of Derek Neill? Just arrogance? In the absence of any forensic evidence, without a confession it was going to be hard to link him to the deaths.

She stood by her office window looking out at the blustery swell. Mogford was still in the interview room but he had lawyered up. It was going to take a lot of painstaking work to build a case against him.

Her phone rang. Frank Bilson.

'Any sign of Mogford in Derek Neill's apartment?' she said.

'That's for your fingerprint people to figure out, dear heart,' Bilson said.

'Dear heart' was a new one but Gilchrist let that go.

'We don't have enough to arrest him so we can't get his DNA or fingerprints because he won't allow us to take them,' she said. 'We're stymied unless we can get a confession.'

'That's for you to achieve—'

'*Dear heart*. Yes, I know. I get that. OK. Thanks.'

She started to put the phone down.

'Are you still interested in the results of the swabs of Mrs Medavoy's house?'

'Mrs Medavoy?'

'The house where Roland Gulliver was water boarded and stabbed.'

'Yes, yes – do you have something?'

'We have a Bill Clinton moment.'

'You're going to have to explain that, Frank.'

So he did.

Mogford sat in the interview room staring at the wall, thinking about what he'd accomplished. God he hated those people and their lifestyles. In Crete one thing he could clearly remember was how they thought he was 'straight' and boring because he didn't go along with their hedonism. And that Rasa was a snooty bitch but they had the temerity to call *him* stuck-up. Gulliver's had been the most laborious killing. He'd been in Gulliver's house when that ditzy woman had arrived with her bottle of wine. He'd doctored both drinks when they'd gone into the bedroom. He was expecting them to take longer but Gulliver had come back almost straight away. Mogford had hidden until he figured the roofies had worked.

But then he'd found her address on her driving licence and thought it would be a good idea to lug them both round to her house without being seen. He got to work on Gulliver in her bathroom with the wet towel so Gulliver would know what it was like to drown. The stabbing was on impulse since Gulliver didn't seem sufficiently contrite. He'd got a bit carried away that evening, one way and another.

The others had been much easier. Ridiculously so and, therefore, perhaps, not so enjoyable. More like ticking them off one by one. Although he'd really enjoyed seeing to that stuck-up bitch, Rasa. He'd decided that instead of her drowning in water like poor Genevra he'd drown her in her own blood.

Frank Bilson peered through the viewing window in the interview room door.

'I won't do the obvious jokes about not recognizing someone with their clothes on,' he said.

'I'm relieved,' Gilchrist said.

'It's the man from the sauna.'

'Thanks, Frank.'

She led him in with Heap and two constables bringing up the rear. Mogford looked up with a supercilious grin on his face. Gilchrist read him his rights then Bilson took the DNA swab from in his mouth.

Gilchrist, Heap, Wade and Bilson all piled into Bob Watts's penthouse apartment. Wade kind of tiptoed to the window and just stared out, seemingly awestruck by the view. Bilson stood close behind her, murmuring 'very nice, very nice' and Gilchrist couldn't work out whether he was admiring the view or Wade's rather nice arse.

'Is it enough to convict him for all of it?' Watts asked Gilchrist once they were all settled with a range of drinks. Wade turned out to be a vodka and tonic girl; Bilson and Heap were both on some exotic bottled beer from some northern microbrewery.

'Well, he pretty much fessed up to all of it except Genevra Flynn,' Gilchrist said.

'Yes – who is this Genevra Flynn?' Watts said.

'She was at the swimming camp with Harry Mogford, apparently left with Mogford on a boat they borrowed/nicked but then disappeared. Mogford told Tamsin Stanhope when she found him alone in Hania, where he'd docked the boat, that she'd died stung by jellyfish, but that was the fate of poor Lesley White. Whether he killed Genevra on the boat or she came back to England and disappeared we don't know. The Greek authorities don't keep track of the comings and goings of EU citizens.'

'She's a sad case,' Heap said. 'Her ex-husband, who abused her, is dead.' He saw Watts frown. 'Natural causes. She had no friends from work as far as we can tell – her husband discouraged that – and no family. DI Gilchrist and I think Mogford probably drowned her somewhere between the swimming camp and Hania but we have no way of knowing.' He shook his head. 'She remains one of the many unmourned disappeared in the world.'

'It's all wrapped up then?' Watts said.

'We never got closer to William Simpson,' Gilchrist said. 'We think he is tangential. And the under-age gang who attacked Kate are up in court soon so that won't be easy for her.'

Watts nodded. 'So how did you get Mogford?'

Gilchrist tipped her wine glass towards Bilson. 'Take the stage, Mr Bilson,' she said.

'It was a Bill Clinton moment,' Bilson said.

'Ah,' Watts said, nodding. 'Rasa?'

'Mrs Medavoy,' Bilson said.

'Ah,' Watts said again.

Gilchrist looked from one to the other. 'How come everybody but me knows what a Bill Clinton moment is?' she said plaintively.

'Only you can answer that, Sarah,' Bilson said. 'I'd like to think it relates to a certain innocence but it also speaks to a lack of awareness of world affairs.'

'Affairs in more than one sense,' Watts said. 'Short version: Clinton was allegedly fooling around when president with a young female staffer. The proof it happened was his semen on her dress.'

'I still find it perverse it was on Mrs Medavoy's dress,' Gilchrist said.

'A multiple killer and perverse do go together,' Bilson said mildly. 'He almost got away with it because he was obviously very careful. The spot of semen is minute – but that's all we need to establish DNA.'

'Mrs Medavoy was drugged, right?' Watts said. 'He raped her while she was unconscious?'

'Mrs Medavoy has no awareness of that,' Gilchrist said, 'and a physical examination revealed no sign of trauma in her vagina. Time has passed but, even so, probably not.'

'Except now she's traumatized at the thought of what went on while she was drugged,' Heap added quietly.

'Masturbation, then,' Watts said.

Bilson nodded. 'Quite commonly linked to criminal acts,' he said. 'Amateur burglars end up either masturbating or evacuating their bowels. Sometimes both. But in this case, I think he was overexcited by what he had done to Roland Gulliver – the stabbing more than the drowning – and needed some other release. Mrs Medavoy was unconscious and helpless but even in his intoxicated state he knew enough not to leave evidence by raping her. So he did the next best thing. And he was obviously careful about that too. Probably he had his handkerchief to hand. Except for this one, tiny amount.'

There wasn't really any way to follow that so they all took sips of their drinks.

'And has he said why he killed them all?' Watts asked.

'I'm not sure he knows why,' Gilchrist said. 'He told me what he called his mantra, the thing that he lived by, but that didn't really explain it.'

'What was the mantra?' Bilson said.

'Never forget; never forgive.'

Epilogue

Kate Simpson trembled as she stood on the pebbly beach at two in the morning. Shakespeare Beach, Dover. The starting point for every modern attempt to swim the Channel. She'd got the call from her boat pilot, Ronny, at eleven p.m. to say the conditions were right and to get herself ready and down to the harbour. She was already ready. Physically, aside from the Vaseline she needed to smear over the parts of her body that might chafe, she was as ready as she was ever going to be. Mentally the best she could be.

She was wearing only her normal swimming costume, her bathing cap, ear plugs and goggles. She had two light sticks attached to her, which gave her body an odd glow. The moon was hidden behind clouds and that somehow made the grating roar of the pebbles as the water rushed onto the beach sound even louder. The water seemed dark and threatening.

Her pilot boat bobbed in the water around fifty yards out, drawn into shore as far as was safe. There was a spotlight on the roof, at the moment pointing up into the black, starless sky. On the boat she could see dear Bellamy and Bob Watts and Sarah Gilchrist and a couple of people from the Channel Swimming Association who were there to monitor her swim. She hadn't invited her mother. And certainly not her father. This was her team. Her support. And they were *such* supporters.

Yet never had she felt so alone. Never had she felt so reliant entirely on herself.

It was twenty-one miles to the beach at Cap Gris, Calais. It could take her anywhere between twelve and twenty-one chilly hours, depending on how she caught the currents and what the weather decided to do. The first five would be in utter darkness, although the pilot boat would be able to keep sight of her because of the light sticks. All those hours for her to see for herself what she was made of.

There were big waves coming in – the sea was what Channel swimmers called *lumpy*. She saw the pilot reach for the spotlight on the roof of the boat and angle it down and back so that it shone down on the water she was about to enter. It was time. She gave a little wave, saw all on board the ship wave and heard the guttural roar of 'Go Katie!'

She stepped into the cold, surging water, dropped down into a low dive. Twenty-one miles. Starting now.